Into The Night & The Glass Demon

Novellas *Volume I*

Jerry J.C. Veit

BLUEWOLF
PUBLISHING
Waukesha, WI 53186

The Complete **Jerry J.C. Veit** Collection:

Apocalypsia
Into the Night
The Glass Demon
Capricorn
Days Gone By
Utopia
The Form

Library of Congress Control Number: 2022919604
ISBN 979-8-9871666-3-5

Books

Into The Night

They will never stop hunting you.

Contents

1

The Drifter

In every century there is one great significance. One great push toward the future, which may be ahead of its time, or beyond the knowledge of the masses. It can be an idea, a story, an invention, or a movement. In the year 1325, England was faced with such a significance. It was the culling of two threats, one foreign, and one domestic. Now, it's not always clear to all who lived in this time that such an event was even taking place, and that's why history and legend often merge to become blended tales of fascination and wonder. Fiction and fact depend greatly on who's telling the story, and the role they played in it. Some will say this was the year the barbarians invaded our homeland. Others will argue that it was the time of a vicious streak of vampire attacks. Only a few will know the truth. This is a time of the two wars. One which we all had to fight, and one that only a few of us were selected to partake in. If it were not for one certain individual these wars could have had a very different ending. If it were not for a single woman, one of them would have been lost. But that's usually how it goes. It only takes one person to change history.

A man in his thirties is traveling on a dirt road with nothing more than a walking stick and a knapsack. His name is Samuel Hall.

Ever since I was a young boy, I was curious about the things others feared. I eagerly investigated the stories about witches, vampires and ghosts roaming the countryside; a fascination that eventually branded me as an outcast. While everyone else crossed their chests, said their prayers, and locked their windows and doors. I would stay out at night hoping to get a glimpse of one of these supernatural monsters. Whether by worry or sheer embarrassment the townsfolk thought it best if I left. I became a drifter, traveling from town to town, from countryside to countryside.

Samuel's solitary journey takes him through multiple countrysides, rocky hills, and along coastlines. His voyage is never-ending with no destination in sight or a home to look forward to. He's seldom welcomed by others and accepts any moment to nap in the shade of a tree when he chances upon it.

I live my life one dream at a time. Everything I am, everything I want, the one I need. They are all gone when I open my eyes. I don't remember now if it was by chance, or choice, that led me to Piketon. My first impression of the town was typical of any town I traveled through. It was small, and secluded, seeped in superstitions and lore. The townsfolk worked by day and drank by night, that's all there was to do in a place like this. It is here that I soon would find myself in the middle of two wars, one that everyone could see, and the other that only a few of us would experience. My first stop, just like every place before this, was the tavern. The name of the place was Townsend, a certain play on words since it was the surname of its owner and the last building at the end of town; right before the meadows that led to Wytchwood Forest. This is where I would meet Valencia. My first impression of her; however, was not typical. She was pretty, but tough, two qualities, that in my experience, never went together. However, it wasn't Valencia who I noticed first—

Townsend is serving drinks behind the bar while talking and laughing with his customers. A lovely barmaid brings Samuel his pint of ale and sets it on the table. He nods and smiles to the point of nearly blushing when she gives him a wink and a smile. He sighs and takes several long gulps before setting it back down. A woman's tantalizing laughter reaches Samuel in the otherwise rowdy tavern. It's not like any laugh he had heard before. This one is soft, sweet, and innocent, but the pitch also carries a dark, mysterious, and seductive tone. It is the essence of lust in the female vocal cords, and it's designed to attract attention.

Samuel searches around for the origin of this captivating laugh. He hears it again, and homes in on the three tables adjacent to his. She continues to giggle and converse with the other men around her while taking turns sitting on their laps and stroking their beards. She has their undivided attention and keeps it well by flaunting her chest out and shaking her hips as she strolls in between her admirers. The men laugh and cheer as they seem to almost worship this woman. Samuel instantly becomes hypnotized by her beauty and carefree persona. The tavern room is crowded and boisterous, but her laughter echoes perfectly in Samuel's ears; her laugh, and nothing else. He doesn't know why, but he is beguiled by this woman. Her blouse is the only color he can see, and her touch becomes desired. What demands her to act out in this fashion with her company? His reserved nature is threatened, and false bravery begs him to join them. His hypnotic stance is suddenly interrupted when the chair across from him is aggressively pulled away from the table.

A black-haired woman, named Valencia Ruskin sets her mug of cider on the table and then takes her seat.

"You do not belong here," she begins. Samuel stares at her blankly but doesn't answer. She turns to look at the woman that Samuel was fixated on before turning back to look at him.

"Do you like her?"

"She's a beautiful woman," he admits.

"You haven't noticed it yet, but she already has her eyes on you." Samuel smiles and shakes his head.

"I don't think she has noticed me. I haven't seen her look at me once."

"You aren't that observant. You're lucky that I am."

"How do you know?"

"She has charmed you; like she has charmed all those poor chaps. It's her spell, her lure, and she has many. The weakness of men is no mystery. I just saved your life. I do not know yet if I made a mistake or not." Valencia stands up and is in mid-reach of grabbing her drink when Samuel puts his hand out in front of him.

"Wait, please. What do you know about that woman?" Valencia sighs and then sits back down and leans back into her chair

"She's waiting for you to leave—"

Outside the tavern is a drunken man stumbling home. The flapping of a loose article of clothing followed by a thump on the ground motivates the man to stop and glare behind him, but only the empty street is seen. Valencia continues her explanation.

"When you make your way through the dark street, she will be following you. She is a skillful stalker, a patient hunter. She will take her time hiding in places you will never think to look."

The drunken man turns down a narrow alley and becomes startled to see the charismatic woman from the tavern standing in front of him. She glares at him with her green eyes with a straight expression.

"All of a sudden, she will be in front of you. How she got there? You wouldn't know. Where she came from? You wouldn't know. She will gaze into your eyes, and you will be drawn into hers," Valencia further explains.

The woman presses her body against the man to force him against the brick wall. She tilts his chin up until his eyes meet her glimmering irises. She puts her arms around his neck and brings her head closer before opening her fanged mouth and then bites into his neck.

"The only thing you are thinking about is how much you want to kiss those lips. Her smell will put you into a trance; you'll close your eyes and fall into her. Pleasure, pain—then nothing. She lifts her fanged mouth from your neck and lets you fall to the street, leaving another corpse to be found in the morning."

The vampire lifts her bloody fangs from the man before letting him fall to the street.

"You're telling me she's a vampire?" Samuel inquires.

"She's a drug, a poison, and her name is Cerbera," Valencia responds.

"Well, I would know if I was being followed," Samuel says before taking a drink.

"You really aren't that observant. You still haven't noticed, have you?"

"What—"

"She's gone." Samuel glances to where he had last seen Cerbera but observes a new group sitting at the table instead of the previous crowd.

"How did you know she had left? You were looking at me the whole time."

"Around here you have to learn to see everything and everyone all at once. If you don't, it won't matter because you will soon be dead. I can tell you are someone who is oblivious to his surroundings. So, finish your ale, get some sleep, and in the morning, leave this place." Valencia stands up with her cider and walks away before Samuel can protest.

Tonight, two women entered into his life, and one of them is said to be a vampire. It is an amusing thought for Samuel's inexperienced mind. If Cerbera had beckoned, he would no doubt have advanced; it's easy to be fearless when one has no concept of danger.

After a hot meal, and several beers, Samuel slowly ascends the creaking tavern stairs. He slides his room key into the lock and steps into his rented lodging for the night. He kicks off his shoes and undresses to his undergarments before climbing into bed and pulling the covers up to his shoulders. A combination of exhaustion, and one too many beers, cause him to drift off to sleep as soon as his eyes close.

An image of Cerbera enters his mind. She smiles while motioning Samuel to come to her with her finger. As he draws nearer, she cups her breasts and says, "Would you like to see them?" Samuel nods and eagerly awaits to get a glimpse, but Cerbera only bares her fangs. That was his dream.

Not many dares venture outside their homes after dark, but not everyone believes in the superstitions about monsters roaming around at night. A man inspects his sparse supply of stored logs before glancing across the street at the full pile his neighbor has. He quickly scans the area and then cautiously crouches toward his neighbor's supply. He gently picks up one log and cradles it in his arm before reaching for another.

WHOOSH! THUMP!

The sound was directly above him, as if a large bird of prey had just perched itself on top of the roof. He remains frozen in place with his fingertips hovering over the next log he was planning to grab. A drop of clear liquid falls onto this very log. He hopes it's nothing more than a raindrop, but perhaps he should have heeded the warnings the town tried to give. The next drop lands on his hand, it's not rain, but saliva from a hunting predator. He doesn't look up; he doesn't want to know if his fears are right. He drops the only log he had and scurries back toward his house terrified. His door gets closer as his legs reach their maximum speed. He's almost there, maybe he can make it. He continues running without looking back or taking his eyes off the door that's now in arms reach. He extends his arm towards the knob, but a dainty hand lightly touches the back of his shoulder. The man is instantly frozen in place, unable to move, paralyzed, his nose just inches from the door. Soon, a woman's arm slowly reaches around the incapacitated man and wraps around his chest. The man sweats, his eyes wide, his mouth open, but unable to make a sound.

"Shhhh—" a soft voice says in an attempt to soothe her victim. Her other hand lands on his cheek and forces his head to the side followed by a snarl, and an open mouth revealing two fangs, rushing for his neck. This is the last memory he experiences.

Valencia suddenly awakes from sleep with a gasp and jolts up to a sitting position. She takes a moment to observe the morning sun shining through her window as she runs her hand through her hair.

"Every night. The same dream. The same memory. I will avenge you; then maybe we both can finally rest," she softly says to herself.

Later that morning, Samuel opens the shutters to his window and observes the crowded street. The town is filled with the clacking of horse drawn carts, the sizzling of hot metal being submerged at the blacksmith, the sawing of wood from the mill, and the smell of freshly baked bread from the bakery. Samuel admires the lively town until spotting an increasing number of townsfolk gathering and murmuring on a street corner. Samuel gives in to his curiosities and prepares to see the attraction for himself.

"A single vampire will never kill twice in the same night," one of the townsfolk says just as Samuel approaches.

"No, there must be two of 'em now," another points out.

Samuel squeezes through the crowd and stops at the body of the man who was attacked the night before. The body is rigid, pale, and with the eyes and mouth still open. The local doctor begins to inspect the cold corpse before making his claim.

"He wasn't killed here. This is just where they dropped him when they were done." He points to the man's head. "Cracked skull, broken neck." He lifts the man slightly onto his side and then sets him back down. "Broken back. This man fell from a great height but was dead long before landing."

"Did I hear right about there being two deaths?" Samuel says curiously. The doctor looks at him while pointing towards the opposite side of town.

"Yes, we found him earlier this morning, some drunkard. I believe he was attacked first and then this poor sap later in the night." The townsfolk slowly begin to depart from the area when a horse pulling a cart approaches. Two men, carrying a stretcher, gather the deceased man and then lifts him into the back of the cart. One of them takes a hot iron, in the shape of a cross, and sears the shape onto the victim's bare chest. Samuel remembers this act from his days as a boy. The belief is that the image of the cross, permanently engraved into a corpse who was attacked by a vampire, will prevent the body from rising after death.

Samuel glances further down the street to notice Valencia standing outside of the bakery. She wipes her hands on her apron before heading back inside, showing little to no interest in either Samuel or the dead man.

Samuel enters the bakery as Valencia removes several loaves from the brick oven. She is lightly covered with flour as she continues her task before finally addressing him. "Have you seen enough yet?" she asks without lifting her head.

"Seen enough, what?"

"Death—" Valencia stops what she's doing and turns to face Samuel. "Or are you one of those crazy people who likes to see dead bodies?"

"No, in fact that was the first one I ever saw."

"Then what are you still doing here?"

"Just thought I would buy some bread before leaving."

Valencia has no real quarrel with Samuel, but she doesn't particularly consider him very bright either. He appears too innocent for the time which he's living in and has a child-like assumption of how the world operates. This adds to her dislike of him, but also an annoying responsibility to get him moving along before he finds trouble.

"What kind do you want?" she says with a sigh. Samuel reaches into his pocket and places four coins on the counter.

"This is what I have." Valencia picks up three loaves from her display and then puts them into a burlap sack.

"So, was it really a vampire? That killed that guy, I mean." Samuel asks as she gathers his order.

"Believe whatever you want to believe." She hands him the sack of bread then picks up two coins and slides the other two back to Samuel. He takes the bread and then puts the remaining coins back into his pocket.

"Thank you. It's just that I've never seen a vampire before."

"You're lucky."

"Have you?" Valencia hesitates while trailing off into a distant thought.

"Yes," she eventually replies in a soft tone.

"I'm sorry, I didn't mean—"

"Don't worry about it," she interrupts. "Good luck on your travels, sir."

"Sam, Samuel Hall."

Valencia doesn't need to know his name; she will most likely never see him again. She's also not too keen on giving hers out to this stranger but replies before convincing herself out of it.

"Valencia Ruskin."

"Nice name," Samuel says with a bashful grin. She remains looking at him without a response or any hint of being amused. "Is that Latin?" Samuel asks.

"I don't know," She admits.

"I can read a little Latin, you know," Samuel continues his failing attempt to flirt.

"Congratulations," she says sarcastically without any change in her expression or tone of voice. Valencia isn't one who's easily impressed, and without any positive results, Samuel changes the subject.

"How far is the next town after the forest?"

"You're going through Wytchwood Forest?" she asks surprised.

"That's my direction."

"Make haste then. You should reach Middleton before dusk." Samuel smiles and holds the sack of bread up.

"Thank you for the bread," he says as he starts walking toward the door. He stops in the doorway and then looks back. Valencia sighs in frustration and glares back. "It was nice to meet you, Valencia." Samuel then takes a deep breath and attempts to sound important. "Well, I suppose I should get going now. Long day ahead of me."

"Good, then I can get some work done," she replies. Samuel smiles and gives one last wave before finally walking away feeling absolutely foolish.

Samuel strolls through the tall grass of the meadow carrying his knapsack, the sack of bread, and his walking stick. He glances back at Piketon one last time before proceeding into the woods. A mysterious and pretty baker and a seductive vampire who visits him in his dreams. What a nice little town that was, he thinks to himself. Like most young men, Samuel lets his imagination create fictional and unlikely scenarios with these two women, which are based so far from reality that it can only be described as a lavish fantasy; however, their images are the only company he has. Maybe Middleton will have something to offer, or someone, maybe Middleton will become home. This is what he tells himself everywhere he heads. Always hopeful, but always wrong. For Samuel every day is filled with possibilities, and every night is another disappointment.

It was a beautiful, sunny day when Samuel first entered the forest, but within two hours the sun had gradually crept behind dark rainclouds. Rolling thunder, in the distance, suggests a brewing storm, but without a proper shelter nearby, Samuel must continue his steadfast hike.

Elsewhere, is another small town in the middle of their workday. The forty townsfolk consist of farmers, carpenters, and seamstresses who have all adapted to their daily routines. One of the men working the fields glances up to see a sight that has never been seen before. A formation stands on the hills holding axes and swords, but this doesn't look like local soldiers. A distant cry sounds out just as a hundred-eighty barbarians sprint toward the defenseless town.

The ground trembles from the stampeding war party, and their unified roars drown out the lingering thunder overhead. The townsfolk take notice of the approaching threat as panic spreads quickly throughout the streets. People scramble to find suitable hiding places or hope that their garden tools will suffice as worthy weapons. Unfortunately, the fate of this town remains grim.

The barbarians collide into the frenzied townsfolk while wielding their weapons. Heads become decapitated, limbs are severed, and intestines coil out of gaping stomach wounds. A light drizzle begins, but the blood pools around the town faster than the coming rain. Women are dragged out or pushed around to the side of their homes. Their clothes are torn off before they are defiled on their backs or bent over fences and barrels. Their screams and cries do not save them from molestation or prevent their inevitable slaughter afterwards. In less than an hour all the men from the town are dead and all the women have been raped multiple times, and then executed. After setting the town ablaze the victorious band of warmongers depart while singing and joking.

Meanwhile, the torrential rain of an early autumn storm blankets Wytchwood forest into an early night. Samuel is soaked and cold as he sloshes his way through the forest in the relentless rain. His path becomes obscured, and his bearings are lost in the fog and wind. The sudden sound of hissing flies past him overhead. He looks up startled, but only sees the swaying canopy through the heavy patter of raindrops on his face.

Lightning flashes followed by a clap of thunder. Samuel thinks he can hear soft footsteps in the underbrush behind him. He stops and listens to the footsteps getting closer. Samuel whirls around, but again finds no one in sight. He remains stationary until he spots a glimpse of a blurry image darting across the woodland turf just ahead of him. He squints his eyes to try to focus on the area. The blurry image flashes past the corner of his eye, but he turns too late to make it out. Low steady growls and snarling seem to surround him now as he inspects the radius around him. His heart begins to pound inside his chest as fear begins to take over rational thought. Are these just normal sounds of the forest during a storm? Maybe it's just the wind through the trees, or the repetitive patter of large raindrops on wet leaves? He cannot deny the fact that he feels uneasy.

Something directly above him descends rapidly just as a lightning bolt strikes one of the trees. Samuel looks up just in time to dodge a thick branch that was struck. Leaves, sticks, twigs, and other branches follow the massive tree arm and lands around him while he shields his head. The clues to run are too many to ignore; he finally succumbs to his fear and bursts into a full sprint. He scales over fallen logs and dashes through a patch of shrubs. His knapsack becomes snagged and torn from his grip, but he decides to abandon it and continue without it. He zigzags around the maze of trees and bushes, but trips on an exposed root. He finds himself helpless when he hits the ground and rolls down a muddy hill while colliding into rocks and thorny branches before hitting the bottom hard. Bleeding and sore he is slow to recover. He spits the muddy water out and struggles to return to his feet. He finds the sack of bread next to him, but he has lost everything else.

He glances ahead and sighs in relief. He can see the hills of the countryside through the next patch of trees. He staggers ahead and takes his first few steps into the vast open field. However, with the threat of lightning Samuel wonders if he's actually better off where he is. There's no favorable outcome here, Samuel does not get relieve from the rain and wind and cannot advance on his intended route. He is so hung up on these two misfortunes that he forgets about the third. Whatever was hunting him may still be doing so, but the odds were always stacked against poor Samuel.

A dainty hand extends and lightly touches the back of his shoulder and then brushes across his upper back. The sack of bread falls from his hand and lands at his feet, Samuel stands motionless with eyes wide, and lips sealed shut. He cannot make any further action or comprehend why he suddenly finds himself completely paralyzed.

2

Vampires and Barbarians

As evening arrives, the first wave of townsfolk, in search of ale, swarm into Townsend. Valencia is content with her usual cider and mostly keeps to herself, but this becomes challenged when she overhears the conversation between a traveling merchant and a farmer sitting at a nearby table.

"Where are you coming from, stranger?" the farmer begins.

"A most unholy place. I fear the images I saw will haunt my dreams for the rest of my life."

"What did you see?"

"Every building burnt, and every man, woman and child slaughtered in the most gruesome manner I have ever laid my eyes on."

"Was it vampires?"

"Vampires? No, not even vampires are this cruel. This is a new evil. One that I hope does not linger."

"Where was this place, friend?"

"This great evil has fallen upon a town that used to be called, Middleton."

Valencia lowers her cider from her lips with a concerned look. "Sam—" she softly utters.

Samuel's eyelids quiver before opening, and his dilated pupils slowly begin to focus on a vast rocky chamber. He's inside some sort of cavern, which is lit by a multitude of torches secured inside sconces. He attempts to take a step forward but feels a resistance that prohibits his action. He inspects his wrists to notice a metal bracelet around them. It takes another moment before he fully understands that he's chained to the wall, and no amount of shaking or pulling can free him.

"Stop that now," a booming deep voice responds to his rattling ruckus. Samuel scans his surroundings until an intimidating man with bulging muscles steps around a bend. There must be another area that Samuel cannot see from his location.

"Where—Where am I?" Samuel asks.

"You do not need to know," the man answers.

"How did I get here?"

"They brought you."

"Who's they?"

"You will find out."

"Why am I here?"

"Look, I'm only tasked with making sure you are still here when they return and nothing more," the man roars in annoyance of his constant questions.

"When will they get here?" Samuel continues.

"How many questions are you going to ask? I hope they change their minds and drain you completely." Samuel hesitates but asks his question anyway.

"Drain me of what?" The man grins to bare his fangs and chuckles. It is his only reply before turning back around the corner. Samuel is a prisoner of vampires and for a reason that still remains unknown to him.

Valencia awakes at the break of dawn and allows several moments to pass as she lies in bed while observing the horizon through her window. She wonders if Samuel made it to Middleton before the onslaught. If he did, he's dead? If he hadn't, then he arrived at a place that could not offer him shelter. Would Cerbera follow him? She has too many questions and no way to answer them. Then again, why does she have them at all? Samuel isn't the first drifter who passed through Piketon. Is he really worth a second thought? She sighs and tosses the covers off her. "Dammit," she whispers to herself. There's only one way to silence the voices in her head, and that's to find Samuel. Dead, alive, or undead, she must know for sure.

Valencia changes into a pair of black pants, followed by a belt, black boots, and then her archer's gloves. Next to be added is a thick, woven vest with a neck guard, and lastly, a long black hooded cape. She opens her wooden wardrobe, but instead of clothes inside there are crossbows, several throwing daggers, swords, arrows and two unique wrist trigger crossbows.

She places the throwing daggers in the sewn straps of the vest, and then places a sword at her side. She attaches the two wrist crossbows to her wrists and adds the small arrows into the loops located on her belt. Lastly, she takes one of the larger crossbows and straps it onto her back along with a quiver of arrows hanging on her shoulder. She flicks her wrists to make the wrist crossbows rotate from their rested state, on the side of her arm, into her hands. The bottom cartridge rotates to bring the bowstring back into firing position and one of the five self-loaded arrows moves into firing position. Only one other person knows this baker is also a vampire hunter.

Valencia strolls past Townsend, who's already behind the bar with a cloth inside a recently washed mug.

"I'll be back later," she says.

"Are you going hunting?" She stops walking and briefly glances back.

"I don't know yet." She continues toward the door while still talking. "I have some day-old bread in the back if anyone asks. Give it to them for half price."

"What if they want fresh?"

"Tell them to wait a day."

"You never did have good customer service," Townsend yells as she steps outside.

"I never liked any of my customers," she responds before departing. Townsend chuckles and keeps a smile on his face as he continues cleaning.

Valencia reaches the spot of the forest where lightning had struck the tree branch. She's an attuned tracker, but Samuel made it even easier for her to pick up his trail. She follows his path and soon stumbles upon his torn knapsack. She retrieves it and peeks inside before tossing it aside. She doesn't need the extra baggage and there's nothing about it that seems to have any value. Several moments later she abruptly stops sprinting to inspect the ground.

"Where did you go?" she says to herself. She doesn't see a sign of him now and fears she may have lost his trail. She backtracks several paces and then glances down the slope. She spots a stick that doesn't quite fit among the other felled branches and twigs and recognizes it as Samuel's walking stick. Valencia carefully inches her way down the slope by lowering her center of gravity and using her feet and hands to control her direction and speed of descent. She slides the last few feet down until arriving at the foot of the slope. She notices the hills of the countryside through the patch of trees and advances toward the clearing. It is here that she locates the burlap sack with three loaves of soggy bread inside. She crouches low to the grass and lightly touches the blades while looking around. "You were here—but did not walk in any direction?" she concludes. She processes her thoughts and then looks into the sky. "You never made it to Middleton." She stands back up and stares ahead in another direction. In the distance is a rocky formation with a cave entrance. "Yeah—" she says almost disappointed in discovering what she always had suspected. Samuel was taken.

Valencia peers into the mouth of the cave and acknowledges the uneasy vibe that she receives. The narrow sloping path indicates it descends underground, but to what depth is unknown. The fact that this cave is inhabited is clear from the torches and sconces running along the side of the cavern wall. The air is damp and cool as Valencia advances with vigilance, and her quick reflexes are posed to strike. She takes note of the ledges that tower above her and how they could make fine places for vampires to organize an ambush. The steady continuous drip of water suddenly becomes interrupted by falling pebbles.

Valencia flicks her wrist crossbows into her hands and aims them above her. A solitary vampire leaps off the ledge and scurries down the wall before lunging at her with a snarl. Valencia squeezes her trigger to send an arrow into his forehead that drops him at her feet. She waits motionless to make sure this disturbance didn't alert any others. After a moment she is confident to continue her descent.

The corridor opens into the vast cavern where Samuel is being held. Valencia stops to thoroughly investigate the area. At first glance the entire place looks vacant, but this is the vampire's living quarters and therefore must be teeming with clan members. Her refusal to advance motivates two vampire guards to drop down from above her, and then charge while growling. Valencia darts her arms forward and shoots an arrow from each of her wrist crossbows in unison. The bolts hit their marks in each of the vampire's necks to end their pursuit.

Her perspective reveals the chamber that was hidden from Samuel's viewpoint. Wooden long tables and ornate chairs occupy the floor, while several vertical red banners with an unknown golden sigil in its center adorn the walls. She also catches sight of Samuel chained to the far wall with his head hanging down. She scans above her swiftly before beginning her way towards Samuel. She advances slowly while always darting her eyes around her. She doesn't know what to expect when she reaches Samuel and still suspects a trap to be sprung on her at any time. Her assumptions prove to be correct when she reaches the middle of the room, and nine vampires drop down around her.

Valencia takes in a deep breath and then lets it out slowly. She regulates her heartbeat and syncs her exhales between the firing of her weapons. Her concentration is now at its peak. Assured of their victory, the vampires attack.

Valencia tosses the small throwing daggers stored in her belt at some of the approaching vampires. Her accuracy is perfect as they penetrate deep into her targets' skulls. She then fires her wrist arrows continuously as she spins around in a circular pattern. One of her bolts enters the open mouth of a vampire, while the others pierce into the middle part of their necks. Valencia never had a use for aiming, but with results like hers, she never had to try.

Samuel is still groggy as he begins waking up and tries to focus on the shadowy images in front of him. Only the imposing brute, Samuel encountered earlier, and one other vampire stand on either side of Valencia, but she's confident this will soon be resolved. She lifts her wrist crossbows and fires them with outstretched arms from her sides. The bowstrings snap forward, but no arrows are loaded to be released. Her only folly was losing track of how many shots she took. "Shit," she says with vexation.

The vampires grin and dash toward her.

Valencia draws her sword with one hand and an arrow from her quiver with the other. She jolts the arrow into the eye of one of her assailants to halt him in agonizing pain. This allows her to put all her focus into the hulking one. She dodges and sidesteps to evade his claws, fists, and arms before dishing out a relentless series of slashes. The vampire's strength and behemoth stature fail him as Valencia's blade slices through his chest, head and finally his neck. She then forcefully jabs the tip into his heart to make the kill. She then turns her attention back to the second vampire by grasping the shaft of her arrow and pulling it out, along with the vampire's eyeball. His screams end with a decapitating blow from Valencia's sword.

His head continues to roll across the floor while leaving a trail of blood in its wake. Valencia can finally relax and breathe a sigh of relief. She allows herself to come out of her increased adrenaline state by closing her eyes and letting go of her intense trance-like state. When she reopens them, she observes Samuel staring at her with a look of complete shock and utter surprise. She sheaths her sword before approaching him.

"Valencia—"

"Be quiet, don't talk; don't move," she orders. Valencia puts both hands on his neck to inspect every inch of it. She then glares into his eyes and checks his pulse. She sighs and pulls out a bolt from her belt loop.

"Wait, what are you doing?" he asks nervously. She raises it above Samuel and then jabs it into the lock of his cuffs to break them loose. With his restraints off, Samuel rubs his sore wrists while admiring the carnage Valencia bestowed on his captives.

"You're lucky," Valencia begins. "Not only did you see your first vampire, but you also survived it." Samuel continues observing Valencia's handiwork.

"I thought you could only kill vampires by stabbing them in the heart?"

"No, anywhere in the neck or head will work."

"Are you sure?"

"They aren't moving, are they?!"

"No," Samuel admits softly.

"Come on now. Unless you want a souvenir." Samuel glances down at the eyeball resting near his feet.

"No, I'm good."

Valencia heads back the way she had come as Samuel follows close behind. He hasn't fully grasped the danger vampires pose and still shows hints of excitement towards entertaining his curiosities. Valencia; however, knows exactly what they are up against and prefers not to linger any longer than she needs to.

Valencia and Samuel exit the cave and welcomes the warm morning sun once again. Samuel glances back into the cave and then at Valencia with a smile.

"So, you hunt vampires?" His tone expresses his fascination with the concept.

"No, I only seek one." Valencia replies.

"You mean that Cerbera?"

"No."

"You should be a vampire hunter."

"Why?"

"Because you can help people."

"I don't like people."

"You helped me." Valencia glares at him and then turns away.

"And I already regret it."

Valencia turns to face the direction of Piketon and then the way to Middleton, as she silently contemplates returning to Piketon or confirming if the Merchant's tale was accurate.

"Are you going back to Piketon now?" Samuel asks.

Valencia finds herself in another situation that will prolong her attachment to Samuel. She knows he's going towards Middleton and her inquisitive nature beckons her to satisfy her curiosity.

"No, I need to make a stop in Middleton."

"Oh, that's where I'm going too," Samuel says with delight. She, of course, already knew this and gives him a retired look. "I suppose this makes us travel partners for a while," he continues. Valencia sighs and begins walking without responding. Samuel is more excited about having company than she is and happily joins her side.

Samuel is a talkative companion, and as he's also curious about vampires, relies on Valencia's experience with them by inquiring extensively on the topic.

"So, does a stake through the heart still kill a vampire?" he asks.

"Yes—but think about it. Why would piercing their hearts be effective when they don't need them? These are cognitive predators who use their minds to plan and trap."

"Okay, so then if their hearts no longer play a vital role in their existence, why would damaging it kill them?"

"It was explained to me like this. When a person transforms into a vampire the last bit of their humanity becomes trapped inside the heart. Piercing the heart releases the soul and destroys its evil shell."

"Hmm, interesting," Samuel says thinking about her explanations. "But now why do you think they didn't kill me like the other two back in town?" Samuel continues.

"If they're the same vampires as the ones back in town then they weren't ready to feed again. They were saving you for another night."

"Can you control what kind of vampire you become?" Valencia shoots a dumbfounded glance at Samuel.

"What do you mean?"

"Well, if you're a good person in life and then become a vampire. Do you keep those qualities?"

"Are you asking me if there's such a thing as a good vampire?"

"Yeah—"

"How did you survive this long on your own," she says with a sigh. "Look, there's no longer a sense of right from wrong once you turn. There are no consequences for your actions. Whatever you want you take. Whatever you need you indulge in until there's none of it left. You have an unquenchable hunger that drives you mad. Super strength, power, and speed that you never had before and no boundaries to limit you. No, you can't be good. You have been freed from moral choices." Samuel received a longer answer than he was expecting and spends the last leg of their journey thinking about everything Valencia had said.

Middleton is just over the next few hills, but the circling buzzards ahead signal a grim scene may await them. Samuel picks up on Valencia's worrisome expression as they scale the final hill that conceals the small town from their sight. The last push to the top confirms the rumors about Middleton. Valencia and Samuel see the aftermath of the barbarian onslaught for the first time in horror.

Middleton is a burnt heap of charred wood, and piles of rubble. Townsfolk are sprawled in the streets or hanging over fences and overturned carts. The slain women are topless or completely naked and lying in the mud, while other bodies are too maimed to be identified. The remains of these citizens, and the livestock are left to decompose disrespectfully in the sun. Middleton has been wiped from the pages of history; there's nothing salvageable to rebuild it and no one left to do so. This land will forever be cursed. Survival of these towns either depend on good leadership or brute force. Middleton had neither.

"Oh-my-God," Valencia says in a soft and distraught tone as she and Samuel walk along the dirt path. The men with spears through their torsos or axes in their backs along with the nude women, paints a disturbing image of what these people endured in their final moments. "Who could have done this?" he asks.

"I don't know, but we can't leave them like this," she says.

Valencia and Samuel cover the dead with hay and then lights each one on fire with their torches. After their task is complete, they respectfully watch the burning bodies from the meadow.

"This land will always be barren. No seed will ever grow. No home build will stand. This plot is tainted," Valencia explains.

There's just enough light left in the day for the return trip to Piketon and much too late for Samuel to venture beyond Middleton toward the unknown. Valencia has little choice but to accept his company for the remainder of the day. Samuel never went back to a place once he's left it, but with the thought of another hot meal, an ale and a bed, Samuel is willing to compromise. At least, that's how he tried to make it sound.

"I suppose I will see you back safely before I'm on my way," he says.

"Please, don't do me any favors," she futilely responds.

The duo proceeds back through Wytchwood Forest and only stops momentarily at a stream. Samuel cups his hands and bring the cooling liquid to his face to wash off the dried dirt and blood from his tumble the night before. He then brings the water to his lips and sips it. Valencia joins him after forging for two apples and hands him one of them.

"Thank you," Samuel says while smiling as he accepts her offering.

They continue their journey while crunching down on their

apples. Valencia may have found a way to keep Samuel quiet, but as soon as he devours his apple, he begins talking again.

"Did you always live in Piketon?"

"Only for the last twelve years. It was Townsend and his wife who took me in when I first arrived. She died two years ago from a fever."

"So, you live in the tavern?"

"That's right. I still live in the same guest room they gave me. Townsend is the only one in that town I care about."

"How did you come to know Cerbera?"

"Cerbera is like a spider to me. I don't like her, but she gets rid of the pests that plague our town; the unruly, uncouth, and immoral. That's why I never went after her; and we have a kind of truce."

Valencia recalls the first time she met Cerbera. She was still a teenager when she stumbled upon the vampire skulking towards a man staggering home. She quickly dashes behind some rising steps and squats down. Cerbera doesn't ambush or attack from behind, she walks around into his path and glares into his eyes. Valencia watches in horror but says nothing as she observers Cerbera's green eyes appear to glow. The man is put into a trance, and this is when she advances. She sinks her fangs into his neck and begins to slurp his blood. When she's done, she lifts her head and lets the man fall lifelessly to the ground. Despite Valencia's best efforts to stay hidden Cerbera finds her. She pounces on top of the landing and peers down at Valencia with a bloody grin.

"Do not worry little girl. I have had my fill tonight. And besides that, I prefer to hunt men."

"She puts all her victims into that trance," Valencia explains after telling her tale to Samuel. "I saw that same look on you at Townsend's. That's when I knew she had you singled out. When I delayed you, I think she just got impatient and decided to go after the first to leave."

"Why me though? She had plenty others around her."

"Because you were alone."

Vampires have no need to try to conceal their activities, but drifters still make the perfect prey. Their disappearance is expected and even if discovered, no one will bother looking into their death.

"It's been so long since I've lived in one place," Samuel begins. "The town I grew up in was very traditional, very strict, very religious and very superstitious. They feared witches and demons more than famine. I never saw any witch, vampire or werewolf kill anyone in that place, but I did watch a mob hang a girl who was prone to convulsions. They said she was possessed, some mistress of the devil. Her illness was unknown to them. I was young, don't know my exact age, but their fears became my obsession as I got older. I was too different from them, I guess. None rejected nor opposed when I was told that I would never have a home among them. That was five years ago now." Valencia feels she may have judged him too harshly. Samuel is just looking for a place to belong.

"Why did you come to Piketon?" she asks.

"Just happened to be at the end of the road I was on, I suppose. That's how everything is for me. I just pick a direction and go. Wherever I end up, whatever happens, doesn't matter. I only live in a single moment." The next few steps are traversed in silence until Samuel becomes more curious about Valencia's life.

"Where were you before Piketon?" She doesn't immediately reply or indicate that she's keen on sharing those moments with him.

"Someplace else," she somberly responds after the long pause.

"I'm sorry, I didn't mean to pry," Samuel says as he turns to look ahead while remaining quiet.

Valencia still remembers the exact moment that everything in her life changed forever, and the worst part of it was that she never saw it coming. With the experience now fresh in her head she might as well try to release some of the grief that has been building up for so long. She uncharacteristically confides her story with a stranger, but Samuel seems to be a worthy audience.

"I was nine when my mother killed my father," Valencia begins. "She poisoned his food in the belief that he was involved with another woman. My mother, not knowing much about poisons, still had some on her fingers as she fixed her own dinner, inadvertently killing herself as well. From then on, it was my seventeen-year-old brother, John who raised and cared for me. He did the farming and I cooked. He chopped wood while I washed the clothes. And for next six years that was my life—until everything about it would change—"

Evening becomes dusk as the sun sets over a tiny farmhouse. A fenced-in garden butts up to one side of the home and leaning garden tools, a chopping block and a barrel of water are on the opposite side. The plot sits just off the main road, that runs through town, and behind it is a vast untamed field. Valencia is carrying a basket of vegetables out of the garden when she looks up to see John returning home from his chores in town. Valencia remains standing with the basket in her arms while watching him approach with an unknown woman hanging on his arm. They never had guests and John never mentioned anything about meeting someone.

"Val, I want you to meet Isabella," John says as he admirably taps the top of her hand. "She's traveling with the gypsies who are passing through."

Many townsfolk are apprehensive about inviting a band of gypsies near their town, much less bringing one of them home. They are known to be immoral and unjust with a tendency to commit a variety of crimes, but to a young Valencia and her smitten brother, they are only performers.

"Hi there," Isabella addresses Valencia. "My, you have such a beautiful little sister, John," she says.

"Yes, just don't make her angry," John adds laughing. Valencia smiles at his joke and has come to accept Isabella's presence whenever John brings her by the house.

Two weeks pass, and she's now observing the two holding hands and cuddling just after sunset. Isabella and John are only seen together at this time, but Valencia believes it must be work that keeps them busy during the day. She spies on them from inside the house as John and Isabella share a kiss. She scrunches up her nose at the sight but keeps watching. Isabella lays her head on his shoulder and slides her fingers through his.

"We are leaving in two days," she regrettable admits.

"Can you not stay longer?" John asks.

"Only through marriage will I be released." John kneels down on one knee and takes her hand in his.

"Will you marry me, my fair Isabella of the traveling gypsies?" She giggles and nods her head.

"Yes." John rises to kiss her again. She puts her arms around him and hugs him tightly against her bosom. "I will take you and keep you forever," she whispers.

Isabella smiles to reveal the fangs that she had been hiding and then punctures his skin with a bite to his neck. John lets out a gasp but is unable to pull away from her hold. Valencia jumps away from the window and hurries outside, but there's nothing she can do to prevent this outcome now. Isabella continues taking in the blood from John's wound while ignoring Valencia running towards her. Once satisfied, she pushes John back, and he falls with blood seeping through his fingertips.

"Aren't you going to welcome me to the family?" Isabella says to Valencia before pouncing on top of her. "Young blood is so sweet." She pins Valencia down underneath her while holding her face down to keep her neck exposed. Valencia's only defense is to scream as long and as loud as she can.

Her wailing soon attracts several townsfolk over to investigate the disturbance with some of them arriving with weapons. A hunter pulls back his bow and sends an arrow into Isabella's shoulder blade. She leaps off Valencia with a snarl as she observes the mob of farmers and hunters closing in. She hisses and then retreats up into the night sky and glides away.

"Check the girl!" one of the men barks. The hunter sets his bow down and kneels in front of Valencia to inspect her neck, face, arms, and legs.

"Was she bitten?" the man asks.

"No, she was not touched," the hunter confirms. A farmer turns his attention to John as he gurgles and gasps while helplessly glaring up at the crowd gathering around him.

"Then get her out of here. She doesn't need to see this." The farmer raises his sickle while two men try to carry Valencia away as she kicks and screams.

"No! Let me go! Don't hurt him! He's all I got! Let me see him!" she pleads. The men around John know what must be done and it comes with a heavy heart.

"May the Lord have mercy on your soul," the farmer says somberly. Valencia's last sight is that of the sickle coming down and then John's bloody hand falling lifelessly to the ground.

Unable to live in her home any longer or around the same people, she leaves with a hard shell around her heart and a cold viewpoint toward the world. She arrives in Piketon to discover she will never be able to avoid vampires, but with the help of one man, she also learns more about them. Under Townsend's watchful gaze, she'll hone the skills needed to pursue the one that got away.

"I never got to say goodbye to him. I never went back. All I want is to avenge my brother's death. After I kill Isabella, my life will be complete," Valencia concludes her story.

"I traveled through a lot of places, and I've seen a lot of bad, but I've also seen some good too. It is out there; it does exist and it's worth finding. Once you lose that hope the world will devour you and spit you back as something that is unrecognizable."

"Have you forgotten where we just came from!? How can you say there's still good left in this world?!" Samuel can tell Valencia is fighting through a lot of different emotions and thinks it best to end the conversation without getting into a debate.

"I'm sorry, Val. Let's just get back to town."

The grassy meadow, swaying in the breeze, can now be seen through the last few trees; however, relief does not come when dark rising plumes of smoke are spotted. Piketon is burning. The duo halts in the field in horror before shock subsides and worry takes command. Valencia takes off in a mad sprint into town with Samuel at her heels.

The same band of barbarians who attacked Middleton were also responsible for this attack on Piketon, but they took the road that curved around the forest. The extra travel time this added onto their journey allowed Valencia to reach a safe distance before their arrival.

Piketon is much larger than Middleton and still has several buildings intact, but all of them have been ransacked and mostly likely anyone who was found inside did not escape. Fires are still burning in some parts of town while others have become smoldering ruins or flame-licked structures. Slaughtered townsfolk litter the streets and stoops of their homes or lie unseen inside buildings or concealed areas not visible from Townsend's tavern. Just like Middleton, Piketon will never again be inhabited.

Valencia storms through the door of the tavern to find men sprawled over tables or lying maimed and decapitated on the floor. Pools of ale and distilled beverages swirled with the blood of the fallen to add further disgust to the grotesque scene. Valencia threads diligently toward the bar and then scales over the counter. She covers her mouth after letting a gasp escape her lips. Townsend is sitting up against the back wall with a lowered head and a hatchet buried in his chest. His bloody sword, beside him indicates he must have wounded one of his attackers but failed at killing him. Valencia slowly bends her knees to kneel beside him. She tries her best to hold back the tears as she softly places her hand on his shoulder.

"Townsend—" she mutters. To her surprise he lifts his head and opens his eyes.

"Val-en-cia—"

"Shhh, keep your strength, you'll be okay. I'm here now," she says while caressing his cheek. He slowly shakes his head and reaches for her hand.

"Our homeland has new enemies. I know what brings them, what drives them. My kin came from the same area once, but we came to build towns. They come only to destroy."

The men Townsend speaks of were once citizens of ill-fated northern villages of foreign lands. Plagued by disease, starvation, and cold weather, they were forced to scavenge farther and farther for natural resources. They eventually discovered it was easier to take and kill than to grow and trade. Once driven by need they are now consumed by greed. They will never go back home. They have become warmongers.

"You must not seek them. Use your wits to avoid them," Townsend's breathing is labored, and wheezing follows every breath he takes. "Go now, you must not tarry." Townsend's grip loosens with one final exhale and then his head falling once more.

"Townsend?" Valencia waits for a response that will never arrive. Her tears can no longer be held back as they stream down her cheeks. She wipes her tears away and takes a deep breath before rising to her feet. Samuel observes her in a respective silence before glances away tactfully.

Valencia heads up to the second floor where the guest rooms are located. All the doors have been broken into and are hanging off their hinges, including her room. She cautiously enters to find it in shambles and completely ransacked with furniture broken into pieces or tipped over and holes and scorch marks deface the walls. She advances to her wardrobe that's tipped over and leaning against the wall and pulls the door open to find it completely empty. Every last weapon she had inside has been taken.

"Goddamn scavengers!" Valencia screams. She picks up broken chair legs and chucks them hard at the wall while kicking whatever her foot encounters. She finally sits at the foot of her bed with her forehead in the palm of her hand. She remains in this state for several moments before lifting her head as if suddenly remembering something important. She carelessly throws debris away from another area of her room and then lifts the rug and tosses it to the side to reveal the wooden floor beneath. She kneels and pries two of the floorboards up and then reaches in to take out a sword, some arrows, and a few throwing daggers. The creaking floor alerts her that someone has just entered her room. She stands up quickly with her sword extended in front of her. Samuel raises his hands while fixated on the tip of her blade inches from his nose.

"It's just me, Val," he says nervously. Valencia sighs and lowers the sword. She then flips the sword to have the handle toward Samuel.

"Here, you will need this." Samuel takes hold of the sword and curiously inspects the entire piece from pummel to blade.

"I never used one of these before. Anything I should know?"

"In the moment when you need it. You'll know exactly what to do," Valencia says while gathering up the other weapons she had recovered. "Get some sleep," she says while motioning Samuel toward her bed.

"This is your place; I don't want to intrude. I can go in another room."

"Nothing here—is mine anymore."

Valencia departs from the room and begins down the hallway toward the room at the very end; this one belonged to Townsend. His room was also invaded and pillaged, but she finds comfort being in a space that was his. She has lost everything for the second time. She doesn't know what to do or what to think, she doesn't even know how to feel. She picks up a tipped over chair, that's still intact, and sits down. She leans forward with her elbows on her knees and interlocking her fingers to rest her forehead against her hands.

Tears begin to run down her cheeks, and she swiftly wipes them away, but they keep coming. She continues trying to wipe the steady stream of tears away, but they don't ease up; she has lost the ability to control them.

"No, no. Don't cry. No, I said!" She stands up abruptly attempting to rebel against her emotions, but she succumbs to them none-the-less. She collapses to her knees, and completely overcome with grief, cries uncontrollably as she curls into the fetal position. She hates crying and feeling weakened with immobilizing sadness, but it becomes too much for her to avoid it. This is where she spends the rest of the night.

When morning dawns, Valencia sheds herself from the life she had in Piketon. She puts a torch to the alcohol-soaked wooden floor and watches the flames spread throughout the tavern. She leaves the burning building behind her and advances into the field where Samuel is waiting. He's now wearing a hooded coat that he found in one of the guest rooms along with Valencia's sword strapped at his side.

"This isn't going to stop, is it?" Samuel says.

"No." Valencia replies.

"What are you going to do now?" he asks.

"There's no place else left to go but north."

"I suppose I will be heading that way too then." Valencia gives him a weak smile. She never thought of Samuel as a companion she wanted to have, but they do have something in common. Each of them is the only person the other knows.

They begin their journey northward, uncertain of what lies ahead. Will there be towns to rest, or will those too be victims of barbarian attacks? Will vampires be stalking them?

Samuel knows all too well about walking into the unknown, but Valencia's displacement is not easily accepted. She now can understand Samuel a little better. Without a destination in sight or a concept of home, one can never truly feel accomplished. Neither knows how much they will need each other as their travels take them further north.

3

The Journey North

Northern towns have larger populations due to their prosperity, trade, and access to amenities, as well as better fortifications. The southern region, in contrast, are occupied by smaller towns and villages with little trading between them. As a result, they are populated less and must produce everything themselves.

Mid-autumn motivates the townsfolk, across the region, to begin harvesting their crops, stockpiling wood, smoking meats, and producing warm clothing before winter transforms the landscape into a barren tundra. Some of the trees are already starting to change into the reds and yellows as planning for the faires are underway. The bigger the town the more lavish the celebration, with games, music, and dancing for entertainment, and apples, roast pig, and ale to indulge the senses.

A lonely road curves through the countryside as Valencia's and Samuel's shuffling feet crunch the stones and dirt beneath their steps. They only stop to read the wooden sign that has the name of the next town chiseled into it, along with the distance:

GUILDSMITH – 15

It comes as a relief to them, knowing they will have a hearty meal and a warm place to stay the night.

Guildsmith is a fortified town with wooden walls and two watchtowers that stand inside the double gates. Each watchtower holds three archers who scout the surrounding countryside in shifts. Samuel and Valencia approach the open gate guarded by two soldiers with long pikes. The guards take notice of them as one holds his hand out to make them stop.

"What brings you to Guildsmith?" The guard asks.

"Just two weary travelers looking for food and rest, good sir," Samuel answers. The guards exchange looks and then waves them through.

"Bellwatch Inn is the fourth building on your right," the second guard says. Valencia nods and thanks him as they enter.

"At least this town has walls," Samuel softly says to Valencia while admiring the height, and how it encloses the entire town.

"I don't know if that will matter," Valencia replies feeling less secured than Samuel.

They follow the main road until arriving at a building with a symbol of a bell being rung above the doors.

"This must be Bellwatch," Samuel observes.

Bellwatch Inn is much like Townsend's Tavern. It's rowdy, but not out of control, and more crowded toward this evening hour than it was a few hours ago. Everyone just seems to be enjoying themselves with food, drinks, and conversation after a long hard day's work. Laughter and drowned out gossip, along with, mugs being placed on the solid oak tables and beer being poured from their casks fill the atmosphere.

Samuel and Valencia find two empty chairs at one of the long tables and settle in with their orders. Samuel has his usual pint of ale, while Valencia prefers her cider. With two rooms secured and food and drinks in front of them, Valencia finally begins to relax.

"I've been meaning to ask you something," Valencia begins.

"Go ahead," Samuel replies with a shy smile.

"How many places have you traveled to?

"Oh, I've been everywhere. Forests, mountains, highlands,

lowlands, coasts—"

"The coast?" Valencia interrupts with a slight hint of excitement. "You mean you lived by the ocean?"

"Only for a little while, but yes."

"I never saw the ocean," Valencia admits.

"It's very beautiful. The smell of the salty sea breeze, and the sound of the waves. Some say, once the ocean has made its way into your bloodstream it never leaves. It just becomes a part of you."

"I can picture it," she says with a faint grin. Samuel takes a gulp of ale and then sets it back down.

"A fisherman once told me, a farmer, doesn't dream about dirt, a logger won't dream about trees, but once you fish, you will always dream about the sea."

"Sounds like you've met a lot of people."

"Oh yeah, I probably met someone from every artisan and profession there is in the world." Samuel lifts his ale, "and after a few of these, everyone has something to say." He takes a long sip and then sets the mug down. "Or a lot of nothing in some cases," he continues with a contagious chuckle that includes Valencia.

"Why did you leave the ocean?" Samuel shrugs his shoulders while resting his eyes on Valencia.

"No one was there to convince me to stay," he says softly.

Valencia takes a sip of her cider while keeping her eyes on Samuel. He isn't like anyone she had met before. She still thinks him as an annoying and oblivious buffoon, but there's also something else about him that's uplifting and sensitive.

"Can I ask you something?" Samuel begins. Valencia's nod is her silent reply. "Why do you only drink cider?"

"That's easy. I consider ale to be for fat, smelly, piggish men with no class." Samuel has his mug lifted to his lips for a moment before setting it back down without taking a drink.

"Oh—" Samuel replies. Valencia smiles but says nothing more.

Someone starts playing a fiddle and then a flute joins in, followed by a lute. The upbeat music silences the room as everyone becomes drawn to the performers at the center table. The tempo becomes faster just as a beautiful young woman hops onto the table and starts dancing. Her skirt sways and spins around her while her breasts bounce rhythmically to her steps. The crowd have their drinks raised and cheer, clap, or drum on the tables with their hands as the jig continues and the woman's chest keeps the crowd's attention. Samuel soon finds himself joining in with the other hooting men.

"Yeah!" he cheers while tapping the table and bobbing his head in support to the girl's dance. Valencia glares at him before rolling her eyes and shaking her head. Just as soon as he started making a positive impression on her, a seductive, well-endowed, blond decides to dance on a table. The talented entertainers are rewarded with applause and standing ovations when their show comes to an end. Samuel looks at Valencia with a huge grin.

"This place is awesome." She stares back at him with a straight face. "What, you don't like music?" Samuel asks puzzled. The room returns to its former blending of voices and clanging mugs.

"This is a debauchery, if you ask me," Valencia responds while standing up. "I think I've had enough hootenanny for one night," she says before climbing the staircase toward her guest room. Samuel doesn't know what triggered the sudden change in her demeanor, but decides not to dwell on it, and raises his mug for one more round.

It's late when Samuel retires to his inn room while attempting to hum the jig he heard earlier. The modest layout consists of a square table with two chairs, a standing armoire, a large bed, and a nightstand. Samuel swings the French casement-style windows out to feel the fresh, crisp night air. The moonlight gleams a soft glow across the covers and the gentle breeze plays with the curtains. Samuel climbs into bed and falls asleep relatively fast.

The calming wind continues throughout the night until suddenly becoming a strong gust that sends the curtains up toward the ceiling. This burst also carries with it a feminine whisper that fills the room.

"Samuel—" Samuel opens his eyes and listens until he hears the voice again. "Come to me—" Samuel directs his gaze to the open window and sits up. The curtains flap and flutter as Samuel tosses the covers off and slides out of bed. "Come, Samuel—" The wind swirls around him like a cool embrace as he glares out the window.

He discovers Cerbera is standing in the street, just outside his room, with her head down and her cloak flapping in the wind.

She never looks up, but he can't deny the slight nudge, from an invisible hand, that beckons him to go outside to meet her. The impulse is too great to ignore, he straps his sword to his waist and leaves the room.

Samuel exits Bellwatch Inn and continues toward Cerbera who has not moved from her spot or looked in his direction. He stops a few paces from her with his hand on the pummel of the sword.

"I know who you are, Cerbera." Cerbera keeps her head down and giggles. "Why are you tracking me?" Cerbera giggles again while keeping her head down. Samuel tightens his grip around the sword and takes a step closer towards her. "I do not fear you. I will not fall for your lures." Cerbera suddenly jerks her head up and focuses her bright green eyes on Samuel. He immediately becomes hypnotized and immobilized when his eyes meet hers.

"Oh, but you have." Cerbera says in a seductive whisper. "You are not immune to my lure, my dear Samuel." She grins and closes the gap between them. She places her hand on top of his and gently guides it away from his weapon. She then puts her other arm around his neck and breathes into his face. Her breath enters through his nostrils and travels down his throat. "Give yourself to me," she continues in the same seductive whisper— soft and sweet. "Shhhh. Breathe my kiss." Cerbera slowly moves her lips closer to his. He thinks about resisting, but his thoughts betray him. Valencia was right. He cannot resist her lips; he can think of nothing else. "This cold night belongs to us." Cerbera continues while caressing his wind-swept cheeks. She presses him against her body and lowers her mouth to his neck. "Do not be afraid. I am here to cure your loneliness." Cerbera's fangs come out and she gently tilts Samuel's head to the side. Her game with him is finished, but an unfortunate event comes as an uncanny rescue with the arrival of several orange flames in the night sky.

A volley of flaming arrows sore over the city walls into each of the watchtowers and setting them ablaze. The archers yell out in agony as their inflamed bodies fall over the edge and splatter on the ground. Thunder collides into the front gates as they grown with every impact from the battering ram. Splinters and shattered shards of wood fly into town after every collision. The locking apparatus can no longer keep the gates shut and the next hit forces the gates open with an explosion.

Cerbera hisses at the interruption just as Samuel snaps out of his trance. The drawing of his sword forces Cerbera to leap back with a taunting smile. "Let's continue this some other time, darling," she says. The streets become a confusing tangle of barbarian marauders and frightened townsfolk attempting to escape. Cerbera takes advantage of the frenzy and disappears into the scrambling crowd of the panicked townsfolk, but Samuel takes off after her with sword in hand.

The barbarians begin setting fires to the nearby buildings and slaughtering those they meet, while others have already claimed their female prize and are carrying them away over their shoulders.

Valencia hops out of her inn room window onto the slanted roof with her wrist crossbows loaded in each hand. She fires at the invading barbarians in quick succession and with deadly precision as every arrow hits their intended targets in their heads or necks. She then notices Samuel chasing someone and focuses on the figure ahead of him. Cerbera glances back and appears to take delight in Samuel's tenacity of pursuing her. She flares her lips into a wide grin that makes her fangs reflect in the moonlight.

"Cerbera?" Valencia whispers to herself. She then tries to shout her warning to Samuel. "Don't give chase, Sam!" He doesn't hear her and soon both Cerbera and Samuel disappear behind a stable. "Damn it!" Valencia hisses between her teeth. She heads to the edge of the roof and then leaps off into a cart of hay. She rolls out of the cart and begins running after Samuel and Cerbera, but her pursuit is cut short when a barbarian intercepts her. He smirks and swings his battle axe at her, but she sidesteps away from the falling blade and then counters with her wrist crossbow that sends an arrow into his eye.

She whirls around only to find several more barbarians who have noticed her. She draws her sword as they close in and surround her. She parries their swords and ducks or dodges their attacks until she finds an opening to drive her blade into their abdomens or slice any unprotected area they may have. The confrontation only lasts a minute, but she fears this may have delayed her too long to catch up with Samuel and Cerbera now.

Cerbera leads Samuel out of town through a damaged section of the wall and into the fields where several town guards futilely fight the staggering numbers of barbarians. The army used to invade Guildsmith is far larger than the party in Middleton and Piketon, which makes guessing the true size of this enemy difficult, since their full force may not have been included. It's closer to the truth, that the armies are organized to attack several locations at once and based on the size of the targets. If that's true, then Guildsmith no doubt received the larger army. Outnumbered and overpowered, Guildsmith's outcome becomes bleak.

Cerbera disappears and then appears somewhere else amongst the warring sides. Samuel is unaware that Cerbera is deliberately leading him into a trap. She has no need to run from him; this is just another one of her games. He tries to keep his sights on her, but there are too many distracting movements, and he loses her again. He was so focused on trying to keep up with Cerbera that he doesn't realize he's now in the middle of a battle.

A nearby barbarian runs his sword through a guard and then turns his attention to Samuel. Samuel has never fought in battle before and doesn't have the skill to go head-to-head with this warrior. The barbarian lets out a mighty howl and then advances toward Samuel.

"Shit—" he says under his breath. Luckily, one of the few remaining guards jabs his pike into the barbarian's side. His bravery becomes his sacrifice when another barbarian severs his arm with a poleaxe. Cerbera leaps on the barbarian's back and digs her fangs into his neck that create a stream of blood jetting out of his veins.

Samuel becomes overwhelmed with the brutality of the barbarians, and with the lack of guards left standing, aid will not arrive a second time. Samuel's anxiety rises and his bravery leaves him. Cerbera's attack on the barbarian may have given him the only chance to escape. He takes it, and retreats from the fray, but he doesn't go unnoticed.

Underneath a twin-horned helmet is a face hidden by a long, wild, black beard. He's tall, husky, and clothed in animal hides and chain mail. He goes by the name, Hagathor, and he's the barbarian chieftain. His eyes observe Samuel leaving the battlefield as he places an arrow into his bow. He lifts the bow and takes careful aim while slowly pulling the bowstring back with a steady hand. Samuel's head is in his sights, and he has the power to ensure his arrow reaches it.

Samuel follows the outside wall toward the main entrance just as Valencia bolts out in front of him.

"What the hell is your problem, Sam!?" She yells while pushing him forcibly against the wall. Her action saves his life just as Hagathor's arrow swiftly strikes into Samuel's left shoulder. He glances at the festering wound before going into shock. His hearing becomes muted, and everything within his sights rushes away from him. Lastly, his legs go numb, and he collapses to his knees. "Sam!" Valencia's aggression immediately becomes concern as she grabs his healthy arm and helps him back to his feet. "Come on now!" Valencia orders while pulling him behind her.

Hagathor scowls at missing the fatal blow and quickly reaches for another arrow, but Valencia and Samuel escape around the corner of the wall before he can reload.

Samuel's temporary daze slowly subsides during his reliance on Valencia's leadership.

"Are they following us? Samuel asks while occasionally glancing behind him.

"The town might be a bigger prize than either of us, but just in case, we need to get to the trees. They won't be able to track us through them at night," Valencia suggests. Samuel leans his back against the wall while taking deep breaths and holding his throbbing shoulder.

"I need a moment, Val," he says with a grunt.

"We don't have a moment," she regrettably admits.

Samuel groans in pain as she inspects his wound by applying some pressure with her fingertips. She then snaps off the shaft with the fletchings without warning.

"Why would you do a thing like that?" Samuel grunts.

"It will make it easier for you to move," she replies.

Samuel still finds the shooting pain unbearable but forces himself to keep up with Valencia's pace as they near the edge of the wall. The trees are only a short sprint away but talking from the back wall stops them from making the dash.

Valencia puts her hand out to stop Samuel as both freeze their backs against the wall. Valencia signals Samuel to remain quiet and stay where he is as she carefully inches her way to peek around the corner.

Three barbarians have their swords drawn to the necks of two men and a teenage boy who are on their knees, while two others restrain two women huddling together. Valencia brings her head back and softly announces her thoughts.

"Damn, Damn, Damn."

"How many?" Samuel whispers.

"Five." Valencia shuts her eyes and then takes a deep breath before slowly releasing it. In the next moment she pops them open with a determined and focused glare.

"I don't know if I can fight them," Samuel says in a nervous tone. Valencia looks at him and replies calmly while drawing her sword.

"Then you can stay here and do nothing." Valencia leaps around the corner before Samuel can muster a response.

"Shit," he huffs. He knows nothing of war or combat but cannot allow Valencia to fight alone either. His avoidance of confrontations expires the moment he draws his sword and decides to follow her.

The barbarians raise their swords as they prepare to decapitate their prisoners. Valencia's sudden appearance catches the first invader by surprise, and the tip of her sword penetrates his sternum. The others turn their weapons on her, but Samuel's yell diverts their attention onto him. He drives his blade through the torso of one of the barbarian invaders just as Valencia takes her second kill. The three men, who were seconds from meeting their end, swiftly begin aiding Samuel and Valencia by punching or choking the two remaining men. Samuel pushes his sword into one of their chests just as the last one elbows the teenager off him and charges behind Samuel. He glances back but cannot retrieve his sword in time to block the oncoming attack. The invader thrusts his sword forward, but his blade stops inches from Samuel's spine. The man's sword slides from his grip, and he falls forward with Valencia's sword in his back.

Samuel lets out a sigh of relief before taking note of the blood dripping from his sword. A new sensation comes over him and a new identity is born. When one takes a life, they can never go back before that moment. It doesn't matter the reason or if it was deemed necessary or not. Samuel will never be the same.

The reunited family members hug each other overjoyed they are still together.

"Sorry to interrupt, but we can't linger," Valencia tells them. She safely leads the group into the trees without further detection as the flames of Guildsmith light up the night sky.

Their escape through the woods is soon slowed when Samuel begins to fall behind and his stride becomes smaller and smaller until he finally stops. A tiny moan exits his lips and his head snaps back. Wooziness sets in, and before he knows it, he's flat on his back with his view on the stars.

"Sam! Sam!" He hears Valencia's voice as the ruffling of underbrush proves his party is backtracking towards him. Her face enters his sights followed by the men they had rescued.

"Keep going. I'll catch up," Samuel softly says.

"Shut up, Sam; you aren't thinking clearly as usual," Valencia replies. She utilizes the glow from the burning town to look at Samuel's arrow wound. His shoulder appears black and green as the bruise shows signs of spreading toward his neck and further down his arm. "Dammit, I need to get this arrowhead out."

"Wait, you're supposed to give me a strong drink first, right?" Samuel says with concern.

"We don't have anything, Sam." Valencia replies.

"Maybe we should wait then."

"If we wait, you lose your arm, or worse."

"She's right. Men have perished with less injuries." One of the men points out.

"Can you hold him down—" Valencia asks while looking at him.

"Gavin, and yes I can," he replies.

"Thank you, Gavin."

"Alistair, find a stick or something." Gavin says to the other older gentleman.

"I'm sorry Sam, but this is going to hurt," Valencia warns. Alistair returns with a twig and places it into Samuel's mouth and then holds his jaw shut with his hands. Valencia glances at Gavin and he gives her the okay with a nod. She forces her fingers into the open wound in search for the arrow tip. Blood oozes out and Samuel kicks his legs up while letting out long and desperate muffled cries.

"Get his legs, Augustine," Gavin tells the boy.

Samuel tries to lift his arms and legs as he twists his body in agony, but the three men are able to keep him adequately restrained while Valencia widens the wound just enough to clear the arrowhead.

"I got it." She tosses it to the forest floor and then applies pressure as blood continues to gush out.

"One moment," Gavin says before getting up. "Sorry, Morgan," he tells his wife just before ripping one of her long sleeves from her blouse. He and Valencia help wrap it under Samuel's arm and over his shoulder and then ties it into a snug fit. Samuel spits the twig out of his mouth while taking several deep breaths.

"I need a drink," he says in an exhausted voice. Gavin and Alistair help him up while laughing at his comment.

"Thank you for everyone's help," Valencia says.

"It is us who should be thanking you," Gavin replies. "I guess we were never really introduced. "That's my father-in-law, Alistair, my son Augustine, my wife, Morgan, and my daughter Paige," he explains.

"Well, you know Sam here, and I'm Valencia." The group politely smile and nod their greetings before continuing marching again.

Gavin is a bit more familiar with this area than Valencia is and knows where to exit to put them back on the road. She lets him take the lead, while remaining close to Samuel as they follow close behind.

"I'm proud of you, Sam," she begins. "You did very well with a sword back there." Samuel chuckles.

"Thanks," he replies. "But I faked it. I didn't really know what I was doing." Valencia giggles.

"I won't tell anyone."

The first signs of light washes across the horizon and revels the long-awaited cobblestone road. The fact that time was taken in its construction means it was intended for more traffic and will lead to prosperous towns with more skilled laborers and possibly a trading center.

Gavin admires the morning sky with a bittersweet reverie. "Dawn for some, but not for all," he softly mutters. The tragedy that took place the night before is still unknown in this region and the ominous signs of it approaching is not yet foreseeable.

The nightly hike through the woods has everyone ready to rest when they discover a patch of rocky hills. Each finds a slab to sit down on while relishing the calming moment. Valencia notices blood seeping through Samuel's bandages and points it out.

"You're bleeding, Sam. We need to find a way to close that wound."

"Well, there is one way," Alistair begins. "But it's not pleasant."

The group helps to gather dried grass for kindling and find suitable rocks to create the spark. After a few attempts a tiny flame comes to life in their campfire. Gavin lightly blows on the flame while Alistair delicately feeds the spreading flame contained in the stone circle. Alistair rests Valencia's sword tip in the fire for several moments before retrieving it and heading towards Samuel.

"Can't we just let it heal on its own?" Samuel says nervously.

"You will lose too much blood or get an infection," Gavin explains.

"I really need that drink," Samuel whines.

Gavin and Valencia take hold of Samuel's arms as he prepares himself for the searing pain about to come.

"Sorry kid, but this needs to be done," Alistair says as he puts the tip to Samuel's exposed skin. Samuel hollers and squirms until the blade is finally lifted. "You will live," Alistair calmly jokes. Samuel once cursed boredom—now he's starting to miss it.

"Are you okay, sir?" Paige asks Samuel with a worried expression. He gives her a weak smile and nods as she shyly returns the grin.

The group returns to the road and continues their travels after resting replenished some of their energy.

"What happened to Cerbera?" Valencia asks Samuel softly so the others can't hear.

"The last time I saw her, she was attacking one of the barbarians," Samuel replies in the same soft tone.

"You shouldn't have chased her. That's what she wanted." Despite her best effort to keep the conversation between her and Samuel, another was eavesdropping.

"Who's Cerbera?" Augustine asks. Samuel and Valencia exchange relinquishing looks.

"Would you believe me if I told you she's a vampire?" Samuel responds.

"I haven't heard stories about vampires since I was a kid. But they were just stories." Gavin cuts in. Samuel just smiles. He knows there's no point in trying to convince them about something they have never seen.

"Forget about vampires. It's Hagathor that you need to worry about," Alistair adds.

"Who's Hagathor?" Valencia asks.

"He's the barbarian chieftain," Alistair answers.

"He's the one that shot me with that arrow. It had to be him. He was dressed differently than everyone else," Samuel recalls.

"Hagathor is a man who was destined to kill, starting with his own mother upon his birth." Alistair begins. "His grief-stricken father considered him a curse and abandoned him to his uncle, who ultimately raised him. He taught Hagathor to be ruthless in taking anything he wanted, whether it was food, gold, or women. You may want to avoid him if possible. He's skilled in war and kills with absolute joy. He has no moral ground to prevent him from enacting the most brutal and horrific acts he's known for. I do believe he knows no other way."

"How do you know all of this?" Valencia asks.

"A long time ago I was a soldier in King Ladislas' army," he explains. "I saw Hagathor when he was still a child during our time in Scotland. If I knew then who he was going to be today. I would have strangled the lad."

"It's best to leave this province while we still have the chance," Gavin concludes.

"You should come with us. There will be plenty of room on the boat," Morgan adds.

"There's no point in staying here any longer. Hagathor will spread like a plague and eat the land like a swarm of locusts." Alistair continues.

"He is the essence of death," Augustine chimes in.

"Won't you come with us? I hear Ireland is very beautiful," Paige asks almost talking exclusively to Samuel.

"You're sailing to Ireland?" he asks.

"Yes, on the western shore there is a shipwright and a friend who owes me a favor," Gavin explains.

"I've always wanted to go to Ireland," Samuel admits.

"Oh, good. So, then you will come with us?" Paige insists.

"I'm sorry, but I can't," Valencia says after thinking for a moment. "I can't forget. I can't forgive. I can't just start over. This is my war now."

"And I have agreed to lend you my aid," Samuel says while resting his hand on his pummel.

"It's okay, Sam. You should go with them," Valencia smiles reassuringly.

"Now who's the one not thinking clearly," Samuel replies smugly.

"With all due respect, neither of you have a chance to overcome what you are up against," Alistair butts in.

"I made a promise to someone," Valencia adds with the thought of John on her mind.

Paige lets the others gain some distance until she's walking beside Samuel. Valencia reads the girl well and speeds up her steps to allow her the opportunity to walk alone with him, but keeps a keen ear tuned to their conversation.

"I am a little disheartened that you will not be joining us," she begins. "I would feel much safer with you in our company."

"You are traveling with many brave people who will not let harm reach you," Samuel points out.

"Yes, but one more couldn't hurt now, could it?" Samuel chuckles as Paige continues. "How long have you been a soldier?"

"Oh, I'm not a soldier." Samuel pauses and then continues in a confident tone. "I'm more of a swordsman, really."

Valencia snickers and then quickly clears her throat to cover up her slip up.

"Oh, well, I must admit, a swordsman sounds way better than a soldier," Paige says enthralled.

"Yes, I mostly work alone. Going where I'm needed. Sleeping under the stars. I have sworn an oath to protect this land, and its people." Samuel's glorified explanation about himself presents Valencia with a difficult task of holding in her laughter. She keeps her arms folded with one hand over her mouth as this conversation is quite amusing to her.

"I wish I had met you under better circumstances," Paige says regrettably.

"That's how life works, I'm afraid. You are either ahead of your time, or behind it."

"Your wisdom is something I will forever cherish."

The parting of the two groups comes when they reach where the road splits in two directions. One path leads to the west as the other continues north. This is where choices need to be made and destinies are determined.

"If I hadn't a family I would join you, but I need to keep them safe," Gavin says while giving Samuel, and then Valencia, a hearty handshake.

"I understand," Valencia nods in agreement.

"I hope fate allows us to meet again," Augustine says.

"I look forward to that day," Samuel replies.

"My blessings go with you," Morgan adds as she warmly hugs Samuel and then Valencia. Paige walks up to Samuel and lands a small kiss on his cheek.

"Do visit us someday soon, okay?"

"I will dream of Ireland until I do," he says. Paige smiles, and then rejoins her family.

"Take this road as far north as it goes, and you will come to Ashborough. It's a few days journey, but you should find places to rest along the way," Alistair instructs. "Ashborough is heavily fortified, and their stone walls reach high above any building. Seek a man named Bartel, he's the steward. Tell him about this barbarian threat and six thousand strong will prepare for battle."

"Here, this will help your voyage," Gavin says after reaches into his pocket and takes out a few coins.

"No, you don't need to—" Samuel begins.

"Please, it's the least I can do," Gavin insists. He takes Samuel's hand in his and places the coins inside before closing his fingers. "And give Bartel my greetings, will you?" Samuel smiles and nods.

"May God watch over you," Morgan says as her family begins their trek on the western road.

"I don't think God can see us anymore," Valencia says reservedly.

"Of course, he can. He brought you to us," Morgan reminds her.

Samuel and Valencia face the northern road with nothing but wide-open fields in their sights. Adding to the complexity of their situation are an army of barbarians and a vampire clan who have no intent of letting them escape again. They have chosen the most difficult path, but for them, it was the only one to take. Samuel jolts his head forward with a smile. Valencia returns the smirk, and the two continue north.

4

Blood Moon Rising

A decrypted castle with a single tower is nestled near a rocky cliff surrounded by a field of dead trees. Long, thin blades of brown grass and spiny thistles are the only thing that grows in these Deadlands. No animal borrows here, and no road comes close to these forsaken parts. Only a long-forgotten race makes this their home. This is where the last of the vampires reside, feed, and nest.

The castle's interior is furnished with plain, shabby tables and high-back chairs that appear to have been out of use for many years. Dust blankets every surface and cobwebs occupy every corner. One might mistake this structure abandoned, but none who entered ever left to tell their tale. Unraveling runners and rugs sprawl across the stone floor, and tapestries, with the same family crest that were on the banners in the cave, decorate the cold walls. Hearths that hold no burning flames stand in desolate rooms that were once great halls, and the windows are all concealed with veils or curtains that no sunlight can penetrate. These dark corridors have memories of lavish, drunken gatherings filled with haunting music and orgies, but all is still now.

Climb the tower to its top, and one will enter a bed chamber that houses a canopy bed enclosed by scallop-edged curtains. Area rugs cover the floor and lit candelabras sit on either side of the bed. This room is occupied.

Cerbera strolls elegantly into her room followed by quickly darting her head to gaze into a darkened corner where someone is standing.

"You have been having fun without me," the female intruder announces before stepping into the amber light. She is one only Valencia would recognize. Her face hasn't changed since their last encounter, on the day her brother was killed. Cerbera smiles as she heads towards her bed.

"Not as much fun as I had hoped, my dear."

"Why do you tease him?" Isabella asks.

"I want to dominate him," Cerbera replies while stroking her bed covers. "I want him underneath me. I want to see his expressions change. I will keep him alive all night to ravish him until my body is satisfied, and then at dawn I will feast upon him."

"And would you deny your own sister the pleasure of having a taste." Isabella says while sliding up to Cerbera.

"You want me to share my meal?"

"I want you to share him," Isabella implies. "Not so much his blood, but his flesh." Isabella runs her fingers through the flames of the candelabra without sustaining any harm. "After all, it was I who first caught him."

"But it was I who found him."

"And he has evaded you." Isabella snuffs out one of the flames with her fingertips.

"He fancies a local girl," Cerbera says.

Isabella lies on the bed while leaning back on her elbows, and with her legs facing Cerbera. "He fancies what all girls have." She slowly parts her legs and places her hand on her crotch. "You just have to show it to him. That should make him forget any face."

"I do not know how he would escape both of us," Cerbera grins. "Very well. We can share him."

Meanwhile, Valencia and Samuel continue their voyage

northward without seeing evidence of a nearby town to spend the night. None-the-less, they chatter back and forth with little worry about the setting sun.

"I think Paige was smitten by you," Valencia jokes.

"Why do you think that?"

"I heard the two of you flirting."

"I wasn't flirting."

"Oh, no? Mr. Swordsman—" Valencia says, prolonging the completion of her words.

"What's wrong with swordsman?"

"Did you not hear her swooning? You are so brave— I wish we met under better circumstances—"

"That was just conversation," Samuel replies.

"Oh-my-God," Valencia sighs. "You really are oblivious."

"Why would she be interested in me?"

"It's only natural. She has identified you as her hero who rescued her. And as you are injured her nurturing instinct is to take care of you. You could have had your way with her."

"She's half my age," Samuel replies with a snicker.

"Does that matter?"

"Maybe not to everyone, but at least to me it does." Valencia smiles, but Samuel is too focused on the road ahead to notice her gaze.

"What really made you decide to stay, Sam?"

"I'm in your debt for saving me, remember?" Samuel says.

"I already said you didn't owe me anything." Samuel is silent for a moment and then looks at her.

"The truth is—this is the first time I'm doing anything with my life. For once I have a destination. What if this is what I was meant for?"

"What if you were really meant to go with them? What if you were only meant to know me until I lead you to that crossroad?"

"That could be true I suppose; but I don't want to be plagued with wondering about this day. The day I could've stayed and done something important. I can live with myself if I decide to act when I didn't have to, I can't live with myself if I failed do something when I should have." Valencia admires Samuel's audacious spirit, but she fears he cannot fully comprehend the severity of the situation that he's in.

"Cerbera has smelled your blood; she will never stop hunting you," she says. Samuel taps the sword strapped to his side.

"I'll be ready next time."

"How did that work out for you last night?" Samuel lacks a response to her question. "That's what I thought. You can't fight her if you can't draw your sword." Valencia notices a small farmland not far off the road with a secluded cottage behind it. "Come on, the best way to kill any vampire is from afar."

Valencia urges Samuel to follow her closer to the farmland. He isn't sure what she's up too but has learned not to question her logic. Valencia stops a few yards from the farm plot that's still in process of being harvested.

"Do you see that bale of hay over yonder?" A single bale of hay is about a yard from the front door to the cottage.

"I do," Samuel replies. Valencia retrieves her large crossbow and then pulls the bowstring up before handing it to Samuel.

"Do you think you can hit it?"

"Psh, of course," Samuel scuffs at the question.

Valencia hands him an arrow and then folds her arms while instructing him as he keeps up with her demands.

"Hold it up higher. Now bring it against your shoulder. Hold it tight. Concentrate on your target. Make sure it's in the middle of your sights. Hold your breath, then squeeze the trigger. Fire when ready."

Samuel follows her guidance and takes careful aim. When he thinks he has his target locked in, he holds his breath and then fires. The arrow flies completely past the bale of hay.

Inside the cottage is a pot of soup hanging over the flames of a fireplace, while an elderly farmer enjoys a bowl of it at his table. Samuel's arrow whizzes just past his window. He glances up to look outside, but gives the whooshing sound little thought, and returns to his soup.

Back outside, Samuel lowers the crossbow and frowns while Valencia continues looking forward in silence.

"I didn't take in account the wind. That's what happened there." Samuel tries to explain. Valencia slowly nods allowing him to think that she believes his excuse.

"Would you like to try again?" She resets the bow and then hands it back with a loaded arrow. "Your last shot veered to the right, so try to compensate by aiming slightly to the left." Samuel aims his shot again, holds his breath, and then fires.

The farmer lifts the bowl up to sip the broth.
CRACK!!
The startled man jumps up while spilling the hot soup in his lap and yelling out in pain. "What the bloody hell!" he exclaims. He glares up to see an arrow embedded in his door.

Outside, Samuel and Valencia bolt as fast as they can towards a patch of trees before they are spotted. They remain hidden behind their tree trunks and peek out just as the old farmer swings his door open with his soiled trousers still on. He scans the countryside but finds no one to blame or scold. "Goddamn Welshmen!" He yells out in frustration and then returns inside with the slamming of his door.

Samuel and Valencia lean against their trees while laughing hysterically.

"Maybe I should just stick to swords?" Samuel forces out when he's able to talk again. Valencia nods while still laughing.

"Yeah, I think that's a good idea."

The last ray of light fades from the horizon to send the countryside into an ultramarine darkness, and the cool autumn breeze plays with Valencia and Samuel's loose clothing. The moon has risen a deep red hue this night, and Samuel takes note of this rare occurrence.

"When the blood moon is high and bright the witches take flight and the vampires bite. Stay inside tonight for the witch's moon is in sight."

"That's a nice, creepy little rhyme. Where did you hear that?" Valencia asks.

"When I was young, my mother sometimes said that to me before bed, But I never saw it until now."

"No wonder you're odd," Valencia adds.

"We're all odd," Samuel replies with a smile. "And it's usually our parents' fault." Valencia snickers at his comment. After several paces in silence Samuel touches on another topic which was concerning him for some time. "Is it strange that we haven't come across any towns yet?"

"Not really, towns are sparse in these inner midland areas."

Valencia's answer makes sense as most people settled near the coastline to make it easier to fish and sail, while ports welcomed increased trading and ships from abroad. Rivers and lakes also provided good land for farming to sustain smaller towns and they sprouted up along these waterways; many of which led to the ocean and the larger towns. An occasional village will take development further from these bodies of water, but they depend on wells for their water supply and irrigation. Other inland areas are occupied by solitary families who fend completely for themselves or hermits who wish to be alone. Some trading routes exist, between these locales, to allow traders to make the required trek to reach prosperous towns. Unlike Samuel and Valencia, who have no supplies to set up camp, these merchants usually come prepared with their own food, water, and shelter.

Luckily, for Samuel and Valencia they are traveling on one such trading route, unluckily for them; however, is the fact they are ill prepared. This becomes even more prevalent when they chance upon a mysterious scene concerning a canvas-covered trader's cart with one missing wheel abandoned just off the road.

"What happened here, I wonder?" Valencia questions.

Samuel climbs into the back of the cart and begins rummaging around.

"What do you think you are doing?" Valencia calls after him.

"Just seeing what's in here."

"So, you're a thief now?"

"It's not stealing if it was left behind— it's recovering." Samuel replies.

Valencia was just about to snap back when she notices a figure darting across the road ahead. She focuses her view but doesn't see anything further to indicate another presence. It could be the night playing tricks on her or perhaps the wind. She doesn't allow herself to drop her guard and brings her hand up to grasp her sword. Samuel continues scavenging through the cart but there's little use for wheat and barley without preparation and production facilities.

Valencia catches another glimpse of a shadowy figure rushing past her peripheral vision.

"Sam, get out here," she orders, feeling as if they are now being hunted. Her assumption becomes undeniable when several blurry figures dash across the field. She draws her sword and prepares herself for an imminent vampire ambush.

"Sam, we aren't alone!" Samuel finally jumps out the back of the cart.

"What did you say?" He asks unable to make out what

she had said, but before a reply can be uttered, a vampire leaps on top of the canvas cover behind Samuel. The cover collapses underneath the force as the vampire hisses and then lunges toward Samuel. He narrowly dives out of its grasp and lands on his stomach. The vampire makes another attempt toward him, but Valencia thrusts her sword into his back with the point exploding out where his heart is. Samuel swiftly picks himself up and draws his blade. Valencia keenly studies the vanquished vampire clad in furs and two fresh puncture marks on his neck.

"I think this is our merchant, and he hasn't been dead long," she observes.

"That means this wasn't an accident—it was an attack," Samuel confirms.

Valencia turns back to the road but stops abruptly. Samuel follows her gaze to see five vampires standing in front of them. Either instinct or worry gives Samuel an uneasy sensation to peer behind him as well. Another group of five vampires stand ready to advance. "We are in a very bad place, at a very bad time," Samuel says in a yielding tone.

After surrounding their victims, the two groups of vampires rapidly close in. Valencia fires her wrist crossbows on her approaching mob, but her arrows miss the rampaging vampires and are easily dodged by these agile hunters. This breed of vampire isn't like the ones she fought before—these are faster and seasoned aggressors. She fires another arrow into the group. The leading vampire leaps up to avoid the arrow, but the one behind him doesn't react in time and is struck in the chest. One is all she eliminates before their foes enter melee range.

The duo slice or jab their swords at the vampires, but a successful attack cannot be landed. Samuel quickly becomes overpowered by three vampires and falls to the ground. His sword extends through the back of one of them when it jumps on top of him. Samuel desperately uses the impaled vampire as a body shield from the other two clawing at him.

"Sam!" Valencia kicks her vampire attacker backwards and then turns around to stab one of the vampire's preoccupied with Samuel. She leaps up and high kicks another vampire coming up from behind her by pushing off her sword, which is still inside the defeated vampire, this acts as her anchor.

She pulls her sword out just in time to stab the vampire she had just kicked back. Samuel crawls out from under his kill, but his sword is still embedded in the body that lies between him and the other vampires. He could try to make a dash for it, but his opponents grow tired of waiting and charge him instead.

"Sam!" Valencia calls out. He looks up just in time to catch her sword by the hilt. He wastes no time to spin the blade down and swoop it around to slice the throat of one vampire.

Valencia must resort to unarmed combat and prepares to defend herself. She spins a kick to a vampire and then jabs her palm into his chest. She rotates her crossbows into her hands and then fires continuously. The close proximity of her opponents gives them less time to react, and two vampires fall with arrows in their chest and head.

Samuel ducks his assailant's sweeping claws and then thrusts his sword into its heart. Valencia flips her vampire over her back and hurls it toward Samuel, who jabs his sword down as soon as the vampire hits the ground. His quick action skewers his target with fatal precision. The last vampire soars toward Samuel, but Valencia fires her last wrist crossbow arrow into the middle of the vampire's forehead.

Samuel and Valencia exchange relieved smiles. He hands her sword back and then kicks his previous kill over to retrieve his own sword.

"Well, that wasn't so bad," Samuel says optimistically. Just then, seven vampires dart inward from the field to encircle them.

"Did anyone ever tell you that you talk too much?" Valencia says with a retired sigh.

"Once or twice," he admits.

Valencia slides her fingers through the holes of her throwing daggers and then flicks them with lethal accuracy. Her attack sends two daggers into each of her two targets' skulls. The remaining five are fought with swords as Samuel and Valencia stand back-to-back. Samuel has become adept with his blade techniques while avoiding incoming blows. Valencia's skills aren't limited to her weapons as she utilizes her swift kicks to stun or knockback her foes to present openings to jab her sword. This fearsome and resilient duo succeeds in culling another threat, but Samuel doesn't dare celebrate this time. It wouldn't have mattered anyway, as the silence is soon broken by someone sarcastically clapping slowly.

"That was im-press-ive," Cerbera says as she glides toward them in midair. "You dispatched my entire hand-picked army." Her feet touchdown several paces away as she continues. "If I wasn't so turned on right now, I would be very upset." Valencia points her sword at Cerbera, but she smiles in response. "I won't harm you, girl," she says. "However, the same cannot be said for your friend."

"I will not stand idle and let you kill him!" Valencia barks.

"My intention was never to kill him, but to keep him. To make him like us."

"I can't let you do that either."

"My, how you have grown," another voice comes from above them. Valencia is overwhelmed with disbelief and anger when she spots Isabella floating effortlessly down to take her place next to Cerbera.

"Isabella—" she detestably utters through her teeth.

"The last time I saw you," Isabella continues. "You were screaming and in tears. Now here you are so forceful and determined," she taunts.

"You killed my brother, you gypsy whore. I will avenge him tonight!"

"I didn't kill your brother. As I recalled, it was the farmer with the sickle who killed him. I was only trying to make him mine forever; and, since we're on the subject, I was never with the gypsies. That was just a fib I knew no one would try to prove."

"You disgust me greater than any pox or rotting remains," Valencia scowls.

"It seems she has made up her mind to kill you, dear sister," Cerbera announces.

"Sister?" Valencia repeats dumbfounded.

"Yes, did you not know? We were alive together," Cerbera begins.

"Then we died together," Isabella continues.

"And now we rule together," Cerbera concludes.

"Do you think you can keep him from our grasp? Just one tap from my fingertips and all men's limbs become stone. My sister has the same effect with her glance." Isabella reveals.

"Our treaty comes to an end. If you stay in our way you will no longer be safe from me," Cerbera tells Valencia.

"It's too bad he was unconscious when we had him last,"

Isabella says disappointedly.

"You see, we like to play with our humans first. It's no fun if they aren't awake," Cerbera adds.

"Why me?" Samuel demands.

"Your blood is rare. To us, it is the same as gold is to you." Cerbera takes in a long, deep breath as she smells the air. "You smell like a fine, aged Cabernet. Tart, smooth, and with a lingering finish."

"John had the same blood. Perhaps, I shouldn't have romanced him for as long as I did," Isabella adds.

"I will cut your voice from your throat!" Valencia yells, but it only amuses Isabella further as she giggles.

"Why resist us, Samuel? Why deny yourself what you've always wanted?" Cerbera says as she turns her attention to him.

"I never asked anything from you," he replies.

"I saw it in your eyes when you looked at me," Cerbera's words are soft as every syllable is given more time on her tongue. "I felt it in your heart when my hand touched yours. You are lost."

"Lost among the rich, who have no interest in you," Isabella chimes in with the same technique of drawing out her words. The two sisters continue while alternating their verses.

"Lost among the brave, who have amazing stories to entertain their guests, but you have none."

"Lost among the beautiful, who never had to experience rejection, but you never belonged."

"Lost among the forgotten, and here is where you become one of us."

"Don't listen to them, Sam." Valencia tells him. Cerbera fixates her green eyes into Samuel's, and he makes the mistake to look back. Her gaze entraps him, her voice flows through his bloodstream, and his essence is slowly pulled out of him. Everything she does urges his mind and body to surrender.

"I can give you freedom; I can give you immortality. Strength—speed—to see everything—to hear everything." Cerbera's soft tone and slight sway of her hips and arms make her spell more potent.

"To fly limitlessly; to give into all of your desires without consequences," Isabella joins in on the beguilement of Samuel.

"To love endlessly—I will share with you, my bed." Cerbera's hypnoses has put Samuel into a deep trance.

"Don't listen, Sam!" Valencia yells noticing his blank stare.

"We will taste your blood," Cerbera continues as she now begins to advance along with Isabella.

"And a leader for our clan you will become." Valencia snaps her fingers in Samuel's face, but it has no effect. The two vampire sisters continue to stalk closer. Valencia stands in front of Samuel with her sword pointing outward, but the sisters are unfazed by her.

"Inside our loins—" Cerbera begins.

"We will be one," Isabella finishes. The sisters reveal their fangs and stretch their arms to grab him.

"Damn it, Sam!" Valencia whirls around and slaps him across the face. This act finally takes him out of his passive state. "Run Sam, you need to run!"

"I can't leave you to fight them alone."

"Their spells won't work on me."

"But they're still vampires."

"Run, I said!"

Valencia pushes Sam into a sprint and then follows close behind him as they scatter across the open field toward the forest ahead. The sisters pursue them as Valencia scurries to load the arrows into her wrist crossbows while running. "Keep running, Sam. Don't stop! Don't look back!" She employs.

Valencia glances back to fire an arrow at Isabella, but she avoids the projectile and continues after them.

Cerbera soars up into the air and then lands beside Valencia. With a swift push Cerbera's hands collide hard into Valencia's ribs and shoulder. She is sent flying across the field and rolling away until she's able to brace herself. She jolts her head up to notice Samuel entering the forest with Isabella and Cerbera directly behind him.

"Sam—" she whispers in concern.

The disturbance of leaves and the breaking of twigs and branches occur behind Samuel as he runs through the forest without looking back. He continues running until the ground ahead of him becomes the edge of a rocky cliff. He immediately stops himself and looks down the thirty-foot drop where a gushing waterfall pours into the pond below. He turns around but isn't given an opportunity to find another escape route. Cerbera and Isabella have caught up and are now in front of him.

"You can't lose us in the forest," Isabella claims.

"This is where we were born," Cerbera adds.

"Where's Valencia?" he demands.

"Don't make us jealous," Isabella says before placing her hand on his chest. "You are ours." Just as before, Samuel becomes paralyzed. Isabella and Cerbera take each of his arms just as Valencia bursts through the patch of shrubs while firing her arrows. Isabella gives Samuel a slight push before she and Cerbera dart up into the sky unharmed. Samuel is unable to shift his bodyweight or grab onto anything to prevent him from falling. Valencia catches a short glimpse of Samuel falling backwards before he disappears from her sights.

"Sam!" She dives off the cliff and descends after Samuel. She collides into him and wraps her arms around him as they barrel roll in midair before splashing into the water. She swims to the surface with one arm and kicking her feet while pulling Samuel up with her other arm.

She breaks through the surface of the water and quickly scans her surroundings while pointing her available wrist crossbow in every direction she inspects. It seems the vampire sisters did not follow them.

Valencia drags an unconscious Samuel onto the shore and then leans over his torso with her arms and chest to keep him warm. She sighs and combs her long black hair back with her fingers. The fear that these matriarchal vampires will eventually get Samuel has already bore itself inside her thoughts.

The morning sun glimmers through the sparse tree canopy and shines on Samuel still asleep on the forest floor. Valencia had almost completely covered him with the fallen autumn leaves to keep him warm throughout the night. The light creeps into his eyelids and turns his blindness into a red void before he slowly begins to open them into this brightness. All the shapes and colors of the sky and forest pour into his sights, and he sits up. His blanket of leaves falls around him as he slowly comes to a stand. He can't recall how last night ended but replays the events leading up to his last memory of Valencia leaping through the bushes.

Cerbera's presence is still strongly felt; everything about her has made a home in Samuel's mind. Her eyes, her voice, her body, and her touch. He knows she's a threat but cannot deny a mysterious pull towards her. He is wholly infatuated with her. None of it makes any sense to him, his logic and his desires are at war with one another, and which one will be obeyed has yet to be decided.

Isabella also presents another level of potency. Samuel may be able to avoid Cerbera's gaze, but Isabella's touch can reach him at any time. Their voices echo in his ears during the day and their bodies dance before him when his eyes shut for the night. He feels a slight inclination to give in, to give up, to take their offer. What Samuel fears more than any army or monster is knowing his affliction may not allow him to protest when they come for him next. A slight glimpse at Valencia, washing her hair in the pond, is the only thing motivating him to continue resisting.

Valencia tosses her hair back and then turns to notice Samuel watching. He immediately adverts his eyes up into the trees to act as though he wasn't paying attention and misses the small smile she lets escape.

Valencia approaches one tree and circles around it while looking up. She then advances to another one and inspects it the same way.

"May I ask what you are doing?" Samuel asks.

"These trees will tell us which way Ashborough is," she replies.

"Do you talk to trees?"

"No, young Samuel, I'm looking for moss. It only grows on the north side; ergo, showing me the direction of Ashborough." She finally locates white moss on the next tree and shows Samuel. "Aha, you see? We have our heading," she says while pointing ahead of her. Samuel looks at the moss and then back at Valencia.

"I knew that. I was just, ah, testing you."

"If you're going to lie, Sam—at least try to sound convincing."

"That was, wasn't it?"

Valencia may not say it out loud, but she's beginning to enjoy Samuel's company. He may be naive, innocent, and oblivious, but he also has an adventurous spirit, passion, and sympathy. He has shown her that hope doesn't live in a place, or a moment, or even a person, but all three at the right time.

Luck allows them to exit the forest on the road near a sign that reads:

ROTHBURY – 7

The relief of a town finally within their reach will guarantee a meal, and sleep in a warm bed. With plenty of light left in the day, there's also time to visit the shops and gather more supplies. The restless slumber, on the forest floor, was far from refreshing, and the long hike and exhausting fight, the night before, have left both Valencia and Samuel with little energy for much else. Their journey to Ashborough will have to wait until tomorrow, as this opportunity can't be passed up.

Rothbury, like Guildsmith is protected by a wooden wall and gate, but unlike Guildsmith, ramparts allow guards to patrol around the entire town. It's also larger and more commerce oriented. Visitors will first notice the blacksmith shaping and selling his armor and weapons, and a fletcher, with finely crafted bows and arrows on either side of the main path near the town's gates. Further along the road is a carpenter offering furniture pieces, and a cooper with his barrels on display. Across the street from them are a weaver with colorful clothes and linens, and a tanner with leather for sale. At the town's center is where the food vendors can be found. The butcher shop and fishmonger showcase their hanging meat or daily catch, and the bakery, with freshly baked loaves of bread, and cheesemaker encircle the cobblestone plaza, along with, the tavern. The streets are flooded with townsfolk, as well as laborers and every store or workshop are fully stocked and waiting for customers. On the other side of town are the residential homes and a stage that provides entertainment.

Valencia and Samuel stand just inside the gate to quickly assess their surroundings and agree on their objectives.

"I'm completely out of daggers and arrows," Valencia begins. "I don't think that has ever happened to me before."

"We should pack some food for us too," Samuel adds. Valencia holds her hand out to Samuel.

"How much do we have?" Samuel digs into his pocket and takes out all the coins he has, including those he had received from Gavin. He then places the small pile in Valencia's hand without bothering to count them. She separates them into two smaller piles before handing Samuel one group and then keeping the rest. "Alright, you get the food. I'm going to talk to the blacksmith and fletcher. Meet me in the tavern when you're done."

While Samuel heads toward the center of town, Valencia visits the fletcher, who's in process of shaping a recurve bow. She sets the large crossbow on the counter as the man leaves his work to meet her. She unstraps one of her wrist crossbows and then sets it next to the larger bow. "I need arrows that will fit both of these." The fletcher picks up the wrist crossbow and inspects it with greater interest than the large bow right beside it.

"This is quite a contraption. I never saw anything like this before," he says.

"It's custom," she says with a smile. He squeezes the trigger making the bowstring snap forward and the bottom cartridge to rotate while bringing the bowstring back into firing position. "Are these self-loading?" he asks with amazement.

"Yes."

"An automatic crossbow—I didn't think this could be possible. Where did you acquire this?"

Townsend had gifted her the crossbows, but where, or how he got them was never explained to her.

"A friend."

"Well, I have the arrows for your larger crossbow right now, but I will need to craft these smaller ones. Would you mind if I kept this here for measurements?" he says holding the wrist crossbow up.

"I suppose that will be okay. Thank you."

Samuel is quick to get his errands out of the way so he can finally sit down with his long overdue mug of ale. He closes his eyes and lets the ale pour through his lips and swish around his mouth. He swallows the long awaiting gulp as more continue to take its place. He gently lowers the half empty mug on the table with a huge grin and a long sigh. "Blissful—" He suddenly becomes aware that people at the nearby tables are intensely focused on him. He brings the mug slowly back to his lips feeling a little bashful from attracting attention.

Valencia steps into the tavern and scans the area until she spots Samuel. She makes her way to him and is immediately welcomed with a foolish grin and a nonsensical wave. She gives him a perplexing look before sitting down and observing two empty mugs next to him and a third in his hand.

"Really?" she begins. "I hope you bought food before spending everything on ale."

"I bought meat—bread—and cheese."

Valencia picks up the knapsack at Samuel's feet and rummages through to see for herself. She then closes the sack feeling satisfied of his choices.

"Did you get everything that you needed?" Samuel asks.

"I have my orders in with the blacksmith and fletcher. I'll pick them up tomorrow before we leave."

Samuel finishes his third ale and then reaches into this pocket. "I think I have enough for one more," he slurs.

"Let me see," Valencia says while holding her hand out. Samuel hands his last two coins to her. She tosses her smaller coin on the table before stashing Samuel's coins in her pocket. Samuel chases the rolling coin on the table and looks at it knowing it has less value than the ones Valencia kept.

"What's this for?"

"For you to get a room," she replies.

These tavern rooms provide guests with a bed, nightstand, and a table with a set of chairs; the inclusion of a fireplace also puts these quarters a grade above many others. Valencia and Samuel are staying in neighboring rooms and mutually decide to turn in early. Samuel waits for Valencia to close her door before walking into his own room. He undresses to his underwear and then jumps into bed. Tired, and aided by the alcohol in his system, he falls asleep almost immediately.

Valencia remains sitting on the windowsill while glaring outside until the sun sets. The luxury of sleep is deprived from those who mistrust the night. She can't help but ponder if the barbarians are planning to attack here tonight, or if Cerbera and Isabella will attempt to nab Samuel again. She stands guard looking for any sign of a looming threat as the hours slowly tick by. Her head begins to nod and her heavy eyes close, but she shakes herself awake at the slightest hint of falling asleep. She gradually begins to drift off again without the ability to resist. She slumps over and succumbs to her exhaustion.

5

Ashborough

Thick clouds roll in during the night to hide the moon, and heavy rain soon hammers down on the rooftops, followed by a dense fog blanketing the sleeping town. Raindrops stream down Samuel's window as he sleeps through the rainstorm. The fog continues to creep across his window and gather into an opaque mass that denies all the ability to see beyond it. The window then begins to open by an unseen force as the cool wind rushes in to ruffle the curtains. Samuel remains sound asleep and unaware as Cerbera breaks through the fog and easily glides into his room before gently touching down on the floor. Her footsteps are completely silent with not even the floorboards creaking underneath her weight as she steps closer toward Samuel's bed.

Isabella is next to pierce the concealing fog and enters the room without making a sound. Cerbera takes hold of the bed covers and pulls them down to the floor to expose Samuel in his underwear. Isabella slips out of her gown and stands naked beside

Samuel, who now begins to feel the chill of the night. Cerbera pulls her gown off and lets it fall to the floor just as Samuel opens his eyes. Isabella places her hand on his chest to restrict his movement and escape from the bed.

"Shhh, we don't want to wake up your companion now, do we?" Isabella says with a grin. She takes his hand and places it upon her breast. "We will take your warmth."

Samuel can only see, hear, and think as paralysis prevents him from running or yelling. He tries to imagine Valencia running through his door, but she never does. Cerbera pulls his underpants off and then slides her fingers up his legs and past his thighs. Isabella forces his hand to her crotch and makes him rub her as she moans softly. Cerbera slithers her way up Samuel and straddles him before claiming her dominance and forcing him into submission. She enacts her will and takes him when she feels her desire to do so.

Samuel's warmth dissipates from the entire length of his body as soon as she forces him inside her. Her touch is cold, and her insides feel like a solid block of ice with tiny needles poking him continuously. Every thrust she makes sends several tiny stabbing sensations into his lower region. Cerbera reveals her fangs and lets out a series of hisses while Isabella joins her. He feels hunted by an army of serpents as panic and anxiety set in. He can't refuse his body's natural reaction, but his release only adds to the intense cold and needle-like piercings in his pubic area to travel throughout his body.

"Are you all done?" Cerbera asks. "As for me, I'm just getting started." She opens her mouth wide and quickly digs her fangs into Samuel's neck while shaking her head violently and digging her nails into his chest. Isabella removes his fingers from her and then sinks her fangs into his wrist. Blood flows down his arm like a raging river, and gushes from his neck and chest, but he can't scream or yell. The attack seems to be everlasting as his body becomes weightless and a sensation of him floating takes over. He feels himself being bathed in his own blood and knows that he's dying.

Samuel finally let's out a bloodcurdling scream and awakes with his eyes wide while gasping for air.

Valencia jolts awake from her place at the window after hearing Samuel's scream. She jumps off the sill and grabs her sword fearing the worst.

"Sam!? Sam?" She yells as she barges into his room. Samuel falls out of bed and hits the floor with a thump. Valencia hurries to where he fell and finds him leaning against the wall while breathing heavily.

"What's wrong, Sam?" He frantically moves his hands to his neck and chest and then holds them up checking for blood in the moonlight. Outside shows signs of a drizzle, but no fog is present. Valencia lays her sword on his bed and then kneels beside him and grips his shoulders. "Calm down, Sam, calm down. You're okay."

"I couldn't wake up," he admits while hyperventilating. "I couldn't move. It felt so real, and I couldn't make it stop," he says hysterically.

"It was a dream. I know how dreams can be, but you're safe now," Valencia says trying to soothe him.

"They're here. They know I'm here," Samuel tries to squirm away from Valencia and flailing his arms. She puts her hands on his cheeks to frame his jawline and forces him to look at her.

"Look at me, Sam. I'm the only one here." She puts her arms around him and gently rocks him in her arms.

Valencia and Samuel somehow manage to fall asleep again while embraced on the floor. The two sleep the remainder of the night without waking until the morning sun illuminates the room. Samuel was just a stranger in a strange place before Valencia, and now he's at war with barbarians and vampires. He wanted a story to tell, and now he has one, but will he live to tell it?

Samuel waits just outside the town gates with the knapsack of food over his shoulder until Valencia gathers her orders and joins him. The road ahead always looks daunting and endless. Samuel has been walking aimlessly on roads like these for a long time, but this one feels different. It feels like there's no way a satisfactory outcome can be reached. He's tired of meandering and desires a stationary home to settle down. His nomadic lifestyle robs him of a sense of stability, but exilement is all he fears he will know.

Valencia is once again fully stocked with arrows and daggers as the two begin the next leg of their journey. They avoid the long trading routes that curve around the forests and rely on the woodland path to cut their travel time down.

"I'm sorry about last night," Samuel says, as they proceed on the narrow passage.

"Why would you feel sorry 'bout that?"

"It's silly to let a dream have such a big impact on you."

"Your mind doesn't know you're dreaming. Of course, you're going to have a reaction to it."

"Well, I feel foolish thinking about it now."

"What was your dream about?" Samuel hesitates before explaining part of it.

"Cerbera and Isabella were tearing me apart with their fangs and fingernails," he responds, but leaves the rest of the details concerning his dream out.

"When I heard you yell, I thought I was the one who was having the nightmare. I didn't want to arrive knowing that there was nothing I could do. I already went through that once."

"You heard me from your room?"

"I'm a light sleeper," she answers with a grin.

The woodland pass was easy to traverse, and the grassy knolls of the countryside, soon begin to show beyond the last patch of trees. The trek may have been gone smoothly, but for every fortune, there is a setback close by. Rising smoke from a campfire drifts above the trees to alert Valencia that something unexpected has been encountered. She immediately grabs Samuel by the sleeve and pulls him down behind the bushes as the two peer through the trees. Six barbarians have gathered around the fire while passing a platter of freshly cooked game amongst them.

"Damn it," Valencia whispers. "These bastards are everywhere."

"Might be a scouting party," Samuel says in a hushed tone. "Which means there could be more nearby, maybe even Hagathor."

"Yeah, but are they going to a scouting point or coming back from one?"

"Either way their report must not arrive to the others," Samuel suggests. Valencia smirks and rotates her wrist crossbows into her hands.

"Let's give them hell."

Samuel exits the woods while looking down at his feet, and with his hood up to conceal his identity. He advances toward the camp with a steady pace, and with a clear desire to engage. The barbarians stand with weapons ready while shouting in an unknown tongue. Samuel doesn't acknowledge them until they begin to charge; he stops walking and lets them come to him. Hiding under his cloak are his and Valencia's swords strapped to either side of him. He closes his hands around their handles and draws them swiftly while duel wielding them rhythmically.

WHOOSH! WHOOSH!

A succession of Valencia's arrows flies out through the trees to pierce the necks and skulls of two barbarians.

Samuel parries the blades aimed at him and then turns his torso sharply from side to side to slice his foes across their mid sections or across their chests. He doubles back around and pushes both swords into the chest of another barbarian.

Valencia's arrow catches up to the last enemy who's attempting to retreat. The bolt rushes past Samuel's ear and hits its mark in the back of the last barbarian's skull. Samuel pushes the hood off until it rests back on his shoulders. Valencia soon joins him as she rotates her crossbows out of firing position.

"Nice work," she says with enthusiasm. Samuel hands her scabbard and sword back and she takes it then secures it to her waist.

Samuel and Valencia begin rummaging through the barbarians' belongings that are lying around the campsite. Valencia finds some smoked meat and rolls and takes a whiff before giving it an acceptable nod. Samuel finds another sword and scabbard nearby and inspects the fine, smooth, shiny blade. This must have been a looted prize as it's too fancy to be one of theirs. It's a sword of status and for the distinguished. He loops the new sword on the opposite side of his other one and now feels more like an accomplished swordsman. He playfully draws both swords at the same time while pretending to be in a scenario where he is needed.

"Do we have a problem here? Because to me it looks like there's a problem—and it needs a fixin'." Valencia glances up at him completely confused. She lets her shoulders fall with a sigh.

"What are you doing?" she asks.

"Nothing," Samuel replies almost embarrassed she had noticed him. "I was just—practicing—never mind." Samuel stops daydreaming and sheaths his swords as Valencia beckons.

"Uh, huh. Come over here." She opens his knapsack and adds the food she had just found to their own supply. "Alright, I think we are done here; unless you want to continue talking to yourself?" Samuel looks at her for a moment knowing that she's patronizing him. He decides to ignore her comment and change the subject.

"I have a new sword?" he says. "Now I don't have to borrow yours next time."

"Good, because you were dulling my blade."

The ascending hillside slopes into a steep knoll, known as, Burton Hill to the locals in this valley. Samuel and Valencia pull themselves up to the climax and spy across the vast valley where endless meadows meet the sky, and an array of wildflowers dot the landscape. The village of Trent, and their farmlands, sit at the foot of the hill without any defense structures, and only a few homes, a general shop, and a tavern. They appear to be mostly farmers and loggers with some horses grazing in the field. Beyond Trent is the sight Samuel and Valencia had been longing for. The silhouette of the distant high stone walls and guard towers of Ashborough prove that it would be a force to reckon with. After a quick stop in Trent, the two might make it to Ashborough before nightfall. With their destination in reach, they begin their descent while silently pondering how to convince Bartel to go to war.

The high grassy meadow clears into a dirt patch that becomes the road into town. It's an uneven, muddy path with trampled vegetation that separates the farm plots lining both sides. The farmers are working hard to harvest their yield of crops as foresters chop wood and then load the logs into carts.

Almost the entire village is built around a solitary well that occupies its center. The Tavern, shop and two big homes surround the well, while several other smaller homes butt up to the path leading out of town and towards Ashborough. In one area is a group of three hunters cleaning their kills and preparing the meat for the smokehouse, which is between the tavern and shop. Logs are stockpiled near every building with the remainder being stored alongside the tavern. Farmers wheel their crops to the tavern and then carried into the storeroom located in the lower level. Trent is too small to trade, so everything they produce must feed and sustain everyone throughout the chilling and bleak winter.

The villagers take brief notice of Samuel and Valencia strolling through town, but they aren't interested in the affairs of visitors and try to ignore their presence. This is a town that changes very slowly, if it does at all, and nothing unplanned is ever considered or accepted. The day-to-day activities have been the same year after year; even the population manages to stay consistent without children being present. An unfamiliar face is not welcomed for more than a single day, and that's too long for some.

Samuel and Valencia step into the awkwardly silent tavern with not a single conversation taking place among the patrons. They get a few cold stares or are ignored entirely as they proceed to an empty table.

"Nice place—" Samuel sarcastically says in a hushed tone as they sit down next to each other on the bench style seating. Samuel raises two fingers to the barmaid leaning against the bar with a look that indicates she didn't want to be bothered. Within moments she plops a plate down in front each of them and then walks away without saying a word or making eye contact.

"An ale too, please. Thank you," Samuel calls after her. Samuel and Valencia exchange disappointing looks at their sparse helpings of the smallest potato and a piece of meat that isn't much bigger. Trent prepares food mostly for its own citizens, and to discourage travelers from staying too long, they are fed very little and charged higher prices. Samuel lightly pokes his slab of mean and then looks at Valencia. "Is this meat?"

"I don't know," she admits while looking intensely at it.

Adjacent to Samuel and Valencia's table are three men discussing amongst themselves who these newcomers might be. Robert is a balding, heavyset man, Richard is a strong, athletic built man, and William is a young lad in his late teens.

"Who do you suppose they are dressed like that?" William asks. "Do you think they are soldiers?"

"More like deserters if you ask me," Robert answers, and then guzzles an almost full mug of ale down to just a few drops.

"No, he doesn't look like a soldier, and the woman he's with seems to be well armed herself," Richard observes. He takes the last bite of his roast and then washes it down with the last of his ale. "If you ask me, they are outlaws. Outlaws who may be attached to a bounty for their capture." They continue watching the two eat as Samuel nods and thanks the woman who just brought him his pint, but she leaves without a response or indication that his appreciation was received.

"This is your call, Richard, but some extra coin can better supply us for the upcoming winter," William says.

"We split it evenly between us then, and this winter we stay nice and warm and plenty fed," Robert adds.

"You're already plenty fed, Robert," Richard replies. "But I suppose it's our responsibility to rid dangerous outlaws from our countryside."

Richard is first to stand as the other two follow him towards Samuel and Valencia. Richard picks up Samuel's mug of ale and places it out of his reach before taking his seat across the table. Robert and William stand behind him with their arms folded to try to look as intimidating as they can. Those who weren't taking an interest in them now have joined the rest of the tavern in silent observance. Samuel finishes swallowing his morsel and then points to the mug with his fork while looking at Richard.

"That's my drink." Robert picks up the full mug and chugs it in one long gulp. He then sits the empty mug down while letting out a loud and lengthy belch. Samuel smirks sarcastically and sets down his fork.

"That *was* your drink," Richard smirks.

"Oh look, the town drunk, the village idiot and their stable boy," Valencia begins. "What's the matter, not much luck with the ladies?" Richard cracks a smile and chuckles. He turns away from Samuel and focuses his attention on Valencia.

"You have a fast tongue as one should expect—given your profession." Valencia stands up and draws her sword with the point to Richard's neck. Her quick action prevents their preparation and the gasps around the tavern proved no one expected Valencia's move. Samuel slowly stands up and pulls back his coat to reveal his swords.

"If you want trouble, then I will appease your request. But first you apologize to my friend for your lack of respect," Samuel says calmly. Richard pushes Valencia's sword away from him with the back of his hand while lifting himself off the bench. Refusing to give up her defense, she immediately brings the blade back to his chest. This is surely more action than Trent has seen in a long time. The entire town is now silently focused on this confrontation when a crowd forms outside to peer indoors. Nobody wants to miss how this will play out while others shake their heads knowing strangers in their town are always bad news.

"I do not show respect to outlaws," Richard says through his teeth.

"We are not outlaws," Valencia replies sternly.

"You dress like outlaws," Richard continues. "In long coats and hoods to hide your face; and carrying concealed weapons to avoid being questioned."

"You accuse us falsely," Samuel responds.

"Then who are you, and what brings you to Trent?" Richard asks.

"What business is it of yours to know ours?" Samuel snaps back. Richard leans forward and places his hands on top of the table.

"I am the leader of the militia here. It is my duty to question suspicious strangers, and my question still remains unanswered."

Valencia does not see a weapon on any of the men who are confronting them, and they did not come all this way to pick a fight over a petty misunderstanding.

"We are on our way to Ashborough."

"What possible reason do the likes of you have there?" Robert asks.

"If you wanted to know, then you should have asked?" Samuel responds.

"I'm asking now," Richard replies. Valencia withdraws her sword and sheaths it. There was a time when she wouldn't have, but the stakes are too high now to let egos run unchecked.

"An invasion from a distant land is upon us," Valencia starts. "We venture to Ashborough to ask for aid."

William glances at Richard with a discerning look and pulls him aside while whispering. "A rider came through here the other day. He spoke of an encampment he saw on the far hills."

"There was faint glow of fire on the horizon two days ago too," Robert adds softly.

"I remember. It looked like Campton," Richard says and then turns back to Samuel. "What do you know of Campton? What's its status?"

"We do not know of this Campton; we were coming from Guildsmith."

"Although, if you saw flames over that town then I'm afraid to inform you their fate was the same as Guildsmith's," Valencia adds.

"We've been in the midst of their onslaught more than once," Samuel begins. "We just killed six scouts beyond Burton Hill not quite two hours ago."

"If you truly are tasked with protecting this town, I suggest you prepare for war," Valencia warns.

"Why should we believe anything these rabble-rousers have to say?" Robert asks, but Valencia answers his question before Richard can speak.

"When those scouts don't return, more will be sent out, and when their bodies are discovered, you can expect them to advance in full force. They could already be on the move." Richard turns back to William.

"You said someone reported seeing an encampment?"

"Yes, he couldn't make out their colors, but thought it may have been a training exercise," William pauses. "What if they were these invaders he saw instead?

The once silent tavern is now humming with muttering and shuffling feet.

"Is it true, Richard? Is an army marching this way?" a man asks after standing up. Richard puts his arms out at his sides and gently moves them up and down to silence the crowd.

"Everyone stay calm. We do not know anything yet," he says while facing the people around him. He then turns to Samuel. "What land did you say these soldiers are from?"

"We don't know exactly where they originated. They came from the north, and they are brutal," Samuel replies.

"Northmen—" Richard begins but doesn't continue.

The people of England know about the raids and conquests on the eastern coastline of their country about three-hundred years earlier. Fear that this is a continuation of what took place then is enough to convince most of the villagers to take up arms and put their winter preparations on hold.

Richard and William walk two saddled horses toward Samuel and Valencia who wait in the town's center alongside Robert.

"These will quicken your journey to Ashborough. If those barbarians attack before your return, we will try to hold them off. This is a town of militias after all," Richard says. "I'm also sorry for my behavior earlier. Robert here gets crazy ideas in his head sometimes."

"Hey, it was your idea. You said there would be a reward for their capture," Robert says trying to defend himself. Richard swirls his finger around his head while looking at Robert.

"The fat around your brain makes you forgetful." Richard turns back to Valencia and bows. "Your forgiveness, my lady." Valencia smirks.

"And I'm sorry for calling you a boy lover."

"Oh yeah—" Richard recalls. "You did say that," he concludes almost regretting his apology now.

The villagers have already begun to sharpen their blades and string several bows, and barrels, that were being saved for food, are now being lined up to create makeshift battlements.

Valencia pulls herself up onto her horse while Samuel rests his hand on the reins.

"Is this your first time?" Valencia says with a smirk.

"Actually, it is."

"There's nothing to worry about. Just get on, hold on tight and follow my guidance."

"Be gentle," Samuel whispers as he pats his horse's neck.

Valencia maintains the lead as the horses gallop along the road of the hilly countryside. Samuel is doing well in keeping up with her pace despite never riding before. The road takes them alongside a river until coming to the only wooden bridge in their sights. Valencia then directs her horse off the path and into the meadow with Samuel following closely. The glorious city of Ashborough is now fully in view and it's something to admire. Samuel has visited plenty of towns and villages during his travels, but none came close to this sprawling capital.

Pure white stone walls and grand towers overlook every structure except for the castle at the hindermost part of the city. The defending walls, towers and ramparts weren't just built to protect, but also to show Ashborough's prestige and prosperity. Archers occupy perfectly rounded additions to the ramparts with chiseled cutouts to peer or shoot out without being exposed. Flowering bushes line the path leading to the gateway, which is adorned with flags and banners. Cobblestone streets begin at the gates and continue throughout, until reaching the white brick steps of the castle.

Samuel and Valencia dismount and then hand over the reins into the care of the young man who meets them. They proceed up the steps toward the two guards standing at the entrance with swords strapped at their sides.

"We've rode from Trent to see Bartel," Samuel says with a

tone that demands urgency. One of the guards turns his head slightly towards the interior of the castle.

"Peter—" he calls. He waits for a moment, but no one comes. "Peter! Peter, get your arse out here boy!" he yells. A moment later a boy in his early teen's hurries from somewhere inside and then stops at the entryway while bowing his head.

"Sorry, sir for my delay," he says humbly.

"I don't care. Inform the steward that he has visitors from Trent," the guard responds.

"Yes sir," Peter says and then runs back into the castle.

Bartel slouches comfortably in an ornamental boarded chair with drapery while gazing deeply into the flames of the hearth. He's an older gentleman with a long white beard that hangs just past his neckline and has a muscular build. The battlefield isn't foreign to him, and he will gladly return to it if needed. Younger men have mistaken him to be a frail man, but soon discovers one with a strong arm and a swift fist. His enemies will not find an easy victory in combat, for when Bartel picks up his sword, he wields it as if he were forty-years younger.

Bartel hears the quickened footsteps of Peter running into his study. "Must you be so loud?" he says while keeping his focus on the crackling fire and the dancing flames.

"My apologies sir," Peter begins while huffing from being out of breath. "Two warriors—from Trent bring a message for you."

"Trent?"

Bartel knows Trent citizens keep to themselves and rarely venture far from their fields. He also believes that the classification of *warriors from Trent*, cannot be true as they do not have an army or training to award any such title. He knows them to be related closer to irritated farmers with pitchforks; however, his duty is to give an audience to whomever wills it.

"Take them to the main hall. I will meet them there, whoever they claim to be."

The hall is used to entertain guests with lavish feasts and festivals or feed the soldiers with their daily rations. Fifteen community tables and benches are placed in three columns with five rows each. Samuel and Valencia wait patiently at one of these tables with a bowl of apples in its center. Samuel eyes the apples with a hungry look before reaching toward the bowl. Valencia quickly slaps the back of his hand while giving him a stern look.

His dinner wasn't exactly filling, but Valencia won't tolerate taking anything from someone without permission either.

Bartel enters the hall and gives them a quick glance before redirecting his gaze around the room. He then looks back at Samuel and Valencia after finding no one else in the vicinity.

"I was told two warriors wished to deliver me a message, but the two of you look like common rogues."

"That seems to be a recent development," Samuel says.

Bartel takes a seat opposite the other two and then folds his hands on the table. "Now, what word do you bring me?"

"Sir, a great threat is in our province," Valencia begins. "Barbarians are invading towns and killing their citizens."

"I've not heard of such things. News of that nature would reach me fairly quickly, I should imagine."

"Most don't escape and so the stories are not told," Samuel adds. "From the southwest to the east there are ruined towns filled with rotting corpses that have no one to bury them."

"And what towns fell to these barbarians, mister—?"

"Hall, Samuel Hall, and this is Valencia Ruskin, sir," Samuel answers before continuing to Bartel's next question. "There are surely many others, but the towns we know of that have been attacked are Middleton, Piketon and Guildsmith."

"A man in Trent also gave suspicion that Campton may have fallen victim to these attacks as well," Valencia adds.

"Campton is like Trent; they keep to themselves. But did you mention Guildsmith?" Bartel asks as the two answers with nods. "Why does that name stick out to me?" he ponders.

"We met a man by the name of Gavin there. It was he who advised us to seek your aid," Valencia replies.

"Gavin—ah yes, he gave council to King Ladislas before his untimely death." Bartel's tone then turns to concern. "What news of Gavin?"

"He and his family escaped, and are now sailing to Ireland," Samuel responds.

"That's good to hear. Do you know where these barbarians are now?"

"I fear they are heading toward Trent, if not already there," Valencia says somberly. Bartel is silent for a moment as he strokes his beard and then slowly nods.

"This tale still sounds unlikely, but it should at least be

investigated," Bartel says as he stands up. "Come with me."

Bartel leads Samuel and Valencia through an archway that connects the castle to a cloister with ornate pillars and then turn off onto one of the adjoining pathways toward a graveled patio enclosed with flowing shrubs and trees. Four stone benches line the edges, and a cherub waterfall sits in its center. They continue past this restful escape to the open field where a few groups of soldiers are gathered while talking amongst themselves. One of them notices Bartel and his guests approaching and assumes a respectful posture while shouting,

"Bartel on the yard!" The other men stop their conversations and take up a rigid pose next to one another.

"Advance guard and patrol to me," Bartel calls out. "All others, at ease and carry on." Several men hurry forward while the others return to their relaxed state. Bartel waits until eight men have gathered around him including the soldier who brought attention to the yard.

"I have been informed of a possible army invasion camped or marching near or towards Trent. Now, I do not want to raise alarm or suspicion, but I do want to know if these claims are accurate." Bartel turns to face Samuel and Valencia. "Where were your last sighting?"

"Beyond Burton Hill near the woodland pass," Samuel answers. Bartel directs his attention back to his men.

"Organize patrols and reconnaissance around the area of Burton Hill and the woodland pass and then extend your perimeter from there. Use caution and report your findings to me at once."

"Yes sir," the men cry out in unison.

"Dismissed."

The men immediately scurry off to prepare for their mission. Bartel returns his gaze to Samuel and Valencia and studies their appearance for a moment. He pinches Samuel's coat and rubs his fingers against the material before looking at the dirt on his fingers.

"If you are going to act like soldiers—then you should at least look like them. And when was the last time you bathed?"

"Bathed?" Samuel says unsure exactly on a precise answer.

"That's what I thought," Bartel says and begins walking back towards the cloister. "With me." Samuel and Valencia exchange looks before puffing out their chests and assuming a marching stance while following Bartel.

Samuel can't recall the last time he found himself in a tub filled with warm water. He leans against the wooden side and closes his eyes as steam rises around him. A hot bath is never appreciated more than when one is unable to access it for a length of time. The door opens and a young man enters with a towel draped over his arm.

"Are you ready for your undergarments, sir?" Samuel could stay in the tub longer but doesn't want to risk the generosity of his host to run thin.

"Yes, I suppose so." Samuel says.

"I shall fetch them," the boy places the towel on a stool and then leaves the room. Samuel climbs out of the tub and dries himself off before tying the towel around his waist. The boy returns with Samuel's undershirt and pants neatly folded in his arms. He shuts the door behind him and then hands the clothes to Samuel before turning around to give him privacy. Samuel unfolds the clothes and holds each piece up to inspect them.

"Excuse me, but these are not mine," he says. The boy slightly looks over his shoulder.

"Um, well, you see," he clears his throat and speaks more gruffly. "Bartel has taken your entire wardrobe and had them torched with due haste. He said they were not even fit for birthing cattle."

"Oh—I see," Samuel says a little surprised by the harsh words. "These will do then, thank you." The feeling of clean clothes against his skin is another luxury he had not experienced in quite a long time and his new clothes allow him to forget about the execution of his old attire. The door opens again, and two guards walk inside carrying leather armor and chain mail. They set it down on the stool and then depart to stand facing out on either side of the doorway.

"Are you ready for the ladies, sir?" the boy asks.

"Ladies?" Samuel replies perplexed.

"Yes, sir. I will send them in and then take my leave. Good luck to you, sir." The boy leaves the room, but the guards remain on the other side of the door. Within a short moment two fine maidens, wearing blue skirts, enter the bathing room. They glance at him in his underwear and then at each other with shy smiles.

"Are you ready for us to dress you, sir?" one of the ladies asks.

"You are—going to dress me?"

"Yes," the other woman replies. It takes Samuel a moment to find his voice.

"—Ok."

The women begin with a pair of leather leggings and secures them by tying a series of strings behind his legs. Samuel then stands with his arms forward as the women pull a leather vest up his arms and around his chest before tying these strings behind his back. Next, is the hard hide leather pants that Samuel places his feet into before the women pull the pants up around him and then ties the drawstrings around his waist. They deliberately pull the strings tightly forcing Samuel to almost fall into them as they giggle.

"Are these too tight on you?" one of them asks sensually.

"No, I'm—comfortable," Samuel replies.

"We know how to care for the areas of men," the other admits in almost a whisper. They women snicker again but stop when they notice the guards peeking into the room while Samuel smiles with blushing cheeks. They share the task of strapping the leather belt around his waist and again, tugs on the belt to make him jerk forward. They catch him in their arms and give him a teasing wink.

"Chain mail," one of them hollers. The guards return to lift the chain mail coat over Samuel's head and position it properly around his torso and then lets it drape around his thighs. The guards shoot the women a glance but say nothing as they return to their post just outside the door. The women lightly push down on Samuel's shoulders to make him sit on the stool. Each picks up a boot and then slides it on his foot before tying the laces. The women take his hands delicately into theirs and pull him off the stool. They put his head through a white shirt with a blue crest and pull it down over the chain mail to signify he's among Ashborough's ranks. They lastly slide his swords into their sheathes on either side of him.

"Thank you, ladies," Samuel says bashfully. The women smirk and curtsy.

"Do come to us again—when you need those clothes off," one of them says with a come-hither look.

"Alright, that's enough," a guard announces as he steps into the room. The women take their leave while snickering and glancing back before turning the corridor.

Valencia is wearing the same leather and chain mail as Samuel, but she's holding an open-faced barbute under her arm. She strolls through one of the many hallways while admiring the framed paintings on the wall. The next painting, she comes to is that of King Ladislas, the lost king of Ashborough. He's showcased in exquisite armor with his hand resting on the pummel of his sword. A white and blue tabard adorns his chest, and a long, flowing cape is illustrated blowing behind him. His eyes are intensely focused on the observer and his cheeks and chin is concealed under a lengthy black beard.

Valencia hears heavy footsteps behind her and turns around to see Samuel walking towards her. It's not often that she's lost for words, and she's never been bashful, but seeing him represented in a new light has her awestruck. *It's amazing what a bath and clean clothes can do for a man*, she thinks to herself.

"From drifter to knight. Now you look like the person you really are," she says.

"Thanks, but it is a bit restricting—" he replies with a grin. Valencia looks away with a smile before recomposing herself.

"I never thanked you for defending me back in Trent."

"You don't have to thank me for that, Val. I will always be there for you."

Valencia had convinced herself long ago to only be driven by revenge, and never let anyone get close to her. She never thought Samuel could be anything other than an annoying leach, but dismissing he who has a fool's heart, also prevents one for seeing their brave soul. He's a hopeless romantic, who was never given a chance to fit in; no one ever gave him a moment of their time. Samuel hides it well, but Valencia is starting to understand some of his strife. Exiled and forlorn for most of his adult life. How does that not affect one's mind? He opens himself up to others in the off chance one of them will welcome him, and there is one who did—Cerbera. Valencia is angry with herself for not seeing it sooner. Cerbera knew how to play with his mind and emotions. The vampire sisters know how to trap him, and there's little Samuel can do to resist their advance. It comes down to Valencia's influence for his last line of defense, but will that be enough?

When desire and temptation meet; does anyone truly stand a chance?

6

Dance of Death

A calm moment in Trent, turns to alarm when the ground begins to tremble, and thunder rocks the earth. The citizens take up their arms and run to their battle stations. Richard looks up at William, who's scouting from a balcony of a modest residence. "Riders from Ashborough!" he shouts down. Richard breathes a sigh of relief and then addresses the crowd.

"Stand down!" The people of Trent observe the eight men patrol unit gallop past their town and head toward Burton Hill. Robert joins Richard's side and shoots him a worried look. "Bartel is no fool," Richard begins while shaking his head. "He wouldn't send scouts out unless he feels there is cause to."

"Maybe it can be resolved quickly. Then we won't have to go to war," Robert responds nervously.

"Don't try to change something that cannot be changed through wishful thinking. You best accept it, Robert. We are most definitely going to war."

Meanwhile, in Ashborough, Bartel joins Samuel and Valencia in the main hall wearing a white and blue cape over his chain mail armor. He sets down a bottle and three mugs on their table, and then pours the liquid into the mugs.

"Enjoy," Bartel says as he takes his seat and then lifts his mug to drink.

"What is it?" Valencia says after picking up her mug. Bartel finishes his drink and then slams the mug on the table.

"It's called mead," Bartel replies.

"I don't usually drink alcohol," she admits.

"Don't worry, it's not at all strong; made from honey and water."

"Is it like a cider?"

"Similar—" Bartel answers without further explanation. Valencia takes a sip and nods to indicate her acceptance of the drink. It's close to the ciders that she enjoys and finds it sweet and easy to drink. Samuel, like Bartel finishes his mug relatively fast, but Valencia continues to gradually sip hers. Bartel pours more mead into Samuel's mug and then hovers the bottle over Valencia's before noticing it's not empty. "How do you have so much left?"

"I'm savoring it."

"Why would you do that?"

"Because then I can taste it."

"I can taste it in one gulp," Bartel replies. He then turns his attention back to Samuel. "Come on Samuel. Let's see who can finish their mug first. Ready?" Samuel and Bartel hold their mugs close to their lips. "Go!"

Samuel and Bartel chug the mead down as Valencia looks at them with disgust. Bartel is first to slam his mug on the table and raises his arms in victory. Samuel sets his mug on the table gently and smiles while wiping his mouth with the back of his hand.

"I think I had more in my mug than you did," Samuel says. Bartel laughs loudly and slaps the table top several times.

"Is this how men prove who's stronger or braver? By silly drinking games?" Valencia points out. Bartel thinks for a moment before smiling.

"Yes," he replies.

"Considering we could very well be going into battle soon. Wouldn't it be wiser to keep a clear head and not get drunk?"

"Ah, but this is battle-ready mead. It makes you alert, strong and your mind sharp. Another round!" Bartel shouts. He goes to pour the mead into his mug, but nothing comes out. He shakes the bottle and then looks inside the opening.

"Oh, I must have grabbed an empty one."

"Clearly, I can see the mead is already taking effect," Valencia observes, but Bartel ignores her comment.

"Peter— Peter—" Bartel cries out. "I swear I need to tie a rope around that kid and drag him in on his hind end." Peter hurries into the room as fast as his legs can carry him, but then trips and slides across the floor on his stomach. "He's also new," Bartel says softly to Samuel who tries to hide his snickering. Peter picks himself up and then bows to Bartel.

"Yes, my lord?"

"Bring more mead."

"Right away, sir." Peter bows again and then runs out of the room as Bartel yells after him.

"And walk, so as not to spill any!"

Elsewhere, Ashborough's riders slowly guide their horses around the dead barbarian scouts that Samuel and Valencia had killed earlier.

"It appears their story holds up," one of them says.

"Where do you suppose the rest of these bastards are hiding?" another one asks. His question is answered with two arrows suddenly striking him in the chest. He lets out a yelp and falls off his horse.

The other riders take notice of the attack and circle their horses around to try to locate the whereabouts of their enemy. A throwing axe sores out through the trees before striking the skull of another rider. He too falls to the ground dead.

The riders cannot pinpoint the exact location of their foes or how many are entrenched. Charging into the trees without knowing this information could result in more casualties.

"Back to Ashborough," one of them yells. Their report is far more important than engaging the threat. They must accept the risk to Trent to warn Bartel. If Ashborough's army isn't mustered, then the barbarians remain unopposed. The scouts turn their horses around and make a hasty retreat. A spear claims another life when it pierces into the back of a trailing scout, followed by a volley of arrows that rains down upon the retreating patrol unit to take one last life.

Meanwhile, Richard is attempting to talk courage into the men as they gather around him in makeshift armor, shields, and weapons.

"We may not have been trained as soldiers of kings, but if they were to open our chests and look at our hearts! They would not be able to tell us apart!" The men cheer as they shake their weapons in the air. "Are our weapons dull!?"

"No!" The crowd responds in unison. Richard taps the shoulder of a man holding his bow.

"Do we folly when we aim!?"

"No!" The crowd repeats again.

"Then let's show these livestock lovers what a town of Englishmen can do!" The group laugh and cheer again, but the sound of horses in full gallop silence them as they observe the remaining scouts riding past without stopping.

"Eight go over the hill—four come back," Richard says softly while watching them riding on. He then turns his attention back to his fellow men. "Gather the women and barricade them inside the tavern." The villagers disperse to ready themselves and secure their loved ones. "Let's pray that Ashborough's army arrives before the barbarians do," he tells Robert.

Meanwhile, Bartel, Samuel, and Valencia remain waiting for Peter's return with more mead when Bartel notices Valencia still hasn't finished her portion.

"Are you not going to finish your mead?"

"I'm no longer thirsty."

"Mead is not for quenching thirst."

"That is where we differ. I drink for nourishment, not for bragging."

Bartel thinks for a moment and then waves a finger at her while looking at Samuel.

"I like this one. Both wise and headstrong." Peter hurries into the room empty handed, but before he can speak Bartel questions him. "Where's the mead, Peter?"

"Sir, some of the scouts have returned."

"Some—" Bartel becomes serious and then stands up with urgency. "Send them in at once," Bartel orders. Valencia and Samuel join Bartel as he holds his arms behind his back until the four scouts march with quickened steps toward him.

"What happened?"

"We were ambushed," one of them begins. "There was no time to counter."

"How many were they?"

"We don't know. They were hidden in the trees," another scout answers.

"They had archers, and threw hatchets and spears," the third reports.

"They took half of us out and we never saw a Goddamn single one of them," the last one admits.

"Ready the men. We move at once," Bartel says.

Valencia and Samuel return to their horses just after sundown as Bartel prepares to send them off.

"We will advance to Trent as soon as possible," Bartel says.

"Thank you. We will ride ahead to help them in case they are invaded before your arrival," Valencia says.

"Godspeed," he says as Samuel and Valencia ride out of town at a full gallop.

"Trust the horses, Sam. They will sense vampires before us," Valencia advises him.

In the looming stillness of night, Trent appears to be asleep, with not a fire or candle burning. The grass stalks begin to sway and rustle despite the lack of wind. Darkened figures crawl closer toward Trent with headgear that imitates grazing bucks. The first few men reach the dirt road on the outskirts of the village before rising to their feet. Another ten follow them until their full force of forty gradually pour into Trent.

A villager slowly rises from his lying position on the tavern's rooftop and carefully draws back his bow. His arrow is sent deep into the knee of one invader to make it impossible for him not to cry out in pain. This signal alerts the villages of the impeding attack, and they run out of their hiding places while yelling courageously. Weapons cling against one another, and pierce flesh, as both barbarians and defenders quickly become casualties.

Richard smashes his mace into his enemies' heads, while Robert prefers to jab his pitchfork into the guts of his foes. His pitchfork is also sufficient at blocking two barbarian swords when they attempt to outnumber him. Before they have time to plan another attack, Richard arrives to send his mace into the back of one of their heads and then the temple of the other.

Several barbarians hurl their spears into a crowd of

unfortunate villagers to strike them down, followed by defenders on balconies and rooftops letting loose a volley of arrows into the gathering barbarians for revenge. Richard cheers at the sight of several barbarians expiring from the attack, but his celebration is short lived when he notices two more charging him with swords and hatchets in hand. "Shit," he utters and retreats farther back into town; however, he's body slammed by another who rushes out from the shadows. Richard falls hard into the muck and hurries to pick himself up, but receives a swift kick into the ribs, that sends him rolling into a wooden livestock fence. He desperately looks around only to notice his mace out of reach and his attacker raising his battle axe over his head. Horror shows in his eyes and his ability to act becomes clouded. The sound of horseshoes on damp soil echo in his ears, followed by the neighing of a horse leaping over him and the fence. Its hooves collide into the barbarian's face as it descends from its leap while also tipping over a basket of bread and spilling the long loaves into the street. Samuel leaps off the horse and helps Richard to his feet.

"You came back?"

"Of course, I came back. Your friend owes me an ale."

"That he does," Richard replies with a chuckle.

Valencia rides through the rear of the village while shooting her wrist crossbows at the barbarians who are in her sights. She dismounts when she reaches the center of town and draws her sword to aid the other villagers in the area.

"Where's Ashborough's army?" Richard asks Samuel as they prevent the army from getting into the back door of the tavern.

"Assembling," he replies.

"So, we are on our own?"

"Basically."

An archer, on one of the balconies, takes a throwing hatchet in his chest, he falls over the railing and lands face down on the road. Robert becomes surrounded by four barbarians and jabs his pitchfork into the nearest one before running back to where Richard and Samuel are fighting. He trips and falls near the tipped over breadbasket with three howling barbarians on his heels. Richard makes his kill before joining Samuel intercepting Robert's pursuers. Samuel blocks a sword aimed at Richard to give him the chance to connect his mace under one of their chins. Samuel stabs another in the torso and then pulls his sword out just in time to block the last foe's sword from slicing him. Richard takes this one down with a swift blow to the back of the neck. Robert sighs in relief and then picks up one of the loaves and takes a big bite out of it.

Valencia forcibly kicks her attacker back then jabs her sword through his sternum. She turns around to kick another one in his kneecap. She runs behind the off-balance man and slices the back of his neck without hesitation. Valencia joins Richard and Samuel as more of the overwhelmed villagers fall in battle.

"There are just too many of them," Richard says in a worried tone.

A village militiaman wields his sword with skillful strokes, and successfully kills three barbarians around him, but fails to dodge the pike from a fourth when it's forced through his chest.

"No!" William exclaims while running out of his home toward the fallen man. Another villager kills the barbarian, holding the pike, and then stands guard in front of the wounded man. William falls to his knees as the man lifts his bloody hand to hold the boy's arm.

"Father, we need to get you inside," William says with tears in his eyes.

"No, my boy. My time has arrived."

"I cannot accept—" William begins but is cut off.

"Listen, my breath will not last long." William's father hands him the sword and ensures William has a firm grip on it. "Take this—carry it with you, and just like it, I will always be at your side." William's father takes his last breath and dies before he can take his hand off the hilt. William sobs as the guarding villager lays a consoling hand on his shoulder.

Samuel, Valencia, Richard, and Robert stand together while fighting in a close-knit pact. Samuel and Valencia share in a kill and then exchange heartfelt looks.

"Maybe we should have taken that boat to Ireland," Samuel says. She smiles wondering if their life would be any better someplace else. What would stop the barbarians from eventually making it into Ireland if there was no one to stop them here? They chose the more grueling path filled with danger and anguish, but neither of them can say it was the wrong decision.

The ground begins to tremble as a distant rumbling grows louder. Bartel leads his cavalry with swords drawn above them as they prepare to charge through the barbarian lines.

"It's not over yet," Valencia says relieved.

"Put all your strength into it, men! Help is on the way," Richard shouts.

The cavalry rushes into the barbarian forces and slices through them with ease. With the numbers now against them, some of the barbarians decide to retreat back into the field.

"Chase them down! Do not let any of them get away! Show no mercy!" Bartel orders. Two groups of riders, stampede through the field in pursuit of the retreating barbarians while the others slay those that become trapped in Trent. The cavalry splits up, one group remains at the heels of their targets, while the other runs ahead before circling back around and then charging forward to force the last survivors into a choke point. Their effective formations and precise tactics prohibit any enemy from escaping. Trent bursts into cheer and celebration. They were the least defended and consisting of the smallest band of citizens, but they were the first to quell a barbarian assault. What will the remaining ranks think when forty of their own fails to return?

Samuel and Valencia meet up with Bartel just as he dismounts his horse.

"Where's the rest of your army?" Samuel asks.

"They're slow moving, but should arrive by morning," he assures him while looking around at the staggering number of slain villagers. "I'm sorry. I wish we arrived sooner."

"It would have been all of us if you didn't come when you did," Valencia says. Bartel nods with a slight smirk.

"Was this their whole army?"

"I didn't see Hagathor, so unfortunately this was only a fraction of his army," Samuel replies.

"He probably thought this town would be easy and only sent a few of his men. He must be planning something bigger," Valencia predicts.

"Well, now they know—they fight unopposed no longer. In the morning we will track the rest of them. Tonight, we care for the wounded and the dead," Bartel says.

The normal morning routine for the citizens of Trent has been forever changed. It's hard to fathom how one day can change so much from the previous. The usual greetings to friends and family are now tearful goodbyes, and preparations for winter are now arrangements for abandonment. Trent may have withstood the Barbarians' onslaught, but it will never again be self-sufficient. With over seventy percent of the population killed, Trent becomes another casualty of war. The people pack up only what they can carry and leave the rest to be forgotten and fall into decay. Bartel offers the survivors refuge in Ashborough, where they will have an opportunity to find work and perhaps make it their new home.

The farmlands of Trent are now a cemetery. Mounds of dirt lay side by side as people stand around with lowered heads as a man speaks his prayers to the crowd. William has his father's sword strapped to his waist as he bends over to take the dirt from the top of his father's mound into his fist. He then slowly lets it shift through his fingers back onto the grave.

Bartel greets the remainder of his army when they arrive, and then organizes an escort to guide the villagers to Ashborough. Samuel and Valencia watch from a distance as the people congregate for their slow and silent migration when Richard joins them.

"I'm going with you. You know that, right?" His choice was not to be that of a defeated soldier, but one who returns to the battlefield. Robert overhears Richard's decision and drags his feet beside him.

"I'm coming too," he says.

"Are you sure?" Richard asks. "Because there will be a lot of walking involved."

"I suppose you will have to carry me when I get tired."

"I don't think a horse can carry you," Richard replies. Robert is not easily offended and lets out a hearty laugh to prove it. Richard glances at William walking a short distance away.

"William's coming with us also."

"Are you sure that's a good idea?" Valencia asks with concern.

"We are all he has now. There's no place else for him," Richard says. "He's young, but he'll grow up fast. It's better if he grows up with us than figuring it out on the road." Valencia and Samuel know what it feels like to be displaced, and neither will object any further.

Bartel leads one-thousand cavalry, three-thousand infantry, two-thousand archers and ten wagons full of supplies. He believes Hagathor and his army may be camped near a water supply.

They march southwest along the Avon River toward the Bristol Channel, along with Samuel, Valencia, and their new friends from Trent. The rattle of armor with every footfall upon the earth and the rubbing of weapons at rest resonate throughout the countryside.

As the journey continues Samuel thinks to himself. *I spent my entire life walking into uncertainty, but this time it feels different. Every step into the night slowly pulls away my blanket of security. Warmth becomes chills and hope becomes shadows. I have a feeling in the very depth of my soul that my life will soon come to an end.*

Bartel observes the sun's close proximity to the horizon and holds his fist up to halt his army. Soldiers gather in their small clicks near the banks of the Avon River, while Richard, Robert and William stay together. Valencia notices Samuel sitting alone while gazing at the setting sun near the bank of the river. She looks away thinking maybe he has chosen solitude for a reason, but then reconsiders and marches toward him.

"What are you thinking about?" she asks. Samuel looks up and forces a smile out.

"You know me, I never do much thinking," Samuel jokes. Valencia snickers, she knows he's deflecting, but decides not to press it.

"We don't have a lot of daylight left," she points out.

"I know," Samuel begins. "And we have two enemies that hunt at night, and neither has given up their locations."

"Is that the cause of your contemplation?" she asks while sitting down beside him.

"I had a different perspective of the world before Piketon."

"And what was that?"

"I saw it full of stories," Samuel pauses. "I wanted to be a bard."

"Really?" Valencia questions while letting out a hysterical laugh.

"It's true," Samuel continues with a smile. "I wanted to tell stories. Stories about far off places and adventure or of heroes and monsters—myths and legends. I wanted something to talk about. Something people wanted to listen too."

"You have a story, Sam. You're living it. How many people can say they fought barbarians and vampires?"

"Not very many I should think," Samuel says after a short moment to ponder the question.

"Not many at all," she says with a smile. Bartel advances toward them as they wait for him to meet them.

"We will be camping here tonight. Tomorrow we should reach Casterham. Maybe we can enlist their army to join us." Samuel and Valencia nod in agreement. "We don't have enough tents for everyone, but I placed a hold on one if you want to claim it."

"Yes, thank you," Valencia says. Bartel smiles and nods.

"I'll have my men set it up for you."

In the fading light, soldiers unload tents and sleeping mats while other begin constructing and staking the tents in place. Sleeping preparations are widely spread out across the field including thirty tents reserved for Bartel, his officers, William, and Valencia. Bartel retires into the largest canopy tent which, besides a sleeping area, also contains a table and chairs in case strategic planning is required. Richard sets up his arrangement just outside of William's tent and Samuel walks past with his sleeping mat rolled up under his arm. He stops at Valencia's tent just as she walks out. She picks up the folded blanket and pillow that was sat in front of the tent and hands it to Samuel.

"Get in," she says. Samuel gives her a perplexed look as he tries to find his voice.

"You—you want me to stay in your tent with you?" he finally says. Valencia narrows her eyes and yanks his sleeping mat from him.

"No, the tent is for you, Sam."

"But where will you sleep then?"

"I'm perfectly capable of sleeping out here."

"But people will talk if they see me inside the tent and not you."

"So, that's what they do. They talk, but you need to listen. I'm not the one being hunted by two vampire strumpets." Samuel peeks inside the tent and then smells the air.

"What's that smell?" He glances around until noticing garlic cloves hanging from the center support beam. "Is that garlic? Where did you find garlic?"

"It naturally grows wild in the forest Sam," she sighs. "How did you survive on your own?"

"Does that really work against vampires?"

"I don't know, but I never heard of it not working."

Valencia is not one for putting trust into superstitions, but believing something won't work and not trying, leaves her open for regrets later. If everything that could be done was explored, then only bad luck and poor odds can be blamed.

Night falls over the countryside like a thick black fog as soft chirps from the crickets and tiny splashes from fish catching mosquitoes fill the air. A few campfires around the encampment are still burning as everyone is sleeping peacefully under the night sky on inside their tents. Valencia has taken her spot near the tree line of the forest which borders the field. She remains sitting up on her mat with her legs crossed over each other and her back against the truck of a tree as she watches Samuel's tent intensely. The light wind plays with her hair and the soothing sounds of night gently rock her to sleep before she's aware that she was drifting off.

The shadow of long slender fingers with long nails slide across the outside of Samuel's tent as he sleeps. They gently scrape along all sides of the tent as this creature circles it, unable to enter, before disappearing. Samuel begins to toss and turn unable to find comfort underneath his blankets. Suddenly, the image of Cerbera snarling with bared fangs awakes him. He looks around and then sighs in relief when discovering he's still alone, but he cannot tell if he was dreaming or if Cerbera was really nearby. Sleep no longer appears to be attainable for him as he lies awake for what seems like hours. He finally throws his blankets off and peeks out of his tent while looking around. The countryside is quiet with no sign of anyone or anything stirring. He dips back inside the tent to light a lantern before stepping outside. He quietly ventures through camp and away from the campfires as he steps into the trees. He inspects his surroundings and then sets the lantern down on the ground near a bush. He fidgets with the layers of his pants and underwear as he struggles to find a way to relieve himself.

"Come on," he whispers a little frustrated.

The sound of flapping and the rustling of leaves behind him cause him to turn around abruptly. After a moment of silent observation, and no further movement or sound, he turns back towards the bush. Finally unhindered he begins to pee, but the flapping of large wings disturbs him again. He looks up just as something lands on the tree branch above him. He tries to focus, but only darkness welcomes his gaze until he finishes peeing. He hurries to fix his pants and undergarments around him and then bends over to pick up his lantern. An unknown thump falls heavy on the forest floor followed by something running swiftly through the fallen leaves behind him. Samuel immediately becomes alert and whirls around while putting his hand on his side to grab his sword. He looks down and realizes he had forgotten to pick up his sheath. He's now defenseless and alone in the woods at night, hunted by something that likes to playfully stalk and taunt him.

"Shit," he says in a nervous whisper.

This creature is now flying with haste behind Samuel. It becomes closer and closer until it's right behind him with him none the wiser. As soon as he senses the uneasy feeling of being watched he turns around just as an owl flies over his head while hooting up into the trees. He lets out a startled yell, but then closes his eyes and exhales a long-drawn-out sigh while laughing to himself. He takes a moment to recompose himself knowing that it was only the usual sounds of night playing tricks on him. He reopens his eyes and takes a step back towards camp when he discovers he was wrong. Cerbera is standing in front of him with a sinister grin before her hands rush forward with curved fingertips ready to grab him.

Back in camp, Valencia wakes suddenly as if from a disturbing dream. She glances at Samuel's tent and spots the flaps swaying in the wind. She is quick to her feet and makes a dash to the tent to look inside.

"Sam!?" she says in a concerned whisper. Fear consumes her when she finds the tent vacant. She withdraws her sword and then hurries to shake Richard from his sleep. He snorts and then jitters from the disturbance.

"What, what is it?"

"Grab your weapon and follow me quickly," she demands. He obeys without question and carefully follows her as they make sure not to step on anyone on their way towards the woods.

"Is it barbarians?" Richard whispers.

"You just have to trust me on this one," she replies.

Bartel hears their whispering while studying his map and tip toes to peek out his slightly parted tent flap. He catches a glimpse of Richard and Valencia walking into the woods with their weapons drawn. He strokes his beard and narrows his eyes. What could they be up to at this hour, and should he find himself involved? Of course, he can't ignore what he has just seen. If there is a threat nearby, he should investigate it too, but if that is true, why would they not have warned the others, or come to him? This mystery cannot go unexplored.

Cerbera takes in a deep breath while swaying her hips and torso from side to side, like the deathly dance of a cobra ready to strike.

"Your heartbeat is so soothing; even when it's beating fast," she says ecstatically.

Samuel can see the forest clearing behind her and predicts if he can get back to camp Cerbera may not want to risk following, but she appears to have anticipated his plan.

"Nuh, uh. Don't even try it, love. You'll never get past me."

Cerbera begins to circle around Samuel like a predator as every step narrows the space in between him and her. Samuel slowly walks backwards in a circular pattern to keep his eyes on her, but she's funneling him into an inescapable situation.

"There's something different about you since the last time I saw you," Cerbera continues. "I guess you can say I'm a girl who likes the knight life."

"Stop the small talk," Samuel replies.

"How else are we going to get to know each other?" she says.

Samuel backs up between two trees as Cerbera steps in front of him. "Checkmate," she says with a smile. Samuel looks over his shoulder to find Isabella has closed off his rear escape. The two sisters slowly advance while exhaling their breaths at him. "You are out of options for escape, my little crusader," Cerbera teases.

"This game of cat and mouse was fun, but your time now belongs to us," Isabella adds.

"There's a whole army in that field. All I need to do is holler," Samuel says.

"Your lips will be emitting all kinds of sounds, of that I'm sure," Cerbera replies.

Samuel's chances are slim, but maybe he can make it to the field, it's the only move he has left. He makes a last mad dash through the woods, but it proves to be in vain when Isabella darts around him and catches him in her arms. She smiles and slides her hand down his cheek and neck.

"Silly boy," Isabella says. "Haven't you learned yet? We are much faster than you." The sisters grin as they sandwich Samuel between them.

"You have proved to be quite difficult to catch, despite just being human," Cerbera says.

"We've been patient with you playing hard to get, but now we want to have our fill," Isabella continues. "Can you pleasure two women at the same time, I wonder?" she adds.

"Betwixt our legs. You will show us equal affection when we take our turns with you." Cerbera demands.

"I want you to smell me when I part myself for you. Sweet words can win a girl, but so can a tongue when no words are spoken," Isabella whispers in his ear.

"But first, a little taste so you may not run from us again," Cerbera says as she and Isabella place their fangs on his neck. Their bite will poison his blood and weaken the circulation through his body. With little blood flow to his legs, he will become immobilized and at the mercy of his new caretakers. He will remain human for as long as they only nibble on him from time to time. This ensures he will be able to replenish the blood that was lost, if more is taken, he will become one of the fold, too much, and he will die. He can feel them starting to break his skin and he relinquishes himself to his fate.

WHOOSH!

An arrow rushes into Isabella's spine. The sisters abandon their task with Samuel to focus on Valencia with her wrist crossbows pointing toward them, and a determined scowl hints at her intent. Isabella's hand slides off Samuel's shoulders to release him from his paralysis and he falls to the ground.

Valencia gives no warning and fires continuously from both crossbows. Isabella takes several arrows in her chest and one through her hand when she tries to protect herself. Valencia empties both crossbows into Isabella and sending her to the ground on her back. Cerbera snarls and hunches forward with her arms out at her sides ready to pounce.

Richard and Bartel soon appear through the clearing as they run around Valencia with their weapons in hand. Cerbera avoids Richard's mace and then leaps up when Bartel's sword draws near to her. She remains securely in place from her vertical position on one of the tree trunks while glaring down at her foes and dear sister squirming while trying to lift herself up. Valencia reloads more arrows into her crossbow and flicks them back into firing position. Valencia takes aim and fires an arrow just past Cerbera's head. She snarls and then leaps higher into the trees before another attempt can be made.

Richard and Bartel help Samuel up as Valencia holds her aim on Isabella as she advances closer. Isabella rises to one knee as she looks up smiling.

"Don't look so mad, little girl. You will always be too late," she giggles.

Valencia maintains her determined glare, and without uttering a word, she fires an arrow into the middle of Isabella's heart.

Isabella lets out a high-pitched screech as her hair grows longer and becomes white, and her face shrinks inward. Her jaw becomes elongated and her eyes recess into their eye sockets. Her fingernails grow longer as the skin on her hands begin to thin down to bone. Her whole body goes through a rapid aging and then decomposing faze until she explodes into a sudden burst of dust. Valencia's arrows fall to the ground as every particle that once resembled Isabella floats up and is carried away in the wind.

"That was for John," she says.

In the distance Cerbera's long, mournful cry echoes throughout the forest. Her sister is dead, but she has chosen retreat for now. Their plan almost succeeded. Samuel was almost theirs forever. Her blood becomes hot with the anticipation of bringing him back to ravage him, now it boils with anger and laden with sorrow. She is fueled with revenge, and Samuel will pay the price for it.

Valencia rests her bows and hesitates before walking up to Samuel. She takes his chin into her hands and forces it to the side so she can inspect his neck. The indentations from two sets of fangs are clearly visible, but the tiny blood spots are not enough to affect Samuel since their saliva failed to enter his bloodstream.

"I think I'm okay," he says. Valencia looks him in the eyes for a moment before swiftly slapping him hard across the face.

"What the hell is your problem! Do you know what you just put me through!?" Samuel remains quiet as she continues. "You knew they were tracking you and what do you do!? You wander off in the woods, at night, by yourself, and you don't even think to bring a weapon!" she scolds.

"I forgot—" he begins in a small voice. Valencia pushes both her hands into Samuel's chest to knock his back into a tree.

"No, I don't want to hear it, Sam! You could have come to me! You could have told someone, anyone! Instead, I wake up to find your tent empty and you're nowhere to be found!" Valencia's emotion wreak havoc on her as anger and fear finally meet to create tears in her eyes. "I heard you yell. And the whole time I'm preparing myself to find you dead, or something I will need to kill. You know nothing about that!"

"I thought—" Samuel begins, but he's immediately cut off.

"No, you don't get to talk. You don't say anything to me," Valencia shakes her head. "You're an idiot. You have no excuses for this."

Samuel gets the hint and remains silent. Valencia huffs angrily and then walks back towards camp without another word. Samuel feels like a child after just being disciplined in public when he notices Bartel and Richard's glare fixated on him.

"Vampires are back?" Richard questions as he places his mace back in its holster. Bartel also follows suit and sheaths his sword.

"They never left," Samuel answers.

"I understand why you may have kept this a secret, but I need to know everything you know—now," Bartel orders. Samuel sighs and looks around, but he no longer desires to be outside.

"Perhaps, that conversation can take place inside your tent?"

7

The Battle of Casterham

Morning arrives as soldiers begin waking up and packing away their belongings in preparation for the march to Casterham. Valencia never went back to sleep and spent the rest of the night sitting on her mat. Samuel had spent his night explaining to Richard and Bartel all the events that led up to arriving in Ashborough, starting with Piketon.

"That is indeed quite a tale," Bartel says leaning back in his chair while stroking his beard. "But I don't think Cerbera will be much of a threat now. Not with an entire army by your side. The barbarians; however, still are." Bartel stands up. "We continue with our plan of marching to Casterham. The duke there should be able to offer us some aid."

"I will prepare my things," Richard says while standing up and then places a reassuring hand on Samuel's shoulder. "And don't worry, what we have talked about will stay between us three, and Valencia, of course." Samuel nods as Richard leaves the tent. News of Samuel talking about vampires will brand him a lunatic, along with his already acquired exile status. He's last to stand and begins to leave the tent when Bartel calls him back.

"Sam." Samuel turns around to face him. "Neither you nor Valencia are soldiers, and I fear our encounter with these invaders will be challenging even for our most seasoned fighters. You don't have to be a part of this any longer. You will be under my protection as a citizen until we locate a safe location to drop the two of you off." Samuel drops his eyes to the floor as he considers Bartel's proposal. He lifts his head again after a short moment and gives him a small smile.

"Well, that doesn't sound exciting at all. I'm afraid you're stuck with us." Bartel snickers and nods his head.

"Then I welcome you into our ranks with the utmost sincerity."

The march carries on along the Avon River before the morning dew has had a chance to evaporate from the blades of grass. Valencia and Samuel walk side by side in silence for several moments. Neither knows how to begin the conversation. Samuel doesn't want to upset her further by saying the wrong thing and Valencia has mixed emotions of anger and worry still fresh on her mind. Underneath it all she's happy that he's okay but forgiving him is still another matter entirely.

"Everyone in my life who meant something to me was taken away," Valencia finally speaks, but keeps her focus ahead of her without turning to face Samuel. "And I never got to say goodbye, not to any one of them. I was afraid that happened again last night."

"Everyone who was in my life walked away. They never came back either. I know—because I waited for them too. I thought that after some time had passed, they would just reappear. All the little things that people argue about or all the imperfections that seem too much to accept would eventually be realized as petty. But that never happens. You hold onto a hope that someone still thinks about you. You dream it every night, that moment when they come back, and all is right again. It's when you wake up that you feel the worse. Maybe I'm just easy to forget. There is no physical pain that can bring more discomfort than that which resides inside the heart."

"I don't know those people, Sam, but I can tell you they

are not worth waiting for. They exist solely to feed off your passions and are only satisfied once they have sapped all desire and euphoria from you. You never meant anything to them. Why waste a thought on them? They leave a poison behind that tricks you into longing for them, but it's an illusion, and when it fades, it becomes clear that it was you who had left them." The two exchange heartfelt glances and small grins.

"Every time I come face to face with death and danger you appear; like a Goddess sent to comfort a man who has lost heart," Samuel says. Valencia smiles and looks away bashfully.

"A Goddess, huh?" Valencia pauses. "Since I've been around you, I've felt renewed. I would have been lost to my vices and vexes if it had not been for you. You brought me hope."

"Then I guess we saved each other."

Bartel halts his army and then sends a three-man patrol unit ahead to survey the landscape. Casterham isn't far but he doesn't want or lead his men into an ambush or be surprised an army is closer than they had anticipated. He also must consider that Casterham may have already been attacked and their journey will be fruitless. The soldiers rest beside the bank of the river while snacking on smoked meat and bread until the scouts return with their report.

Richard holds a roll out towards Robert and then points to a piece of pork on his plate. He nods and makes the trade only to find out that the inside had been scooped out. He chucks the hallow roll at Richard's chest who has just devoured the piece of meat. William rolls back laughing as Richard smiles, but Robert fails to find the humor in the misleading trade and remains pouting.

Meanwhile, Bartel's scouts halt their horses near a bloody patch in the field. After careful inspection they discover the remains of a wild boar and conclude it could be hunters from Casterham. One man jumps off his steed to comb the scene for any further clues. He's almost satisfied with their assumption until an uncommon arrow tip is spotted in the ribs of the beast. He retrieves it and studies it intensely before handing it to someone else.

"What do you make of this?" he asks. The second scout looks it over and then shakes his head.

"This is no English arrow tip." He hands it to the third man while gazing into the distance. If this kill wasn't hunters from Casterham, then the only other possibility is barbarians, and the kill is still fresh. Going any further puts them at risk of becoming ambushed or waste valuable time in advancing to Casterham if an attack is imminent. The scouts ride back to Bartel's tent to find him leaning over his strategy table. One of the men hands the recovered arrow tip to him as he inspects it with a keen eye.

"We found this among a slaughtered boar."

"It's not like anything I'm familiar with," adds another scout.

"It's foreign—" Bartel ponders. "How far away was this found?"

"Just over yonder," a scout points in the direction they had rode.

"The kill is maybe three hours old, perhaps less," a scout explains.

"Casterham is about a two-hour march from here," Bartel thinks out loud while guiding his finger to the town's location on the map. "Which means we are already late—I fear my assumption may have been correct after all. The barbarian army is planning to breach Casterham's walls." He leaves the tent with quickened steps and then turns his attention to the field to shout his orders.

"We're moving out, men. Double time!"

The shuffling of feet and rustling of armor take over as everyone senses the urgency in Bartel's tone and prepares for a hasty departure.

Casterham is located at the meeting of the Avon and Severn Rivers, and four miles to the south is the Bristol Channel. If the barbarians reach the waterways, they can sail anywhere and become untraceable until they attack again. They also could decide to set up a stronghold and wait for reinforcements to arrive to sack larger targets that are better defended with better spoils. They must not be given the opportunity to prepare, lest the entire country will fall under their rule.

Casterham's guards patrol to and fro on the stone ramparts while holding crossbows or with long swords strapped to their belts. A single wall mounted ballista is positioned on top of the gateway to ward off the occasional band of bandits, but Casterham never planned for a large invasion.

The castle, and its surrounding area are lavishly decorated

with banners, gardens and water works while clean, white cobblestone walkways lead to its steps. The rest of the town; however, is mediocre at best, with most of its population living in poverty and poorly maintained and unkempt homes with muddy paths and murky drinking water drawn from two wells.

The duke and his chosen few sap all the riches, and the best food from the citizens to leave them with scrapes and prone to disease as they stomp through feces and urine barefoot when off the main road.

Bartel leads Samuel and Valencia along with five of his soldiers toward the castle steps while the rest of his army, and Richard's group wait patiently outside of Casterham's walls. Word of the steward's army approaching has reached Duke Bennett and he waits at the top of the steps ready to meet him. He's clothed in a long ornate robe, and gold rings and bracelets adorn his fingers and wrists. He stands with his nose up while taking the stance of one who is too important to be bothered. His reputation is that of a snobby, self-centered man; drunk on power and in love with riches, control, and most of all, himself. Bartel nods respectfully, but Bennett only smiles smugly.

"My name is Bartel, steward of Ashborough."

"Duke Bennett," is all he says for an introduction.

"Duke, the reason for my presence is simple. We have been tracking an invading army of barbarians and we believe your city may be in their sights."

"Barbarians, you say—do you wish to entertain me with your fantasies?" Samuel attempts to intervene to defend Bartel's words, but Bartel places a hand on his shoulder to delay him. He wishes to deal with this man on his own terms and pace.

"I have personally encountered this threat, duke."

"I see, and where are these barbarians now?"

"We have yet to discover their current location."

"Well, perhaps you should first find their forces before assuming my city is in any sort of danger," Bennett responds in the same carefree attitude as before with little urgency and no desire to put more thought into the matter.

"My scouts inform me an attack on this city is very plausible if not already planned. I feel consideration in the plausible should be heeded. It may be wise to alert your army and set up your defenses."

"What I should do—is not listen to a *steward* telling me how to run my city!" Bennett barks. The thought of doing anything, is an annoyance in itself, but being instructed by someone he deems lower ranked than him is just insulting.

"With all due respect sir, you should consider the safety of your citizens. They will pay a heavy price for your inactions," Bartel snaps back as his calming nature and patience wear thin.

"War has come to this province before, some will survive it."

"I don't like this guy," Samuel whispers while leaning close to Valencia.

"Peace, Samuel; neither do I," she softly replies.

"You would rather sacrifice human life than to take proper measures in order to protect them?" Bartel asks in frustration.

"If you are wrong, I would have wasted resources and time for nothing," Bennett replies in a self-indulging tone.

"If I'm wrong, you're lucky. If I'm right, you are unprepared."

"I have no further words for you," Bennett says with a careless wave. "Go on your scavenger hunt if you must, and leave my city, but most of all, my presence." Bennett ends this conversation on his terms and departs back toward the castle.

Bartel turns to face his men still fuming from the ordeal. "If we were outside these walls, I would have cut his useless tongue from his pig face." Bartel observes two children running and laughing around a man who holds the fish he had caught up proudly to his wife. Bartel turns his attention back to his men after taking a moment to calm down. "Scout the nearby terrain. I need a detailed report." The men nod and rush to their horses. He then turns to Samuel and Valencia. "We aren't leaving."

Bartel's men ride back through the ranks of the waiting army, but stop their steeds when Richard signals them.

"What's the word?" he asks.

"The word is that Bennett is a fucking bastard."

"He want's proof of the barbarian army," another man says.

"Proof? Should we take him to Trent?!" Richard shouts.

"Trent—" one of the men thinks out loud while scanning his surroundings. Richard remains waiting to give him a moment to explain what he's thinking. "There was mention that their army split at Trent."

"That's what we believe, yes," Richard replies. The soldier then comes to a startling conclusion.

"We were following the Avon, but they are following the Severn. They are coming from the north. Using the trees for cover to avoid detection. They will then continue unchallenged south to the channel." Richard slowly nods his head after taking in the scout's assumption.

"That makes sense."

"What's our plan?" another scout asks.

"We already know there's a barbarian scout skulking nearby. That boar kill proves it. I'm going to find him."

"I'll ride with you," Richard says as he mounts a nearby horse. Bartel's men nod in acceptance of his offer being happy to have one more in their party.

"Watch William," Richard says while looking at Robert.

"Of course," Robert agrees.

Richard then takes off with the other men as they ride north in search of the elusive barbarian scout.

Meanwhile, Bartel has invited himself inside Bennett's throne room to find him slouching in his throne with his feet up and drinking a goblet of red wine. Bennett hardly seems to care as he swirls the wine around his goblet.

"I thought I told you to withdraw from my city," he says.

"I will not depart when so many lives are in peril," Bartel answers. Bennett ignores Bartel's heroism and changes the subject back to his wine, as if flaunting his riches will impress him.

"Have you ever had red wine? I got this as a gift from France, one of many actually," Bennett takes another sip before continuing. "As a Duke I am rewarded with many bounties from both near and far. I find red wine more palatable than white. The reds have a robustness to them that lingers on your senses." Bartel allows him to finish but brings the topic back to what truly is important.

"How long are you going to hide behind your title? You act high and mighty well enough, but when the time demands leadership, you lack action. Having power is easy when war isn't lurking outside your walls." Bennett straightens up and sets his wine down.

"Your words will bring a rope around your neck! You are no king, steward. You cannot speak to me as you do to your underlings. I outrank you!" Bennett leans back and picks his wine up again. He sips it slowly hoping to make Bartel envious before speaking again. "Speaking of kings, what happened to yours? I heard he drowned."

"King Ladislas was on a trading vessel as he attempted to open new trade routes with foreign civilizations. Upon his return, however, they were caught in a powerful tempest. It's believed that all went down with the ship, but that remains a theory. Next time get the full story before you decide to comment on it."

"The full story? Like you, trying to scare me with barbarian invaders, yet not even knowing where they are." Bartel can tell by the posh decor of the main hall that Bennett is a man who prides appearance and status above all else.

"You live quite well inside your palace while the rest of your city deteriorates. Your riches would be of better use to cure the disease, famine, and hovels you so proudly reign over." Bennett stands up brashly and scowls.

"Do not tell me how I should use my possessions! Everything you have is borrowed. Maybe you are the invader that I need to worry about."

"Does your stupidity have no end!"

"That's it! I will have you flogged and banished." Bartel reaches for his sword, but only manages to slide it out partially before screams are heard in the city. Bartel pushes his sword back into his sheath and then rushes outside without hesitation.

Bartel meets his scouts outside with Samuel, Valencia and Richard standing off to the side. Several townsfolk in the nearby area are keeping their distance with a look of shock and disgust. One of the scouts holds up the severed head of the barbarian scout just as Bennett steps outside.

"We brought proof, duke!" the scout shouts, before tossing the head at Bennett's feet. The head rolls toward his toes as he attempts to step back to avoid the grotesque object from touching him. The scout then turns to Bartel to give his report.

"We found his camp in the woods."

"Was he alone?" Bartel asks.

"He was, but he was hunkered down and biding his time." Bartel lets a moment pass before asking for clarification.

"What do you mean?"

"After further exploration we saw several thousand barbarians marching in the lowlands. They'll be here before nightfall." Even though Bartel assumed this was the barbarians plan all along, he did not want to hear the news of it being true. Bennett is silent as he looks from the head at his feet to Bartel.

"Perhaps we may reason with them. Offer them a bribe of some sort," he says now changing his attitude from smug to frightened.

"You want to try diplomacy—with barbarians?" Bartel questions.

"I have gold and silver." Bennett's riches have always bought his way into or out of every situation he was ever in. He thinks it will again under these circumstances as well.

"They will take your gold and silver, but they will also burn this city to the ground, rape every woman and girl, and murder everyone—even you," Bartel explains the harsh reality of the approaching danger. Bennett nervously looks around but seems unsure of what to do. Bartel waits for him to act, thinking maybe he has some hidden leadership qualities to him, but without a word from him, he decides to offer him some advice. "I strongly suggest you fortify the gates, rally your soldiers, and then change your attire. That colorful robe of yours will not stop an arrow or spear."

"Yes, I—I will get ready," Bennett says as he runs back into the castle. Bartel shakes his head knowing Bennett does not have what it takes to lead an army to war. The fate of Casterham, and her people, fall upon his shoulders. He orders some of his men to the ramparts, but for a city that was so poorly ran, preparing it to resist such a force in such a short time frame will be challenging. With no time to waste, he joins Richard, Samuel, and Valencia at the front gate.

"The barbarians are well equipped and armed from their plundering rampage. We will need to use everything this place has if we are to have a change against them," he tells them. Suddenly, a flustered Casterham soldier sprints toward the group seemingly out of breath and concerned.

"Sir! Sir," he begins.

"Yes?" Bartel responds patiently waiting for the man to take a few breaths before talking again.

"It's Bennett sir, he was just spotted riding hard into the fields with some of his gold and silver. He has abandoned us, sir."

"Goddamn coward!" Bartel shouts.

"And here I thought my opinion of him couldn't get any

lower," Richard says.

"We may be better without him," Samuel adds.

"What do we do, sir?" the soldier asks.

"It seems you're completely in charge now, Bartel," Valencia says.

Bartel's original plan of warning Casterham of a potential attack and aiding them, if necessary, somehow turned into assuming full responsibility of its defenses, citizens, and taking command of their army. He discovers the entire town, and every last one of Bennett's soldiers, watching him while waiting to hear his decision. In a short amount of time, he has earned the town's trust and the soldiers' respect. None seems to show any loyalty towards Bennett or morn his swift departure. Many actually feel they have a better chance now with Bartel.

"Alright, I want every able-bodied man rallied at these gates five minutes ago. Spread the word!" Bartel yells.

Casterham soldiers visit all the homes to enlist the men and older boys while equipping them with weapons and armor. Many of the mothers and wives try to protest, but their pleas are not debatable. They watch helplessly as their loved ones are taken and geared for war. Bartel would rather not involve or force citizens into this fight, but the army they will be facing is extensive and he fears his army and that of Casterham's may not be enough to repel them. The outlook is grim either way, for if their resistance fails the town will be lost and none will escape unscathed. Every home cannot be watched but the only entrance into the castle can at least be manned. For this reason, women and children are led inside where they are securely barricaded in case the walls are breached.

Bartel explains his strategy to his calvary while pointing into the southern woods. They then stampede across the field to wait for the time to enact Bartel's plan.

"Bring everyone into the city!" Bartel orders as infantry and archers flood through the open gate before soldiers close them and then place thick wood planks through the steel brackets.

"Since the front gate doesn't have an iron drop gate it will need to be reinforced; if the barbarians come with a battering ram this will not hold for long. Infantry will charge as soon as it's breached," Bartel explains.

The archers position themselves along the entire length of the front wall as Bartel gives them instructions.

"When your targets are in range you are authorized to fire on your own accord."

The last few citizens are led into the castle before the doors are shut and then barred from the inside. Bartel paces in front of his and Casterham's soldiers and the men from town that were chosen to fight alongside them.

"The silence before battle, and the unnerving wait can take their toll on our morale. We have time to think and worry. We start to doubt our abilities and fear sets in. If this happens, we are already defeated. I want all of you to look around!" Bartel says as the men obey and glance at one another.

"You are not alone! You are brave men who will look into the eyes of these barbarians and tell them; today, I will deprive you of your victory! And you will feel the sharp sting of my blade!" Bartel holds his sword high for all to see. The men raise their weapons and cheer.

While Bartel is giving his pep talk, Richard is away from the crowd while observing William with his father's sword strapped to his side. William picks up a coat of chain mail from an armor rack just as Richard meets up with him.

"What do you think you are doing, squire?"

"Getting ready like everyone else." Richard puts his hand on William's shoulder.

"You have not yet reached the accepted age for enlistment. You don't have to fight this one."

"I have to! I will avenge my father's death whether you approve it or not." Richard stares at him for a moment and then chuckles. He knew William was going to grow up fast, but he also wants to make sure he does grow up.

"Alright, but you stay by my side at all times. If I can't see your breath, you are too far away."

"Okay," William agrees. Richard takes the chain mail from him.

"You don't even know how to dress yourself in this, do you?"

"Not really," William admits.

"Come here." Richard pulls the coat over William's head and lets it drop down around him. "There, now practice walking and swinging. You'll need to get used to this armor fairly quickly." William obeys as Richard watches and provides as much advice as he can in the short training session they are given.

Samuel is standing on the rampart looking across the countryside as the sun becomes increasingly lower in the horizon. Two younger townsfolk boys stand near him in armor and with their swords resting at their sides. He glances at them and can tell they are afraid.

"Are you two okay?" he asks.

"We are not soldiers," one of them says in a shaky voice.

"Neither was I," Samuel admits.

"But you are now, right?" the other boy asks.

"No, someone gave me a sword, but never said I had to use it."

"So, what do we do?"

"When the time comes—you just know," Samuel answers with a smile.

Samuel leaves the boys to ponder his words as he joins Valencia on the other side of the wall. "I've been waiting for an adventure my entire life," Samuel begins. "What the hell was I thinking?" he continues softer.

"You got what you wished for, Sam," Valencia laughs. Samuel gazes at Valencia sincerely.

"A result of a restless mind, I'm afraid. I wish for more important things now." Valencia returns the gaze.

"And what is it that you wish for now?"

"I never want to walk alone on a long road ever again." She shyly smiles and directs her eyes back to the field.

"I tried to convince myself that I didn't need anyone," she begins. "It was a failed attempt to make life somewhat bearable. The irony; however, is that without someone—life *is* unbearable." They share the urge to embrace each other and imagine their lips pressed together, but they also share the assumption this thought is not shared by the other. Their soulful moment becomes interrupted by the deep blow of a horn as Casterham's lookouts warn of an impending attack. The barbarians have started to assemble near the tree line and are standing in formation as many more are still pouring out of the forest.

"To arms! To arms!" Bartel yells. Infantry hurry to their designated locations and archers line the walls while bows loaded and raised. With the element of surprise lost the barbarians now rely on brute force and relentless assaults.

On this late autumn, at twilight, the barbarians invade Casterham. Outmatched, and with less than sufficient preparations, they stand ready to counter. The future of the province lies in the hands of mostly unseasoned warriors, led by a steward with no king, and two drifters who all the countrymen never cared to know.

"I'll see you when this is done," Samuel says with a smile.

"Yes, you will," Valencia replies.

The barbarians howl and begin their charge. Casterham's archers let loose a volley of arrows into the mob and a deadly black rain descends upon the advancing army. The unharmed men continue their stampede over their fallen comrades disrespectfully as they tenaciously carry out their intended plans.

The ballista squad works swiftly to load and fire their main offence. The large arrow carries enough momentum to impale three barbarians while sending them flying backwards into others behind them.

The barbarians also have a siege weapon in their arsenal, and the releasing of their catapult hurls a large boulder toward Casterham's walls.

"Catapult!" Bartel warns at the top of his lungs. Luckily, the boulder smashes into the ground before reaching the walls.

"Where the hell did they get that?" Samuel asks surprised.

"It's one of ours. They could have taken it from anywhere," Valencia says.

The archers send another volley of arrows into the barbarians to cut down more of their numbers, but it does little to slow or scare them. Arrows alone cannot win this war.

Bartel looks at the soldiers operating the ballista and points toward the catapult. "Take that out!"

The soldiers nod and aim the ballista towards their new target. The catapult hurls another boulder toward the walls. Learning from their previous shot, this one was better planned as it explodes through the front gate and all its reinforcements. Splintered wood and metal fly up and fall in a large radius as debris and dust fill the air.

"Breach!" a soldier cries out. As the dust clears it's obvious the barbarians now have a direct path into town.

"Infantry to the front gate!" Bartel orders.

The infantry rush into the field and collide into the first wave of barbarians with Richard and William among them. Weapons clash against one another or slice and stab through flesh. A barbarian's axe chops a soldier's leg off and leaves him bleeding to death in agonizing pain. Richard's mace tears half of a barbarian's face off and part of his eyeball. Bodies from both sides quickly soak the grass with blood and entrails with neither side proving to have an advantage.

The barbarians are loading the catapult with another boulder at the same time as one of the ballista's team attaches a black bag to the end of the arrow and lights it. The bag flames up just before it's released. The timing of both weapons being fired just happens to be in sync as both sides have their sights on the other's war machines. The boulder and arrow sore past each other as they continue onward to their destinations.

"Incoming!" Bartel yells, but his warning cannot change the outcome that is soon to follow. The boulder crashes into the wall and part of the ballista. The ballista's operators are blown off the wall with some of their limbs separating from their bodies. The stones from the wall are blasted into town and into the field. The ballista slides down to hang over the edge of the damaged wall with an arrow loosely in place.

The ballista's last shot was well aimed as well and explodes violently into the catapult. The nearby barbarians, along with iron and wood are blown outward around the expanding plume of fire and smoke.

The fields near Casterham show a gruesome scene of blood-soaked soil, intestines, maim limbs and decapitated victims. This is far from an easy victory the barbarians have been used too, but they refuse to retreat or surrender and push harder into town. William stabs a barbarian through his thigh, and when the foe falls to his knees, Richard smashes his mace into his chest. The barbarians break through the line of defending infantry and begin to climb the stone steps of the ramparts. The archers must abandon their posts or risk being slaughtered. Samuel meets them with both swords in hand as Valencia alternates from fighting with her sword and firing her wrist crossbows when she has time to aim. While the two can easily defend this area, the barbarians begin to outnumber Bartel and Robert on the opposite set of steps.

"Go to them. I'm fine here," Samuel says. Valencia nods and hurries to their aid.

At the broken gate, Hagathor effortlessly makes his appearance and kills several soldiers with a large claymore with surprising speed and strength.

Bartel signals to the last group of archers to fire with the wave of his hand. Three men each shoot a flaming arrow into the sky and lands in the field with no target sought out. Few enemies bother to take note of this seemingly useless move, but this wasn't an attack, it was a cue. Thunder roars and the ground trembles as Bartel's cavalry charge toward Casterham behind the barbarian force. The cavalry closes in from behind as the infantry continues to push forward. Richard and William share in another kill and give each other accomplished smirks. Now that the invading army is being attacked from both ends, their offence is slowed as the disoriented mob plans where they need to turn to defend

Hagathor; however, cares not of his men in the field or any technique that doesn't involve brutality. He glances up towards the ramparts and isolates Valencia fighting next to Bartel. He narrows his eyes and snarls; he remembers her from Guildsmith. She was the one who robbed him of a kill when she helped Samuel escaped, and now he wants her to pay for it.

Hagathor forces his way up the steps by killing the resisting guards and then pushing them off as he proceeds with a might none can prevent. Valencia is unaware of him advancing behind her. She aims her crossbows and strikes down several barbarians surrounding Samuel. When she's satisfied of bettering his odds, she returns to her sword to slice the neck of a barbarian as Bartel stabs another. She then fires a shot from her opposite wrist at a barbarian behind Robert. The man topples over the front wall and lands on top of the soldiers fighting in the field below.

Hagathor is stalking closer towards Valencia, no other target is more sought after. He only kills those who are in his way and doesn't deviate from his glare. The ongoing battle drew her farther from Bartel and Robert's quick support. Samuel takes his last kill before earning a break with nearby assailants. His concern now turns to Valencia as he checks on her status. At that moment, a horned helmet rises above the side of the staircase followed by fur covered shoulders. Horror grips him when he understands who is behind her as this monstrosity draws his sword back. Samuel's voice becomes trapped in his head, but his expression begs Valencia to turn around. Hagathor thrusts his blade into her stomach to force her whole body to jolt back. She opens her mouth, but no sound comes out, her grip loosens, and her sword falls silently on the stone floor. Shock prevents sound from being processed and numbs pain and feeling throughout her limbs. For her everything is slow, for Samuel everything has stopped. Hagathor grins sinfully as he pulls the bloody sword from her. She places her hands over her bleeding wound and collapses to her knees. Her hair fans out as she falls and then gently wraps around her eyes when she hits the ground. Samuel finally finds his voice.

"Valencia!"

She feels herself falling again as if in a dream. She does not feel the cold, hard stone when her back hits it, just the view of the sunset lit sky until Samuel's face appears in her view. Bartel and Robert direct their attacks on Hagathor to distract him away from her. She wraps her arms around Samuel's neck as he picks her up and then carries her away from the scene to the lower level. He sets her down near a quiet flower patch and holds her against his chest with his arm supporting her back. He combs her hair to the side with his other hand as she places her cold hand on his cheek.

"You're going to be okay," he says fighting back the tears.

"You saved me," she says with a weak smile.

"I'm going to take you to the coast, Val. I want to show you the ocean." Samuel holds his hand over her wound as she gasps in pain.

"You showed be so much already," she says in a whisper.

"I love you, Val. I don't know why I never said it before. I don't know why I waited—"

She brings his head toward hers and touches his lips with hers. She uses the last of her strength to form a kiss. Samuel lets his tears run down his cheeks as he cherishes the moment he's been dreaming about even before he met her. She was the one in his dreams. Her head falls back, and he eases her down.

"Don't leave me." Her hand falls from his face and her eyelids close. Samuel lets out a mournful howl as he holds Valencia in his arms.

Robert body slams a foe as he makes his way toward Samuel.

"Robert! Robert!" Samuel carefully hands Valencia over to his waiting arms.

"Get her out of here. Keep her safe."

"I will," he promises as he heads toward the secured castle

doors. A guard peers through a peep hole before the doors open to allow him passage. They then quickly shut the door after he has entered.

Samuel wipes the tears from his eyes and then glares at Hagathor still fighting with Bartel on the wall. He draws each of his swords individually and closes his eyes. He steadies his heartbeat and focuses his mind, he hears everything— yelling, grunts, swords colliding— and then silence. He opens his eyes and only sees Hagathor alone in a vacant town. "You're mine," he growls. Samuel calmly climbs the steps as he instinctively rotates his blades around his body. The blades seem light, but deal heavy blows, as they fly glide through the air to strike his opponents. They feel more of an extension of his own arms as his hand does not loose grip or slide down the handle. Samuel advances toward Hagathor with determination. There are no second thoughts; he's not afraid of challenging this behemoth; only to kill the brute who thought going after Valencia was a good idea.

Hagathor's upward swing collides hard into the side of Bartel's sword and flings it out of his grip and over the wall. Hagathor kicks Bartel to the ground and then brings his claymore down upon him. Bartel closes his eyes while holding his breath.

CLING!

Bartel looks up to see both Samuel's swords crossed above him and blocking Hagathor's claymore.

"Take a break, Bartel," he says without taking his eyes off Hagathor. "Do you remember me, you bastard? I will not allow you to live beyond today," Hagathor retracts his sword and faces Samuel eager to finish another who escaped his wrath. He grins as if taunting Samuel was his plan all along. The stage has been set, Samuel's challenge has been accepted, no one is allowed to intervene, this is their last stand.

Hagathor's swing is fast and carries a powerful force when Samuel parries it. Knowing he can withstand his attack; Samuel unleashes his counter with both swords. Hagathor blocks one and then sidesteps to avoid the other.

Those that witnessed this duel will say that their swords sounded like thunder and created sparks of lightening with every deflection, but Bartel admits only seeing arcs of red flames, which was probably the result of the reflecting light from the setting sun.

Samuel's assaults are fast and keep Hagathor on the defense, but Hagathor finds his opening and delivers a barrage of deadly combos that normally would have solidified his victory, but Samuel halts the long blade with both his swords. Two blades can withstand Hagathor's hash swings where one would be forced away to leave his opponent temporary defenseless. Both continue exchanging stabbing techniques and horizontal swipes while trading between offence and defense. It's clear that Hagathor isn't used to lasting fights, since none of his adversaries remained standing this long.

Their fighting has now moved them across the ramparts and to the hanging ballista. Samuel blocks an attack, but this one proves to be the most his sword can take as one of them snaps in half. Samuel swiftly penetrates Hagathor's left shoulder with his second sword, but the successful blow does nothing to slow him down. Hagathor sends a swift kick into Samuel's gut to force his grip from the sword and knocking him back into the ballista.

The ballista rocks back and forth as loose pebbles from the crumbling ledge descend below. Hagathor grabs the blade embedded in his shoulder and yanks it out with little more than a growl to reveal the discomfort. He then flings it into town to leave Samuel defenseless. Hagathor thrusts his claymore forward leaving Samuel with only one escape route. Samuel climbs on top of the ballista and begins making his way to the opposite side, but the disturbance sends the ballista rocking and grinding closer to the edge. Hagathor climbs onto the ballista and follows relentlessly. Bartel observes the ballista sliding and scraping more of the loose stones from the damaged wall.

"Sam!" Bartel calls out while rushing to help his friend in peril. The damaged wall begins to crack and crumble from the abuse of the two men shaking the ballista as they hurry over it. Samuel extends his hand to Bartel just as Hagathor lunges toward him. Samuel's fingers fall through Bartel's when Hagathor falls onto the arm of the ballista while pulling Samuel back by the ankle. It's the last tremor the contraption can withstand. Samuel and Bartel lock eyes only for a moment before the ballista disappears from Bartel's view as it takes Hagathor and Samuel down with it. The shock of this sight freezes Bartel in place as he stares in distress at the empty spot on the wall.

Hagathor is jerked off the ballista while Samuel holds on tight to the wooden arm as they plummet to the field. Hagathor hits the ground on his back just before the falling ballista arrow pierces through his torso followed by the full weight of the ballista crushing him moments later. Samuel is thrown off the ballista when it splinters apart, and a large wooden shard rushes into his lower stomach before he hits the ground on his back.

Samuel lies motionless on the blood-soaked grass among the broken shields and daggers with the large fragment protruding from him. The sound of his own heartbeat is all he hears as the last bit of sunlight fades from the horizon.

The alliance between Ashborough and Casterham's forces finally overwhelm the bulk of the barbarians at dusk. With their leader dead, and their numbers severely reduced, the remaining barbarians give up trying to take Casterham, and call for a retreat; however, the bloodthirsty infantry and calvary units, now confident of their victory, pursue them far into the woods to eliminate all they find. No prisoners and no mercy, this band of Northmen have been repelled and England's cities can now grow and prosper without fear of invasion—at least for now.

Cheers resonate through Casterham as soldiers pat or hug one another while waving their swords above them. It is a costly victory, but a victory none-the-less. Richard smiles and ruffles William's hair. The boy has survived his first war while also avenging his father's death. Bartel doesn't take part in the celebrating as he hurries down the steps and then hastily through town. Richard observes the urgency of his movements and fears this victory came with a price. He has yet to locate Valencia or Samuel and suspects Bartel may be heading towards his answer. Without another thought Richard hurries after him.

Samuel opens his eyes to see a woman leaning over him. His eyesight is blurry, and her face is out of focus.

"Valencia?" he asks softly. The face leans in closer to his eyes to reveal that it's not Valencia.

"Not quite, my dear," Cerbera says. She slides her hand up his chest and rests it on his cheek and then lowers her fangs to his neck. "Your heartbeat is faint. You are dieing. Maybe now you will give in to me. I can save you, and in turn, you will belong to me," she whispers. The puncturing of flesh is the last sound Samuel hears and all feeling escapes him. Cerbera slowly lifts her head from him to see the dagger inside her heart, held in place by Samuel's bloody hand.

"Sorry, but my heart belongs to another," Samuel admits. Cerbera's death is not as violent as Isabella's. Her skin slowly flakes away, piece by piece, and blows away in the wind until there is nothing left—Samuel's neck remains untouched.

Let me show you the ocean, Val— Samuel's last thought is a vision of Valencia standing on the sands of the coast. His eyes close before Bartel and Richard make it to his side.

Bartel and Richard kneel beside Samuel as other soldiers begin carrying their wounded on stretchers. Bartel places his hand on Samuel's chest while lowering his ear to his mouth and nose. He cannot feel his breath or hear a heartbeat.

"Get this man medical treatment at once," he orders.

"Casterham is out of room to care for any more injured," a soldier replies. "The wounded are now being taken to Deerhurst. A cart is about to leave."

"Make sure he's on it then," Bartel says.

Richard puts his hand on Samuel's shoulder. "You fought brave and true, my friend. I will not forget you."

The death of Hagathor marked the end of the barbarian threat. The small pockets of straggling Northmen were later sought out and culled to prevent them from regrouping. Bartel claimed Casterham under his watchful eye and appointed Richard as the commander of its army and governor of its people. The citizens were eager to welcome the new leaders who took matters such as health, hygiene, security, food, and construction seriously. Casterham did not disappear off the map, instead it expanded and became a grand city.

Bennett couldn't take all his riches with him when he organized his swift evacuation. Most of his stockpiles of gold was then spent to rebuild Casterham and provide its citizens the amenities they desperately needed. Clinics, roads, gardens, sturdier homes, barracks, and more farmlands were just a few of these updates Bartel and Richard focused on. The citizens also now earn a salary for their chosen field of work. Several survivors of Trent settled to Casterham while others stayed in Ashborough and the site of Trent became a memorial to all who fell in the battle of 1325.

As for Bennett, he was found in a fortnight, hanging by his neck from an oak branch with nothing on except his long underwear. No bandits have been discovered anywhere nearby and no one has come forth with being responsible for this action. Whoever robbed and hung him remains a mystery, but why waste precious resources and time to solve it?

Most people will never believe vampires ever existed. They will say they were the result of an uneducated mind and unknown sciences. They will say vampires were just stories, born from an overactive imagination in a time when superstitions and legends were believed. But let me tell you this—no matter how the world evolves; old beliefs and ancient powers will never die out. Vampires too will evolve into a form that differs from how history had painted them. To say they are gone would be a mistake, to say they were never here would be foolish. Vampires will always exist in one form or another.

Two months have passed since the battle of Casterham, and England enters a mild winter. Deerhurst sits on the cliffs overlooking the Bristol Channel and remains one of the few towns that were untouched by the barbarian army. This would not have been true if Casterham had fallen. It is a town that promotes education and medical advances; it is a town of scholars and professionals, and it has prospered very well with libraries, schools, and clinics. Deerhurst's doctors are some of the most skilled medical practitioners who are known to heal impossible wounds and ailments. On the night of the barbarian battle they saved a great many who would have perished elsewhere. Samuel was no exception.

The pub is mostly empty save for two old men and one still recovering from his brush with death. Samuel stares deeply into his cider without an expression and with his stomach still wrapped in cloth bandages. Someone enters the pub and stands in the doorway before the pair of feet begin to advance towards Samuel. He doesn't acknowledge the stranger behind him or when the chair across from him is pulled out and the person sits down.

"You do not belong here," Samuel lifts his head from the cider and lays his eyes on a familiar face. One who has lived in his dreams, one who never left his consciousness, his every waking moment and every restless night the same smiling face materialized in his head—and now she is once again sitting before him.

"Where is it that I belong then?"

"With me," Valencia says. The two stand and embrace each

other while engaging in a long passionate kiss that has been long overdue.

"I love you, Sam," she finally admits.

"I loved you since the moment I first saw you," he responds. Valencia smiles.

"It took me a bit longer," she chuckles. Samuel strokes her cheek as his gaze falls into her eyes.

"Every day in that God-forsaken bed I was overcome by worry. I had dreams of returning to Casterham and finding you dead," Samuel says.

"I never once stopped thinking about you, Sam. I told myself that as soon as I was released from care, I was going to find you. It didn't matter how long it took or how far away I had to go; I was going to find you." Samuel and Valencia sit back down while keeping their hands interlocked across the table.

"What's with the cider?" Valencia asks when she notices his drink.

"Someone once told me that ale was for fat, smelly, piggish men with no class." Valencia laughs hysterically.

"Now—who would say such a thing as that?"

Samuel and Valencia ride into Casterham on a trader's cart being pulled by a single horse. Bartel, Richard, Robert and William cheer and clap while taking turns welcoming Samuel back.

"We had your name on the memorial plaque, but Valencia told us to remove it," Richard says.

"She threatened to put my name on it if it was not taken off," Robert admits. The reacquainted group shares in a laugh.

"Somehow, I can actually picture this," Samuel says while laughing.

That night, Bartel arranges a great celebration at the castle for all the people of Castaham. A great feast of the town's harvested vegetables, pig roasts, and of course, plenty of ale and mead, with a cask or two of cider. It is not only to honor the town's expansion but also the return of a servery missed hero of war. Bartel stands up at the head of the hall and gathers everyone's attention as the noisy room slowly becomes quiet.

"Citizens of Casterham, soldiers, officers, and friends," Bartel begins. "I have heard people speak of a man who saved all of England, slaughtered the barbarian army, and rebuilt a town. A man who kicked Bennett's arse up a tree and then pulled down his trousers." The hall is suddenly filled with laughter. "I have seen the paintings of this man and have come to realize he looks a lot like me." The hall becomes filled with cheers and raised mugs, but Bartel raises his hand to silence them once more. "I do not doubt I love to be praised when praise is deserved, but I must admit to all of you now that I am not the hero of this tale.

Let me tell you about a man. An ordinary man, a man who is no different than any man here now. He was not a soldier, not a person of status. He didn't even have a permanent home. He was called a drifter, a pariah, a rebel and a rogue. None of which are considered very heroic, I know. But when this barbarian plague fell upon our land, he joined another to form a solid duo to combat a great number of risks. And they did it alone, until they knew they could not any longer. They could have run, but they didn't. They could have hidden, but they didn't. No, instead of leaving or giving up, even against tremendous odds. Odds that would have made the bravest and mightiest of all men lose faith and nerve—they continued. They walked through the night without food, water, or rest. Deprived of sleep and tired they traversed the countryside to seek me out. To gain my aid in a war I did not even know was happening. Did I believe them? No, they did not look like warriors. Am I to be coaxed by two vagabonds? I can live with myself if I were to be fooled into investigating a false claim, but could I live with myself for doing nothing if a message ended up being true?

I am the messenger now. And these two warriors fought a great war. A war that none here will ever be able to fully understand—not even if every one of their battles were documented. I give to you our heroes," Bartel extends his outreached arm to where Samuel and Valencia are sitting. "Samuel Hall and Valencia Ruskin, the true heroes of the barbarian conflict, of Casterham and of England!" Richard stands up and begins clapping followed by Robert and William. Before long the entire hall rises to their feet in applause as Bartel also joins them. Samuel and Valencia were never ones for attention, but they keep up appearances by smiling with the hope this attention doesn't last long. "Now, bring the mead!" Bartel shouts and then takes a long drink from his mug. An upbeat jig begins playing as food and drink are widely accessible and consumed without moderation.

Music, songs, dancing, and merrymaking will continue throughout the night and into the first few hours of morning. Stuffed, drunk and still singing many of the attendees begin heading and stumbling back home.

"What a glorious night that was," a man howls.

Samuel sits alone outside while gazing into the night sky. He smells the crisp air and closes his eyes as he surrenders himself to the calm and peaceful ambiance—there is no further fear of being hunted. Valencia joins him and sits next to him as they exchange smiles.

"I like the calm surrender of night. There's a mystery about it. How it can make you ponder thoughts that cannot occur during the day. A magic that allows you to tap into another part of your mind." Valencia chuckles after Samuel finishes.

"Maybe you are a bard, or maybe you just had too much ale," Valencia jokes as Samuel laughs. "There could be one vampire still out here, you know," she continues.

"Then I shall introduce them to my sword—" Samuel taps his hand on his hip and then looks down before lifting his head back up. "I forgot my sword again." Valencia smiles while shaking her head.

"You're still oblivious to your surroundings, I see."

"You can be the vigilant one." Valencia smiles and rests her head on his shoulder.

"What do we do tomorrow, Sam?"

"Well, being so close to the channel it would be a shame not to visit the beach."

"I always wanted to see the coast."

Extensive green hills and meadows occupied by wildflowers are surrounded by white stone cliffs with a touch of shrubs and trees, all leading to a white sandy beach and then the deep blue sea. The soothing sound of the surf coming ashore along with the salty ocean breeze brings with it the smell of seaweed, and in the horizon is the setting sun. The ocean reflects the red and orange glow from the horizon as Samuel and Valencia sit in the sand observing the sunset. They kiss each other passionately and then return their gaze outward.

"Beautiful—everything—is beautiful," Valencia says.

Samuel and Valencia eventually return with Bartel and make Ashborough their home, but frequently visit Richard and the others in Casterham. Valencia returns to running her own bakery and Samuel becomes Bartel's advisor with an occasional story to tell at the inn.

"Let me tell you about a time when the only path I had before me was the one that beckoned me into the night," he begins while acting out his scenes on stage in front of a full audience. Valencia smiles as she relives their adventure through his words. Finally, Samuel can say the last words of his tale and know them to be true.

"Everything I am.
Everything I want.
The one I need.
They are all—
in front of my eyes."

———

"I'm not out of touch with reality. I'm a writer; I create it."

THE GLASS DEMON

There is much unrest here—

Contents

1

The House with Green Shutters

A great hunter once said, there's no greater predator than mankind—he was wrong. He was known to have hunted and killed over three-hundred big game and dangerous carnivores throughout his career. He did it for sport, he did it for profit, and he said he was the best at it—then one day, he disappeared. After several days of searching, his body was finally discovered in the dense jungles of South America. His wounds indicated he was mauled by a tiger and his rifle was located nearby without a shot being fired. The events leading up to his final end remains unknown; however, it's clear that the best in his field finally met his match.

Some experts in their chosen fields will develop a condition of misjudged confidence where they believe there's nothing they cannot overcome or achieve. Victories in less challenging tasks with too little experience in much else gives them a false sense of accomplishment. It is assumed that a professional, with years of experience, must always be victorious; however, that is never a guarantee. They say pride comes before a fall, and there is no one more hubris than William Corgel.

William Corgel was born in a small mid-western town where nothing out of the ordinary ever occurred. He soon discovered he had the ability to talk to those no one else could see, that is, he could commune with the dead and see things as they were years ago. He made this his profession and traveled often to help others while making a decent living in the process, but he wasn't without his vices. He often consumed large amounts of alcohol and developed an addiction to pills; this was his way of dealing with the *real* world.

Every time his phone rang, he knew someone needed him to debunk a suspected haunted house, or to tell an old man to move on. Most cases took a few hours, some less, some slightly more, but he always succeeded with little difficulty. That is until he was hired by the Glass family. This experience would test him profoundly and push William's expertise to the brink of doom. This will become his most challenging case and his longest, lasting over the course of several weeks, but taking months to recover.

This is not some case involving a lost spirit or a playful poltergeist. This one opens the bowels of hell and releases a demon upon him. Not a hackling imp in a darkened corner, but a powerful entity bent on wreaking havoc on the innocent, and especially on one who thinks it's a good idea to challenge it. This case will toy with William before ultimately defeating him. But before we get to that we must begin earlier. When William was still a child—

William Corgel is an eight-year-old boy growing up just outside of Stevens Point, Wisconsin. At night he opens his window just enough to let the early autumn breeze blow into his room. The sound of the wind through the trees acts as a soothing lullaby that eases young William gently to sleep. William has already had several encounters with communing with those who have passed on, but at his young age he doesn't consider it unique or abnormal. Sometimes it's difficult for him to tell a real person from a spirit, until someone gives him a perplexing look, or the spirit becomes translucent.

He slides under the covers and then positions his extra pillows around himself as if building up a soft security wall. Now that he's comfortable he waits for his mother to arrive to read him a bedtime story from a collection of Grimm's Fairy Tales. His mother doesn't make him wait long and soon strides up to his bedside and sits down with the book in hand. William smiles as he listens to the new story his mother has chosen.

"And they lived happily ever after," she ends the story and closes the book before setting it down on William's nightstand. She glances at the digital clock, 7:55PM. She sighs and seems upset but tries her best not to show it. William knows happily ever after is usually the end of every tale but tries to convince his mother for one more.

"Can you read another one please, mommy?" His mother smiles and turns her focus away from the clock and back to him.

"Not tonight, dear; it's your bedtime." She stands up and kisses his forehead. "Goodnight, sweetie."

"Night, mommy." She dims the light down to a soft amber glow and then walks out of the room.

William's clock ticks by to show 3:19AM, and distant arguing stirs William from his sleep. He slides out of bed and sluggishly makes his way down the hall and then down the first few steps before spying through the banister spindles to discover his mother and father pacing back and forth while yelling at each other in the living room.

"You were supposed to be home eight hours ago," William's mother screams.

"I told you I had to work late," his father fires back.

"That's bullshit. I called your phone, and no one answered."

"I'm not always in my office. You know that."

"Yeah, I know you weren't in your office because I read this." She bounces a piece of balled up paper off his chest. He picks it up and begins unfolding it to see what the fuss is about. "Who's Vicky?" his mother continues.

"What gives you the right to open my e-mails?" his father scolds. William's mother begins crying while shouting.

"The fact that I'm your wife and I have the right to know where my husband is—or who he's with. How many times have you lied to me to be with her?!"

"Don't talk to me like you're a fucking saint. Every time I come home you are reading or watching TV or too fucking tired to even look at me!"

"You son-of-a-bitch, your responsibility is here with me and Will, not with some office tramp."

"You're the one who got pregnant. I said I didn't want a kid; I wasn't ready for one."

"You cheating, arrogant bastard. I hope you burn in hell for this. Get out of this house; I can't stand the slut smell that your clothes are drenched in!"

William's father shakes his head while stomping towards the front door. "Fine, I hate coming home anyway!" He slams the door behind him with little concern of his wife's response. William returns to bed with tears in his eyes. He's not sure the reason for his parents' fight, but tries to go back to sleep, nonetheless. In the morning everything will be back to normal. At least, that's what he tells himself. Unfortunately, the normal William was accustomed to, and hoped would return, was not meant to be.

The next morning, William dresses and then heads downstairs to have his breakfast before catching the school bus at the corner. William usually meets his mother in the kitchen who has eggs and toast waiting for him, but today no one is in the kitchen and no pan is on the stove. William climbs back up the stairs to see if she might still be sleeping.

"Mom?" William asks as he makes his way down the hallway. "Mom? Where are you?" He passes the closed door to his father's study before entering his parents' bedroom. "Mommy?" he says in a whisper just in case she's trying to sleep.

The bed sheets are neatly folded down and the pillows are undisturbed from the headboard; it looks like no one had slept in this bed at all last night. William turns back into the hallway and stops at the closed door to the study. There's no place else to look. He slowly lifts his hand to the doorknob, but someone quickly grabs his wrist. He looks up startled to see his mother.

"You know you aren't allowed in your father's study," she says. William lowers his eyes before glancing back up.

"Is he coming back?" he asks terrified what the answer might be.

"No, he's not," she confirms.

"Why not?"

"Because you don't need him. Now go downstairs and get your cereal. You don't want to be late." William doesn't try to ask why he must settle for cold cereal. He just obeys his mother and prepares his own breakfast this morning. The time is getting closer to when he knows he should be heading to the bus stop, but his mother has remained upstairs. He grabs his backpack and then opens the front door. He glances back indoors and yells.

"I'm leaving." He waits for a response but receives none. He shrugs his shoulders and closes the door to begin his walk to the bus stop. On most days she's standing beside him until the bus arrives, but this is the first time she completely failed to see him out.

When William returns home that afternoon, he's relieved to see his mother sitting on the couch, although she still appears to be distraught, she at least acknowledges him.

"I'm sorry, William, I wasn't thinking," she says in a hushed, spaced-out tone.

"It's okay," he replies. "What's for dinner?"

"Oh, I forgot about that, hun. You know how to make mac and cheese though. Why don't you do that," she replies in the same distant voice.

"Okay, do you want any?"

"No, I've lost my appetite."

That evening, William is again waiting in bed when his mother arrives to read another fairy tale, but this one is very different from the others with an ending that lacks happily ever after.

"Turn back, turn back, thou pretty bride. Within this house thou must not bide. For here do evil things betide." She sets the book down and then runs her fingers through his hair. "Go to sleep now, my dear." William has been forcing himself to stay awake until the end of the story and now allows his eyes to shut.

William is sound asleep when a shadow passes in front of his open bedroom door. The floorboards creak and groan, and thumping and knocking come from the walls. He abruptly opens his eyes just before a door slams. He gasps and sits up.

"Mom?!" he calls out.

A loud thump explodes on the other side of his bedroom wall followed by a continuous squeaking. William gets out of bed and hurries into the hall where his mother is leaning against the door to his father's study with her back towards him and her head down.

"Mom, I'm hearing strange noises," he says hoping to be comforted. His mother remains silent and motionless with her gaze fixated on the floor. William takes a few small steps toward her. "Mom?"

"I'm sorry, William. I'm so sorry, I wasn't thinking."

His mother turns around to reveal her eyeballs are bulging out of their sockets and blood is oozing from her eyelids, mouth, and nose. It's William's last memory as a child, but as an adult, this memory had already been forgotten.

William is now a man, who awakes suddenly in bed before jolting up and breathing heavily from a recent nightmare. He's thirty-six and have moved from his childhood home to take up residence in Stevens Point as a bachelor.

Every furniture surface in his room is littered with empty or half empty liquor bottles and pill containers. He has adopted a dependency on alcohol and pain killers while being addicted to sleeping pills at night. He has crafted his cocktails to knock him out fast or numb his senses.

His cellphone begins to ring, but he shows no urgency to answer it. He finally sighs and gets out of bed before heading to the dresser. He ignores the vibrating phone nearby and picks up a container of pills and then tips it up to swallow several tablets. He glances down at his still ringing phone but reaches for a bottle of whiskey instead and takes a few healthy swigs. He sets the bottle down and stares at the ringing phone for another moment before finally answering it.

"William Corgel, paranormal medium and investigator," he begins. William listens to the person on the other end as he searches for a pen and pad of paper on his cluttered dresser. He finds a pen but must resort to jotting down his notes on an envelope he had torn open previously. "Alright, I have an opening early this afternoon. What's your address?"

Later that day, William slowly drives alongside the curb while checking the house numbers until finding the one belonging to Mr. and Mrs. Peters. William folds the paper with their address and sticks it into his shirt pocket. It's a typical residential neighborhood on a quiet side street, the homes are older, but most are well maintained. From the sidewalk he studies the exterior of the house and yard intensely. He begins walking up the path towards the front door while taking note of a small pink tricycle on the lawn. He rings the doorbell and looks back as he waits for his clients to answer to discover that the tricycle is no longer there. William's observation of the rest of the yard is interrupted when the front door opens.

"Good morning Mr. Peters, I'm William Corgel." Mr. Peters extends his hand to shake William's as he lets him walk through the doorway into his home.

"Thank you, Mr. Corgel for coming so soon." Mrs. Peters also advances to welcome William when he gets to the family room. She politely takes his hand and squeezes it gently.

"Yes, thank you. We really don't know what else to do," she says.

"It's no problem at all. Can you describe to me again what you've been experiencing?"

"Sometimes we hear a little girl laughing, as if she's right beside us, but we never see anyone," Mrs. Peters begins.

"We'll also hear the patter of little feet running up the stairs or down the hallway, but after searching the entire house we can't find any explanation," Mr. Peters adds. William nods.

"And you don't have any children of your own, is that correct?"

"That's right," Mrs. Peters confirms.

"Has this experience ever felt threatening?"

"Well, no, but it can be unnerving when something moves right before your eyes without anyone near it," Mrs. Peters admits.

"What kind of things have moved?" Mr. Peters points to his spinning globe on a stand.

"My desk globe will begin spinning rapidly at times. There is no way a draft will be able to do that. It looks like someone is physically hitting it over and over for it to reach that speed."

"Okay, let me walk around the house for a bit," Williams suggests.

The Peters' hang back as William calmly makes his way through the house while looking around. He nears the staircase that leads to the second floor and places his hand on the banister. He looks at the banister as if he's lost in a distant memory. Something feels important about it, but it doesn't seem to be connected to this house or the current series of events. He ignores the feeling and looks up just as the image of a seven-year-old girl appears at the top of the steps. She quickly turns away and disappears around the corner.

William ascends the stairs to reach the hallway. A doll, a teddy bear, and a beach ball suddenly appear for a short moment before the hallway returns to vacant. He then turns his attention to the guest room; it transforms into a little girl's room in an instant. Pink bedding and drapes take the place of the plain white ones, and a rocking chair is replaced with a small table with a tea party set on top.

He enters the room while observing the tea party table and chairs. The little girl peeks out from behind a toy chest just as William notices her and smiles before squatting down.

"Don't be afraid. What's your name?" She crawls out from behind the chest and then stands up.

"Sarah."

"Sarah, that's a beautiful name. How old are you?"

"Seven."

"Do you like the people who live here?" Sarah nods. "Yeah, they seem nice. My name is William. Do you know why you are here? What happened to you?" Sarah ignores the question and sits down at her table.

"Would you like to have some tea with me?"

"Sure." William sits down and picks up the tiny cup after Sarah hands it to him. He pretends to take a drink while Sarah giggles. She then looks up and notices Mr. and Mrs. Peters standing in the doorway.

The Peters see William sitting on a footstool in front of the rocking chair, and with his hand clasped, but nothing inside it.

"They never want to play with me," Sarah says. William looks behind him at the couple and motions them to come in.

"It's alright."

"Is there someone here?" Mr. Peters asks.

"Yes, her name is Sarah; she's seven." The couple hold hands as they walk into the room and sit at the foot of the bed.

"What's the last thing you remember?" William asks Sarah, but she changes the subject again.

"You should stay with us, William."

"You don't have to be lonely anymore, Sarah. Tell me what you remember." Sarah looks down and remains silent for a long moment. "It's okay. I can help," William assures her.

"I was playing in the yard with a beach ball," Sarah begins. "I kicked it too hard. The wind took it away. I chased it. It bounced into the street. I heard screeching tires. That's all. Then I was back here. And my parents moved away without me."

William stands up and takes a deep breath with his hand on his chest.

"What is it, William? Are you okay?" Mrs. Peters says concerned.

William can see the little body of the girl under a white sheet on the floor with Sarah's mother grieving over it. William cries out while gasping for air. He clenches his shirt below the collar and collapses to the floor in tears. The Peters' stand up and hurry to William's side.

"Mr. Corgel?" Mr. Peters says trying to get him to respond to them, but William is still living out his moment in the past. Outside the bedroom window are flashing red lights from the ambulance and paramedics hover over the lifeless little body lying in the street surrounded by heartbroken onlookers. The last thing William observes is Sarah looking out the window at her parents following the moving truck. She is alone in a house with a for sale sign in the front lawn. None of it makes sense to her. All her screaming and pounding on the window never caused either parent to glance up.

The room begins to fade back to how the Peters' have it decorated and the cloudy sensation around William's head slowly dissipates. He finds himself in the arms of Mr. and Mrs. Peters as they guide him to sit up. William takes a moment to regulate his breathing and wipe away his tears.

"Mr. Corgel—" Mrs. Peters begins.

"I'm fine," he replies.

"What happened?" she asks.

"Memories and emotions can sometimes be embedded and resonate in the air and land. These emotions can surge through me as if I'm actually experiencing an event and feeling the sensations that go with it or those who had felt them." William accepts the glass of water Mr. Peters hands him. "Thank you." He takes a sip and then stands up. "This was Sarah's room. She was hit by a car in front of the house.

"Oh-my-God," Mrs. Peters expresses. William turns to find

Sarah by the window.

"Sarah—your parents didn't leave you—" William begins.

"I know—" she admits while dropping her eyes to the floor.

"You don't have to be here, Sarah. There's another home for you, one with lots of friends you can play with."

"I'm afraid," she says. William takes her hand into his as she looks at him.

"Trust me. All you have to do is close your eyes and wish for it." Sarah squeezes his hand and closes her eyes. "Wish for it, Sarah. It's time to go home." Sarah's image becomes transparent and then slowly fades away into a dim light that jets upwards. William lets out a long sigh and bows his head.

"Did she move on?" Mr. Peters asks.

"Yes. You will not be experiencing any further disturbances in this home."

As soon as William returns to his home, he heads straight to the bedroom. He uncaps a bottle of sleeping pills and shakes three into his hand before shoving them in his mouth. He swigs a good amount of whiskey to wash them down and then stumbles toward his bed. He falls onto the sheets and passes out within minutes. William will be the first to say nothing bothers him, but his increased sensitivity to emotion brings him too much pain for him to bear alone. He would rather be in comatose than hear all the crying and shouting that are forever seared into his mind and heart. Drowning these voices in a bottle or being passed out are the only ways he copes with reality.

In the center of a peaceful cul-de-sac is a well kept Dutch Colonial with green shutters, and a decent amount of floral landscaping. The garden lights, along with the nightly breeze, cast dancing shadows of the fauna on the siding as the sweet aroma of the roses waft through the open windows. This is the home of Timothy and Emily Glass, and their nineteen-year-old daughter, Elizabeth. This close-knit Irish family works hard for what they own and never speaks ill of anyone. All who know them agree they are a fun and kind bunch who are happy to help anytime there's an opportunity to do so. How could such a happy and loving household ever fall upon turmoil and troubled times? Good-natured, modest, and charitable, the Glass family is only guilty of having no visible faults. They cherish friends and family above all else and never desired excessive fortune or fame, but the

Glass name will soon become infamous.

Elizabeth is getting ready for bed as she stands at the bathroom sink in her nightgown. She turns the faucet on to full blast and then squeezes a generous amount of toothpaste onto her brush. As she prepares to lift the brush to her mouth the toothpaste slides off and plops into the sink.

"Crap," she utters softly to herself.

Elizabeth begins washing the toothpaste down the drain just as a gruesome, pale severed head appears behind her from the reflection in the mirror, but Elizabeth is focused on applying new toothpaste on her brush and does not notice it. The bathroom door, that's ajar, is suddenly swung open to make Elizabeth jolt her attention to her father walking in. The disturbance behind her has vanished, and neither were aware that it was ever there.

"You don't need to run the water full blast, especially when you aren't even using it," he says while turning the water down to a gentle stream.

"It's not that big of a deal, dad."

"It is a big deal when you're paying for it," he replies before kissing the top of her head.

"Sweet dreams, hun."

"Night, daddy."

Timothy exits into the hallway and spots a snarling black dog in the far corner of his perception. He turns his head to view it more clearly, but nothing is there. He shakes his head and then pinches his eyes to the brim of his nose before continuing to the master bedroom. He assumes it's nothing more than a shadow, or a glare playing tricks on his exhausted mind.

Emily is reading a magazine in bed and looks up to give him a smile as he enters.

"What were you and Elizabeth fighting about now?"

"We weren't fighting. I just, very calmly, pointed out the fact that she was wasting water." Emily gives him a smirk.

"That's not that big of a deal, Timothy."

"That's what she said. I think both of you are plotting against me." Timothy takes off his robe and drapes it over the back of a chair. He glances up at the nearby wall clock to notice that it has stopped. "This thing needs batteries again," he says with a sigh. He taps the face of the clock several times, but the hands remain frozen in place. Emily lowers her magazine to look at him again.

"What are you fretting about now?"

"I think this clock is broken." Just then the second hand begins ticking counterclockwise. "What the—" Timothy glances at Emily. "It's moving backwards now."

"Tim—" Emily begins.

"We just need to get a new one. This one has more issues than National Geographic."

"Forget about the damn clock and come to bed," Emily says growing weary of his obsession with such an insignificant thing as a busted wall clock. Timothy drops the subject and makes his way to his side of the bed and then crawls under the sheets. Emily places her magazine on the nightstand and then leans over to kiss Timothy.

"Still think I'm plotting against you?"

"Now, I think you're plotting to take my clothes off," he says anticipating her to continue further, but her teasing smile turns into a frustrated sigh.

"Damn it, I forgot about the clothes," she says before tossing the covers off and stepping out of bed.

"Where are you going?"

"I forgot to switch the clothes to the dryer."

"So, do it tomorrow."

"If I leave them in the washer overnight, they will stink and I will have to redo the load," she replies while putting on her robe and slippers.

"Now who's the one with a hang-up," he says while letting his head fall heavily on his pillow.

"I'll be right back, dear," she grins and then leaves the room.

Emily flips the basement light on before walking down the old wooden steps into the dank unfinished basement. Her steps fall heavy on every creaking step she descends upon, and the musty smell enters her nostrils. She shivers from the damp, cool air when she reaches the bottom while rubbing her arms underneath the robe sleeves. This dilapidated space could benefit from some paint, carpeting, and more lighting, but even a full remodel would not take away Emily's uneasiness of this area.

She opens the lid to the washer and begins taking the clothes out and tossing them into the dryer. A leaning broom against the wall behind her unexpectedly slides to the floor. She lets out a yelp and whirls around to see the broom's final resting place. She takes a few quick glances around the floor hoping they don't have a rat lurking nearby. She decides to ignore the event and turn back to the washer, but when she does, she lets out a horrified scream while observing all the clothes suspended in a bundle above the washing machine. This cannot be so easily ignored or brushed off. Unlike a falling broom that could be a victim of gravity, there is no explanation for this defiance of physics. The washer's metal lid aggressively slams shut, and the clothes are hurled at her by unseen hands. She screams again and bolts up the basement stairs.

Meanwhile, Timothy pages through Emily's magazine when the sound of running water is heard. He lifts his head and listens for a moment. Thinking it is his daughter again he shouts out of the room.

"Elizabeth, I told you not to have the water on so high." The sound continues. He sighs and gets out of bed. "Why do I talk if no one ever listens," he mutters underneath his breath. Timothy makes his way to the lit bathroom and walks inside.

"Eliz—" he begins to say, but the water is gushing from the faucet to a vacant bathroom. He reprimands her from the bathroom in a raised voice. "Elizabeth, you forgot to turn off the water, and you left the light on." He gives it no further thought as he shuts the water off and then turns back to flip the light switch, but the water suddenly starts flowing out again. He freezes and slowly turns back to glare at the sink. His first thought is another broken thing that needs to be fixed, but his peripheral vision catches a figure rushing toward him from behind. He turns around and yells just as Emily bumps into him.

"Jesus, Emily," he says when he swallows the lump in his throat.

"This house is cursed," she says franticly, and at the brink of tears while embracing his shoulders.

When something is trying to get your attention and fails to get a solid reaction, that thing tries a little harder. Our natural tendency to denounce the unexplainable or rationalize some eerie sight or occurrence as nothing at all, creates a challenge for frequent happenings or larger and louder signs that cannot be disregarded. Unknowingly, the Glass family has succeeded in provoking an unseen force starving for attention, but what lies in waiting is much more sinister.

2

Stay Out of the Basement

On this cold night, howling wind rattles the old windows and rustles the leaves of the sugar maples outside William's office window. Many prefer to keep this chilling breeze outside, but William welcomes the cool air in. He lets the wind circulate around him and catches the whiff of the musty window screen that it flows through. He often stays up late while skimming through his emails that have poured in throughout the day. There's a certain calm, quiet serenity at night that allows William to focus. The rushing and noise of the day has settled down and a peaceful mystery takes over; no distracting sunlight from the outside or risk of interruptions; just William and his thoughts.

He has grown accustomed to fake and amateur videos that try to claim a supposedly haunted home or location. Seventy percent of his emails are from those who are too quick to jump to the assumptions of ghosts, fifteen percent are from people looking for attention, and ten percent are faked with Photoshop to modify photographs or splicing video clips to make a convincing effect, but William has seen it all. However, every once in a while, William comes across something that attracts his full devotion. He will study it over and over and read the sender's message four to five times. This time such an email comes from the Glass family residence. He clicks on the link, in the body of the message, and a YouTube video opens in a new tab.

William immediately tries to look for anything that could be controlled by a variable. There are many creative ways to make something appear supernatural. A blowing curtain or closing door, for instance, is ignored because making wind is too easy. Even sliding furniture isn't that impressive anymore. William is looking for something very hard to fake, and he finds it in this video.

The green hue of the video shows it was set up to record overnight. The scene is that of the dining room and part of the kitchen. At first nothing seems to happen until a subtle tug of the tablecloth is witnessed. Then a cabinet door opens in the kitchen followed by another one. The tablecloth seems to be slightly pulled towards one side, but then is suddenly yanked aggressively to the floor. William moves in closer to his screen to make sure he doesn't miss anything. A little girl suddenly appears to crawl out from underneath the table and then glare straight into the camera while remaining motionless. The camera focus jitters before falling to the floor to show the view of the staircase leading upstairs. A tiny beam of light streaks up the banister before taking the form of a woman's head and torso, but then quickly disappears.

There's a lot going on all at once in this video. William never saw so much activity in one place before, let alone at the same time. He's a little apprehensive to believe it completely, but this required a fair amount editing skills and time to complete if it is indeed fake. He watches the entire video again and again before pausing it on the little girl when she's looking directly at the camera. William closes his eyes and touches the screen. "Who are you?" he whispers. A vision appears in his mind of the tiny body submerged under water and her lungs filling up with liquid as she tries to breathe. William begins coughing and gasping for air but keeps his eyes closed. The girl now appears with drenched hair and a pale, pruned face. She opens her mouth to release a long continuous stream of water flowing over her bottom lip, down her chin and to the floor. William forces his eyes open and takes several deep breaths. If the video was faked, he wouldn't have been able to connect with the girl. This is worth investigating.

When morning arrives William phones the Glass family to set up a time to do a preliminary investigation. They are all too happy to accept his help and make it for that day. To date all his correspondences came from word of mouth or his website and Linked-In page. William has investigated forty-five cases around the area of central Wisconsin for over ten years, but still remains mostly unknown—that is about to change.

William pulls up to the front of the Glass family's home and gets out to study the exterior of the house and yard from the sidewalk. Neither the house nor the yard trigger any sensations or offer William any sights into its past. The first appearance of the residence makes it appear to be a normal and restful home. He then begins to advance to the front door and rings the bell; a short moment later, Timothy arrives to answer it.

"Good morning, I'm William Corgel. We talked on the phone."

"Yes, of course, please come inside," Timothy says while shaking William's hand.

William follows Timothy into the living room and suddenly becomes overwhelmed with a strong feeling. He stops his advancement and puts his hand on his chest just as Timothy glances back.

"Are you okay, Mr. Corgel?" William smiles and nods while recomposing himself.

"Yes, I'm fine. The air is a bit heavy right here. It's almost as if I'm walking knee deep through mud." Timothy directs him to the couch.

"Please, have a seat." Emily joins them from the kitchen and Timothy introduces her.

"This is my wife, Emily.

"Nice to meet you, Emily," he says while gently squeezing her hand.

"Likewise, Mr. Corgel."

"Just William is fine."

"Can I interest you in some tea, William?" Emily asks.

"Sure, thank you." Emily leaves for the kitchen as Timothy takes a seat in his armchair. William takes a moment to observe this room is exactly like it was in the video with the dining room table and the entrance to the kitchen in front of him, and the staircase to the upstairs directly to his left. "You mentioned you have a daughter too, right?" he asks after turning his attention to Timothy.

"Yes, Elizabeth is still at school. She's pursuing a degree in art."

"That sounds exciting. I tried drawing, but I'm quite limited to just circles and squares, and even those are hard to tell apart," William admits while sharing a laugh with Timothy.

"We don't know where she got her talent, but it didn't come from either of us. I can tell you that much," Timothy says. William pulls out his pocket notepad and a pen and then flips through several of the tiny pages until he gets to the notes, he had written down surrounding this assignment.

"On the phone you mentioned that you haven't lived here that long?"

"That's right. We moved in here—about four months ago now, but it's just in the last two weeks that we've been experiencing things that seem to defy explanation."

"Well, it's not uncommon for hauntings to begin after living in a place for a while. Sometimes it takes time for the spirits to sense your presence. Have you done any renovations lately?"

"We had to change the water heater, but that's about it," Timothy admits. Emily returns with a tray and sets it down on the coffee table.

"Yes, when we first moved in here there wasn't any hot water throughout the entire house," she adds while pouring tea into a cup and then handing it to William.

"Thank you very much, ma'am," he says as he accepts it. Emily gives him a smile before pouring another cup.

"We've tried to ignore it, but it seems impossible at times. That's when we decided to look for help and found your website," Timothy says and then accepts his cup of tea from Emily. "Thanks, dear."

"It's never a good idea to ignore it. Most spirits want to be seen and heard. If you ignore them, they tend to try harder to get your attention." William takes a sip of his tea as Emily pours herself a cup and then sits down at the other end of the couch. "I've seen my fair share of doctored photographs and videos with added effects in them," William continues. "In fact, I have a collection of pictures with images of people fading into the background, which can easily be done with any camera and a long exposure. One would just simply need to move out of the frame before the lens close and their body would not be fully developed. What interested me about your video was the feeling of an intelligent energy."

"What do you mean by intelligent?" Timothy asks.

"There are two types of hauntings; intelligent, which indicates that the entity is aware of their environment and of you. They can, and will, interact and react with what we do and say. The second type is residual, which is more like a replay of a past event. The occurrence is usually in the same place at the same time and with no acknowledgment of interference from the surrounding environment."

"When you first walked in you mentioned that the air was heavy, what does that mean?" Emily asks.

"It usually indicates a strong, powerful presence. I don't want to alarm anyone yet, but typically it represents anger or hate."

"Oh-my-God," Emily exclaims.

"If I may ask, what kind of things have you been experiencing?" William asks.

"My first encounter was in the basement. I was taking the clothes out of the washer but became distracted. When I turned back around all the clothes were suspended in the air above the machine before being hurled at me by an unseen force."

William presses his lips together while wrapping his fingers around his chin. "Hmm."

"The water in the bathroom sink will also turn on by itself to the point that it's gushing out. At first, I thought Elizabeth may have forgotten to shut it off, but it seems to be a frequent occurrence now." William takes another sip of his tea and then jots down these accounts on his pad.

"Speaking of Elizabeth, how old is she?" William asks.

"She's nineteen," Timothy answers.

"Okay, I only ask because some people in my field believe teenagers can develop psychic abilities and start affecting objects around them, many times without knowing they are responsible."

"Is that when you developed your ability?" Emily asks curiously.

"No, I believe it's been with me my entire life. Sometimes it's difficult to tell a real person from a spirit unless the environment interacts with it. As a child I didn't fully understand it until someone questioned me. I didn't even realize my ability had a name until later, even though I've been using it."

"Do you think Elizabeth could be developing a similar ability?" Emily continues, but William shakes his head.

"No, I don't think so. I was just stating that if this extra sense isn't born with you, it can grow and mature along with you; however, in those few cases it's usually during puberty, and I believe Elizabeth is too old to just be starting now."

"So, how will you know if something is here?" Timothy asks.

"Well, there is most definitely something here. I just don't know to what extent yet. I'm a clairvoyant medium, meaning I can communicate with spirits without entering into a trance. I'll be able to see them, talk to them and even see what the house looked like at the time they lived here. Nothing can hide from me."

"What if it is hostile?" Emily asks with a worried expression.

"You can rest easy. I never dealt with anything I could not handle. What I'm going to be doing first is just walking around the house to get a feel of it. I'll let you know what I pick up."

William leaves Timothy and Emily in the living room as he explores their home inch-by-inch. He carefully walks around the kitchen with his hands out as he feels the air around him. He makes his way around the room until he gets to the basement door. He looks intensely at the knob as an unsettling feeling washes over him, eager to reveal the cause, he reaches for it. A woman spirit suddenly appears behind him.

"Don't go down there," she warns. William turns around to look at her.

"It's okay, I'm here to help," he responds, but the spirit fades before William can question her further. He directs his attention back towards the basement and flips the switch on, but the dim beam of light fails to illuminate much more than the first half of the staircase. He gets a familiar whiff of stale air that's synonymous with an enclosed and undisturbed space with slight undertones of death. William begins walking down the creaking steps and immediately begins to feel his chest tightening and his heart pumping faster. He takes long deep breaths while leaning heavily onto the railing. When he reaches the bottom, he takes a moment to rest. His legs feel like lead as he slides his foot forward to take his next step. *I've never felt this intensity before*, he thinks to himself.

His steps are slow as he drags his feet further into the basement. The walls and floor become covered in blood as bodies with missing limbs or heads hang from the ceiling, or on meat hooks bolted to the walls. William cries out but continues his investigation.

A figure dressed completely in black and with a hood to conceal its identity appears next to him and peers into his face. William cries out again and holds on to a support beam as he hunches over. Several more hooded figures stand in a circle with candles at their feet while mumbling in unison. A shadowy figure darts out from the center of the circle and across the floor to disappear into the wall.

William nears the stationary tub and looks inside to see it's filled with blood. A severed head, with its eyes and mouth open, rises to break the surface and then bobs up and down.

William must get back upstairs before he passes out. He sluggishly makes his way to the steps and crawls up them on his hands and knees like a toddler. He slams the basement door before falling on the kitchen floor while sweating profusely and having a hard time regulating his breathing. He crawls to a sitting position and leans his back against the wall just as the woman spirit appears beside him.

"This place is not safe," she says.

"Who are you?" William asks in an exhausted tone.

"My name is Angie, I'm trying to shield them, but what dwells here is very strong."

"What's here?" William whispers. Alerted from William's actions, Timothy enters the kitchen and then hurries toward him. He unwillingly passes through Angie's image, and she disappears.

"William, are you alright?" He puts a hand on his shoulder as Emily rushes in.

"Emily, get a cold washcloth," Timothy requests. Emily runs a cloth under the faucet and then takes it to William.

"Thank you," he says as he dabs his forehead and cheeks.

"What happened?" Emily asks with concern.

"I'm not completely sure," William says as he struggles to stand up. Timothy offers his hand to help him the rest of the way up and William nods his gratitude before continuing. "There's a benevolent female spirit here named Angie. She appears to be protective of your family, so you can take some comfort in that at least."

"Well, I didn't really want *any* spirits here, but I suppose a good one couldn't hurt," Timothy admits.

"That being said, I would stay out of the basement until I return. I must do some research."

William spends the rest of his afternoon at city hall looking at the public records and making copies of old newspaper articles that mention the address of the Glass' house. He scrolls through pages of property history online while looking up past occupants of this residence and then prints his findings. He compiles all the research together and then begins studying through the stack more in depth and with an uncomfortable look. "I never liked history, and this house has a lot of it." He has gained invaluable insight about this house and what has happened inside it. Tomorrow, he will present this information to Timothy and Emily, but nothing can prepare any of them as to what is about to come or warn them before it strikes.

Later that night, Timothy lifts a framed picture of tall ships in the spot where the assumed broken clock was. He decided no one really needs a wall clock in their bedroom since they have phones charging beside them.

"What do you think, love?" he asks. Emily looks at the painting with little interest.

"It's kinda manly for our bedroom, don't cha think?"

"What's manly about fifteenth century galleons on the ocean. This is art."

"Why do I bother?" Emily says with a sigh. Timothy studies the picture as he holds it against the wall.

"Or maybe this is sixteenth century." He turns it around to show Emily. "What do you think? Is this fifteenth century or sixteenth century?

"Do I look like a pirate to you?" she responds. Timothy gives Emily an intrigued look.

"Hmm, now that is an interesting picture. I would love to see you as a pirate."

"Hush," Emily says with a sly smirk. Timothy begins looking around him while holding the painting up with one hand.

"Where's my hammer?" Emily gives him a look of dismay and

hesitates with her answer.

"I took your tool bag to the basement," she finally admits while biting her lower lip.

"Really—" Timothy says in the most disappointed tone he can muster.

"Just leave it for tomorrow," Emily begs. Timothy sighs and places the picture down.

"Nonsense, it will take but two minutes," he replies while tying his robe around his waist, and then slides his slippers on.

"But William said to avoid the basement," she pleads.

"I'm not going to live in a house where I can't use my own basement, Emily." Emily stretches her neck to peek into the hallway as Timothy descends the staircase to the first floor.

He turns on every light switch he passes as he makes his way through the living room, dining room, kitchen and then beyond the door to the basement. He pretends not to be suddenly overwhelmed by an unknown and primal fear at the top of the steps. He stares into the dark space but convinces himself that his nerves are due to outside influences and not actual experience. He's sure if he walks down there, grabs his hammer, and then leaves, absolutely nothing out of the ordinary will occur. He ignores his jitters and begins down the steps to the partially illuminated dungeon-like basement, but his anxiety remains even if it's not acknowledged. When he reaches the bottom, he takes a quick account of the expanse before heading to the workbench on the far wall.

Several crackling sounds, like plastic being crushed, enter Timothy's ears. He looks behind him and darts his eyes to every corner of the area but seeing nothing of concern motivates him to advance deeper into the shadows. The sound of metal scraping against concrete and something heavy being dragged now accompanies the crackling followed by a deep throat gurgling.

Timothy pans his sights across the basement; what he believes will turn out to be nothing is starting to prove itself as something and his body reacts. His heart thumps faster, the hairs on his arms stand on end, a chill runs down his spine, and in one of the darkened corners he catches a glimpse of a pale, slender woman with long gray hair who's missing her lips. He redirects his attention back to the spot, but the woman is not there now. Timothy notices his tool bag two steps away; he's too close now to give up. He advances toward the workbench and digs into the bag until he pulls out his claw hammer. He doesn't linger any longer and returns to the staircase, but the basement door slams shut before he begins his climb. The scraping, shuffling, crackling, and gurgling sounds return; louder, closer now. Something is moving across the basement floor towards the staircase. He chooses not to investigate and hurries up the steps and then tries to open the door, but it seems to be stuck. The light begins to flicker, and Timothy's uneasiness forces him to throw his shoulder into the door while frantically turning the knob.

"Emily! Emily!" he shouts. "Emily, the door is locked!" The light continues to flicker rapidly until finally going out and leaving him trapped in a completely dark stairwell, but worse than that are the sound of footsteps thumping up the steps behind him.

"Emily!" he desperately cries out again. The dim light fades back on as the thumping behind him progresses and he reluctantly turns to glance behind him. The pale figure of the woman, without lips, diligently slides her drenched feet up the stairs toward him. Her rotted gums and yellow teeth give him a creepy, everlasting grin framed by her gray wire brush-like hair. He screams and throws himself against the door continuously. "Emily—" The lights begin to flicker again as the grotesque woman eliminates his escape and closes the gap between them. He doesn't want to be in the dark with this creature and finally resorts to drastic measures by smashing the hammer against the door with all his might. Preserving the state of his house falls second to his sanity. Splinters fly off as he continues to break through the door. He doesn't want to ponder what she will do to him if he fails to get out. Will he die, will he go mad, or will he be tortured? The hideous woman is three steps away when the light fades out. He screams as gurgling sounds surround him and icy fingertips grip his arm.

The door opens at this moment and Timothy bolts into Emily's arms.

"What the hell do you think are you doing, Tim!?" she scolds horrified at the sight of their damaged basement door. Timothy slams the door closed and backs away as fast as he can.

"Where were you? I was calling for you!" he shouts in distress.

"The only thing I heard was you hammering our door into smithereens!" she yells back, but her anger subsides when she sees the sweat beads on Timothy's panicked brow. She places her hands on his cheeks. "You're freezing. What happened down there?" His mind went into the highest level of survival and his body feels as if it had just been hit and buried by an avalanche.

"I think we should stay out of the basement," he softly says while trying to force his feet to carry him upstairs, but sleep seems all but impossible for him tonight.

It's early afternoon of the following day when the doorbell rings. Timothy answers the door to find William with a folder underneath his arm.

"Good afternoon, I was able to dig up some insight into this residence if you would like to see it," William says.

"Of course," he replies and then steps aside to let William enter. William sets the folder on top of the coffee table and then takes a seat on the couch.

"Sorry for not calling first, but I was in the neighborhood already."

"It's quite alright, William. I'm glad you are here," Timothy responds.

"Is Emily home?"

"No, she and Elizabeth went to some crap— I mean craft fair," Timothy grins. William chuckles and opens the folder as Timothy takes a seat next to him. He begins with a copy of a newspaper article and hands it to Timothy as he explains it.

"In 1959 a man by the name of Adam Faust owned this house. This guy was a sicko. He was found guilty of kidnapping and butchering his victims before hanging them on meat hooks on the basement walls."

"You got to be kidding me," Timothy says in shock.

"His targets were mainly females between the ages of nineteen and twenty-four. They recovered six bodies, but he had claimed of killing seventeen."

"Where's the other eleven?" Timothy asks.

"They were never found but given their tragic deaths I doubt all of them moved on." William digs through the pile before slapping a police report in front of Timothy.

"1964. A group of kids were arrested for breaking and entering. According to the report they were practicing satanic rituals in the basement. I caught a glimpse of that during my investigation yesterday. It's my belief that they may have opened a door."

"So, my house is cursed?" Timothy says in a somber tone.

"It does have a disturbing past, but a blessing could remedy most of it if you know someone."

"We do, but— well, I don't know if he would talk to us anymore."

"Why is that?"

"We aren't exactly model Catholics. We haven't attended mass in three years."

"I've never set foot inside a church in my whole life." William admits. "So, three years is hardly something to have a grudge against."

"Yeah, but you aren't Catholic," Timothy chuckles.

William smirks, "no, I suppose I'm not." William then picks up a stapled packet and hands it to Timothy.

"That's the last home inspection report I found dated in August of 1994. The entire house was completely renovated, almost nothing original remains; new floors, walls, windows, fixtures, everything. The house sat unoccupied for several years after the commissioned work." William places another piece of paper in front of Timothy. "In more recent history, this house has been on the market six times in the last four years." Timothy picks up the paper and takes note of all the times his house was sold and then relisted.

"The realtor said the previous owners just couldn't afford the taxes, and that this property's value would increase by ten percent in a year."

"It's funny how the lure of a commission can find the best sentence in the worst book," William says. A moment of silence passes between the two men before William continues. "What I experienced in the basement supports some of my research, but this house still has a great deal of secrets I haven't uncovered yet."

"What if the house was rebuilt?"

"With a report card like this I don't think it will matter."

"Why not?"

"Because all this negative energy has seeped into the foundation. It's the land that's haunted now." Timothy looks down at his hands as he rubs then together.

"I had an experience last night," he begins. William focuses his attention on him.

"What was it?"

"I went in the basement."

"The basement?" Timothy stands up and walks to the middle of the room."

"I know you said to stay out of the basement, but I needed a hammer, and I didn't think anything was going to happen." Timothy can feel a shiver run down his spine from the mere thought of last night's experience.

"What happened, Timothy."

"I saw a woman—pale, long hair, no lips, just gums and teeth. She walked with this jittering limp. The lights were flickering, and I couldn't open the door—" Timothy stops and looks away to try to recompose himself. William stands up and takes a step towards him.

"Let me see your hand."

"Why?" Timothy asks while holding his hands out.

"If an energy has attached itself to you, I will be able to pick up on it." William holds his open hands over Timothy's and closes his eyes before gently lowering them until they touch.

William's body jerks back when the woman, Timothy saw last night, appears in his vision, but she's not alone. The living room suddenly becomes crowded with several dismembered and maimed people. Some are missing limbs while others are just floating heads with empty eye sockets or bleeding mouths as they swirl around William. The little drowned girl from the video also makes an appearance, but she remains standing in place with the same eerie stare as before. A dark shadowy figure darts up one of the walls and then rushes down another. It takes the shape of a large, scraggly, black, furry beast with red eyes, and saber-like fangs, before lunging at William. He snaps out of his meditative state with a jolt and a gasp.

"Did you see her?" Timothy asks. William takes a moment before answering.

"You can say that—" William doesn't want to tell Timothy everything he had witnessed. He doesn't want to concern him any further than he already is. Even William has a hard time believing all these spirits are attached to this house; some of them feel much older than the history he had discovered. There's also something else here that William cannot completely make out, but one thing is for sure—it's in charge.

William leaves the folder for Timothy and Emily to review through it later.

"Feel free to call me if you have any concerns or if there's an escalation in activity," William says as he rummages in his pocket for his keys.

"I will," Timothy agrees while walking William to his car. William advances around to his door, but Timothy stops him before he gets in.

"I do have one question."

"What's that?"

"What did you mean back there?"

"What?"

"What you said?"

"What did I say?"

"When you were touching my hands."

"I said something then?"

"Yeah, don't you remember?" William slowly shakes his head and gives him a puzzled look. "You said, they all come here—and I let them."

"I said that?"

"Yeah."

William feels his blood freeze. He now knows his assumption are correct. Timothy's house is sitting on a portal that is allowing the dead to enter whether they are connected to the property or not. The fact that something used his voice without him knowing also means the puppet master behind all of this is very powerful. It's usually easier for spirits to interact with William than someone without his abilities. They can even talk or act through him but doing so without him feeling it happening or knowing about it is something else entirely. It means he was overtaken.

"Call me, for anything," William says before getting into his car and avoiding Timothy's question. Timothy doesn't know why he avoided the question but decides not to press it. William lowers the passenger side window and leans over the center console. Timothy slightly hunches over to look inside. "And stay out of the God-dang basement," he says with a smile. Timothy chuckles and waves as William drives away. This time he might actually take his advice.

Later that evening, William is returning home from his weekly grocery shopping. He's nearly home when he spots flashing emergency lights ahead of him. As he nears the scene, he slows down to see a smashed car on the side of the road and several police cars blocking the lane. The driver is also standing near the car with a deep gash in his head. Their eyes meet and remain locked, but it's no surprise that he still appears to be dazed. Just then a police officer walks toward the injured man before continuing through him. William sighs and continues driving past the accident.

William pulls into the garage and grabs his two bags from the backseat. He then taps the opener, on the wall, to close the garage door before entering his home through the fire door. He puts the half gallon of milk in the fridge but leaves everything else in their bags on the kitchen table.

He heads straight to his bedroom and uncaps a bottle of sleeping pills from the dresser. He tips the container in his mouth and lets three pills fall on his tongue. He then chugs the nearby whiskey and painfully swallows the pills before heading to bed. He doesn't bother undressing or pulling down the covers. He just wants today to end.

Meanwhile, Elizabeth is sitting at her desk littered with artist materials. Graphite pencils, erasers, markers, charcoal sticks, colored pencils, paints, and pads of drawing paper almost occupy every flat surface. To everyone else it might look cluttered, but to Elizabeth everything is right where it needs to be. Her colored, and black and white sketches are framed on the walls around her room and her current drawing is that of two horses grazing with a barn in the background.

Several blood spots drop onto the picture. Elizabeth puts her finger to her nose and then looks at the blood on her fingertips. She holds her nose close and makes her way to the bathroom. She spirals a tissue into her bleeding nostril and then washes her hands. After a few moments she removes the tissue and then checks to see if there's any blood on a clean spot that she inserts. The bleeding seems to have stopped. She tosses the tissue in the garbage and checks her face one last time in the mirror before walking away, but in the mirror her image remains, except her skin is pale and her eyes are white with yellow pupils while her lips sport a malicious grin.

The mystery of midnight and the silence of this hour has long since been believed to hold some uncanny power. The floorboards creek when all is supposedly asleep, as a being manifests out of thin air only to dart across the room, then disappear. The morning convinces most that their nightly visitors were nothing more than dreams in the mist, but this one will be hard to dismiss.

The basement door gently swings open followed by a horrible twisted clawed footprint appearing on the kitchen floor. In the dining room the hangover of the tablecloth is blown upwards. Deep claw marks gouge the wall near the stairs and continues up to the second floor.

Elizabeth's bedroom door slowly opens, a short moment later it begins to close until it latches. Something is watching her from above as she sleeps unaware of this presence. Her bed sheets are pulled downward to leave her exposed. Her nightgown is pulled up and her legs are forcefully spread apart. She awakes and tries to scream, but no sound is uttered. Her eyes are fixed in a wide-open gaze and engulfed with fear. Her arms become pinned against her backboard and sweat runs down her face. Her body is pushed violently up and down as some entity thrusts itself inside of her. She feels the experience, but still cannot find her voice. The onslaught continues with no sign of ending as she's harshly jerked upwards on her bed. Unable to move or whisper she wonders if this is really happening. She feels the weight of someone on top of her and her loins has the sensation of intercourse, but her fear, and the aggression shown takes away any sense of pleasure.

She begins to levitate and rise higher toward the ceiling before she is slammed back onto the bed. The assault finally ends. Her eyes are open, but she appears to be in a comatose-like state.

The next morning, Emily stretches and yawns as she heads to the bathroom for her morning urination. She doesn't notice the claw marks on the wall and throws the bathroom door closed behind her. It's only after she opens the door again to leave does she notice the horrifying indentations.

"Timothy!" she yells. Timothy jumps out of bed and hurries into the hall. He follows Emily's gaze and becomes awestruck at the alarming grooves. They make a startling and disturbing realization that the marks lead into Elizabeth's room.

"Elizabeth!" Emily shouts. She knocks on the door, but there's no answer. "Elizabeth!" Emily shouts again. There's still no response. Emily gives up and opens the door to find Elizabeth sitting in a chair facing a corner of her room. "Elizabeth?" She says in a soft voice, but her daughter does not respond. Emily takes a small step forward. "Elizabeth?" She says again in the same soft tone. Elizabeth lifts her bloody hand and slaps it against the wall to leave a bloody handprint.

"Elizabeth, what's wrong?" Emily approaches her with urgency. As soon as Emily's hand falls upon Elizabeth's shoulder, the girl darts her head around to look at her mother. Elizabeth has a sinister grin, and her mouth is covered in blood from the constant biting of her hand. Her pupils are yellow, and the rest of the eyes are white and hollow looking. She lets out a snarl and swipes her curled fingers to scratch Emily. Emily darts back to avoid the attack while screaming out in terror. Timothy observes from the doorway helplessly. The demon has made its move; what follows now is a war no one was prepared to fight.

3

Not a Typical Haunting

Emily climbs the familiar steps of the old catholic church she and Timothy used to frequent as her blue dress flaps against her legs from the wind. Her high heeled shoes echo as she makes the long trek to the confession stand with the open certain awaiting her arrival. She draws the curtain close and then sits down before the priest slides the small window opens and Emily begins.

"Bless me father, for I have sinned. It has been three years since my last confession."

"That is a long time, my child," the priest responds.

"Yes, I'm sorry. I do not have a good excuse for my absence."

"Please continue."

"You may not remember me. My name is Emily Glass, my husband is Timothy." A moment of silence passes.

"I remember you."

"I am here today on behalf of my daughter. Do you remember her?"

"Yes, It's Elizabeth, right?"

"That's right. She has come under a horrible plight."

"Is she ill?"

"No, her mind and body are no longer hers." Emily dabs a tissue in her eyes while sobbing.

"What do you mean?"

"She has been stolen from God. The devil has her now." The priest immediately exits his booth and then slides the curtain away to see Emily face-to-face. She looks up at him and begins sobbing uncontrollably.

Father Victor Brahmer is a heavyset priest with a strong desire to be in service of his congregation; no matter how long they may have been away.

"Take me to her," he says assertively.

The time is 11:08AM and the bright sun shining through William's blinds still hasn't stirred him from sleep. His ringing cellphone finally does the trick as he moans and turns toward the nightstand almost tempted to ignore it. With his eyes still closed, he reaches over to where he thinks it might be but doesn't feel it. He's forced to sit up to look around until locating it on the floor. Seeing that it's Timothy Glass who's calling, he accepts the call without further delay.

"Hello, Timothy," he answers.

"William, you said I should call for anything, right?" he begins with a soft and timid tone.

"Absolutely, is everything okay?"

"No. It's Elizabeth—it has escalated—" William continues to listen wondering if Timothy will elaborate, but he remains silent.

"I'll be right over," he replies. He ends the call and slides out of bed toward his dresser. He lifts some of his pill bottles up to read their labels before setting them back down. He has a dangerous supply of pain killers, sleeping aids and stimulants, but eventually finds the one with Ephedrine on the label.

Through one of his connections, he's able to purchase this banned drug that used to be known for weight-loss; in his case it's taken to boost energy. With little care to his health, he downs the large pill with a swig of whiskey and then sets off to begin his day.

William parks his car and then gets out while taking note of the other car parked outside the Glass' home. Timothy is already holding the front door open and waiting for William to reach him as he makes his way up the walkway. When he enters the home, William immediately notices the gouges in the wall and looks at Timothy with a worried expression.

"Is this what you were referring too?"

"We'll get to that. There's something else I need to show you first," Timothy answers while leading him into the kitchen and to the spot where the claw print is still visible. "What does this look like to you?" Timothy asks. William studies it for a moment and then crouches down to get a closer look.

"It looks like some wild animal," he thinks out loud. He carefully brings his outstretched fingers closer to the mark and gets a flash of a dark, horned monstrosity standing in the doorway to the basement along with a rumbling demonic growl. William quickly withdraws his hand and stands up.

"Did you see something?" Timothy asks. William doesn't respond right away as he's still trying to process what just happened, but he knows what he saw.

"You don't have a typical haunting, Tim. There are two types of intelligent hauntings, human and nonhuman, and this was made from the latter. This is evil. What you have is a demon."

"Why couldn't you pick up on that before?" he asks with a retired sigh.

"Because demons are very good at hiding. I think it's best to rent a hotel until this entity can be removed."

"I'm afraid it's a little late for that," someone says from the dining room behind them. William turns around as Timothy introduces the two men for the first time.

"William, this is Father Victor Brahmer. Father, this is William." The two men shake hands to honor formalities, but William assumes he's only here to do a house blessing and has no intention of working with someone else on his case.

"What happened last night?" William asks concerned.

"Elizabeth—" Timothy begins but cannot continue his explanation.

Father Brahmer agrees to take William into Elizabeth's room but not without some friendly advice first. "I must warn you. What you are about to witness must be met without fear or doubt," he explains. William nods, but brushes Victor's warning off as nothing more than an overreaction. Victor open's Elizabeth's door as William follows him inside and then he gently shuts it behind them.

Elizabeth is sitting upright in bed with her wrists bound to the spindles of her headboard and the hand has been treated and wrapped with a cloth bandage. Elizabeth appears to be herself and in a relaxed state as the two men stand at her bedside.

"She wouldn't stop biting her hand, so we had to restrain them," Victor says trying to explain the reason for her condition.

"Good morning, Elizabeth. We finally meet," William begins. Victor carries two chairs over and places then down so they can sit and talk with the girl. "My name is William Corgel."

"I know," Elizabeth responds.

"Your parents must have spoken about me then." Elizabeth shakes her head.

"No, not from them."

"Then from who?"

"Something else—"

"Does this, something else, have a name?" William pries.

"I don't know." Elizabeth says and then turns her eyes away from William while attempting to pull her arms through the straps.

"What's wrong, Elizabeth? Is it talking to you?" Victor asks.

"Yes," she groans.

"What's it saying?" Victor continues as she squirms while moaning in discomfort.

"Disgusting things."

"Like what?" Victor asks.

"I dare not repeat. I don't want to say." Victor stands up and places his hands on her shoulders to still her. He then brings his head close to hers and whispers.

"What's it saying to you, Elizabeth?" She glances at William and then whispers into Victor's ear. She looks at William again, but then turns away. Victor turns to look at William and then turns back to Elizabeth.

"Do not listen to it. You are stronger than it," he continues softly. William gives Victor a curious look, but Victor shakes his head and sits back down.

William doesn't understand the meaning behind their looks or why he was the subject of their exchange of words. He cannot fathom the severity of the situation and is still too bullheaded to accept methods that differ from his own, but he will soon become deeply involved. If there was ever a time, he wanted to drop this case prior to this moment, he should have, because it just became too late to do so. He doesn't know it yet, but the demon has taken an interest in him.

"Do you know the Lord's Prayer, Elizabeth?"

"No father, I have—forgotten it." Elizabeth begins squirming and arching her body in a way that looks to be painful. Her legs and hands also start shaking and her head falls back to reveal the white of her eyes. Victor stands up while holding a cross in front of him. Elizabeth turns her head to face him, but immediately looks away with a snarl.

"Elizabeth. Elizabeth, look at me. Ask the Lord to deliver you from this menace," Victor demands.

Elizabeth becomes agitated and shakes her whole body violently. William stands up to reach for her, but Victor puts his hand out to stop him.

"What is wrong with her?" William asks.

"She's fighting."

"Fighting what?" Elizabeth stops shaking just as suddenly as she began. Father Brahmer and William stand in silence while watching the still girl with her head resting on her arm as if she just fell asleep.

"She has calmed." William says. Elizabeth suddenly darts her head to look at William with a grin that is so diabolical that it could vanquish all innocence from all who witness it. Her voice is no longer her own but deeper and with a raspy snarling undertone.

"Good morning, William. We finally meet." Victor opens his bible to one of the ribbon bookmarks and begins reading.

"Almighty Lord, word of God the Father, Jesus Christ, God and Lord of all creation, who gave to your holy apostles the power to tramp underfoot serpents and scorpions and the authority to say, Depart, you devils!"

Elizabeth growls and leans forward. She clenches her fists and uses all her might to try to pull her arms through the loops as Victor continues his prayer.

"And by whose might Satan was made to fall from heaven like lightning. I humbly call on your holy name asking that you grant me the strength to confront with confidence and resolution this cruel demon!" The straps begin to tear and loosen. Elizabeth jolts her torso at William, but the last knot of the strap holds her at bay.

"Lick my clit, bitch," she roars. Victor intercepts while holding the cross near her face.

"Silence your fowl mouth, unclean creature." Elizabeth growls and becomes more restless.

"Fuck! I'll fuck you," she says to William. She opens her mouth and chomps her teeth down with tremendous force several times as if trying to tear into William's flesh. "I'll devour you whole." Victor places the cross against Elizabeth's forehead and she lets out an unnatural howl. Victor sets down the bible and reaches into his pocket to take out a small clear bottle of holy water and flicks his wrist to sprinkle it onto the girl.

"Depart demon! Loosen your hold on this child of God!"

"Malchoota hai deelukh mid-til. beesha min passan illa. I'nissyoona I'illan la oo," Elizabeth growls.

Victor presses the cross against her cheek. She begins seizing before finally going limp. Victor sighs and welcomes the silence in this moment of peace. William doesn't know what to say or even what to think. What could make this girl become so lewd and violent so suddenly? He wonders if she's suppressing acts of sexual abuse or if oppression is causing her to find an outlet to act out. Victor interrupts his thoughts to enlist his aid.

"C'mon, William. Let's secure her straps again and get her comfortable. She needs to rest." William helps Father Brahmer getting Elizabeth situated before they leave her alone to sleep.

William never had an encounter with a possession or experience with a demon. While he knows about them, it's easier for him to suspect something else may be the cause of Elizabeth's affliction. He knows some spirits will claim to be demons to appear stronger than they really are. He doesn't anticipate this creature will pose too much of a challenge to him, it won't be long before he changes his mind.

Mr. and Mrs. Glass, along with, Victor and William are sitting at the dining room table without uttering a word for several moments. They each hold a warm cup of tea in front of them, but no one has taken a sip. Finally, Victor breaks the silence.

"I need to document and send my report to the Vatican before an exorcism will be allowed."

"Do you believe she is indeed possessed?" William asks.

"I observed at least seven signs relating to demonic possession." Victor responds and then looks over at Emily. "But I will need her medical records to prove that she doesn't have a history of mental or physical illness." Emily nods and gets up from the table.

"How long will it take for the Vatican to respond?" Timothy questions.

"Unfortunately, it can take quite a while. In the meantime, we should do our best to keep her comfortable and say prayers for her."

"We never enforced religion onto Elizabeth. We wanted her to develop her own beliefs," Timothy admits. Emily returns to the table and hands a folder containing Elizabeth's medical records to Victor.

"Is that why this is happening to us? Because we've stopped going to church?" Emily asks concerned that their parenting decision may have damned their daughter.

"No, absolutely not," Victor replies while shaking his head. "Not everyone is active in their religion. I know people who cheat and steal every chance they get. Yet they are in church every week, singing louder than everyone else and adorned with crosses. They live a double life. They warn against the dangers of lust and greed but are guilty of both themselves. Going to church doesn't make you a good person. As long as one lives a good life and provides for their family and loved ones, they live with God in their hearts."

Emily feels somewhat comforted by Father Brahmer's words and sits back down. Victor could have used this opportunity to direct blame on Timothy and Emily or guilt them into coming to mass more often. In the past the Catholic church did use fear to fill their pews, but Victor is part of a newer generation of priests. He doesn't think God will hold a grudge against one who has never read his book.

"I apologize in advance, but I have to ask," William begins. "Is Elizabeth taking any drugs like Lithium or Prozac?"

"No, no, nothing like that," Timothy responds.

"Were there any signs of her attitude or personality changing prior to this? Any peculiar or eccentric behavior?" William continues.

"She's an artist, she has mood swings," Emily answers.

"But nothing like this. This is different," Timothy adds. William nods and then takes a very noticeable sip of his tea.

"Typically, entities will try to communicate through dreams. Did she mention any strange or lucid dreams she may have had recently?" William pries.

"No, but sometimes she will draw them," Emily chimes in.

"Do you think you can gather some of her illustrations for me to look through later?"

"Sure, if you think it will help," Timothy agrees. William then turns to Victor.

"Do you know what language she was speaking?"

"It, William, and yes, it was saying the Lord's prayer—backwards—in Aramaic."

"And I'm assuming Elizabeth doesn't know Aramaic?" William asks while looking at Timothy and Emily. They both shake their heads in unison.

"She didn't even know the Lord's prayer in English, William," Victor points out.

William doesn't know it yet, but this case will test every fiber of his being and will require all his skills; and even those he has not acquired yet. The demon will ensnare him, toy with him, and then it will defeat him. William could stop popping pills and drinking, he could listen to Father Brahmer and bury his pride, he could take this case more seriously and drop his taunting nature, but some lessons are hard learned.

Later that night, Timothy peeks into Elizabeth's room and is relieved to see her sleeping soundly. He heads down the hallway towards his and Emily's room. She's already under the covers and lying on her side when he crawls into bed and puts his arm around her while spooning.

"How do we sleep here?" she asks without turning around.

"Father Brahmer said we shouldn't show fear."

"But I am afraid, Tim. I'm afraid for Elizabeth and sometimes I'm even afraid to look around the corner."

A section of the hallway is reflected in the dresser mirror that's against the wall behind the couple. A bloody corpse with no arms and an unnaturally long open bloody mouth reflects in the mirror. The Glass couple are engaged in consoling one another and do not notice the image's reflection behind them.

"William said it gains energy from fear and anger. I can be

strong, but not without you," Timothy says. Emily turns around to look at him while putting her arms around him as he wipes her tears away.

"This is an awful nightmare, Timothy." The wall behind Emily begins to bulge out into the figure of a head. Since they remain focused on each other they do not notice the demon's second attempt to unnerve them. "But I'll try to be strong with you," Emily continues. The wall returns to normal when they kiss. Timothy rolls over to turn off the light but stops in mid-reach before turning back to embrace Emily.

"I think I'll leave the light on tonight," he says, and Emily doesn't protest.

During the night, the light fades out, and Emily rolls over to begin running her fingers through Timothy's hair.

"Timothy," she whispers in his hear. Timothy remains sleeping on his back without stirring.

"Tim—o—thy," She whispers again, but he remains in a deep sleep. She climbs on top of him and straddles him. Her pelvic trusting slowly wakes Timothy from his coma-like slumber. He tries to focus his eyes in the darkness, and just barely makes out the outline of his wife's body.

"Honey—" he says somewhat surprised of her action.

"Shhh," she says as she continues rubbing herself against him. Timothy submits to her and slides his hands up her ribs as she pushes his penis inside her. He sighs and lets his head fall to the side. He doesn't understand why he's seeing the back of Emily's head beside him if she's on top of him. He suddenly concludes that she's not the one trying to satisfy him.

"Emily?" he whispers. He turns back to look above him. "You are not—Emily." He still can't make out any particular features of this being on top of him. A type of paralysis sets in and talking becomes difficult as his strength seems to be extracted from him. "Who—are—you?" The foam begins to descend through the night air towards him. It comes into view in an instant as a scaly head with four fang-like teeth and a forked tongue as it hisses in his face. Timothy screams and kicks wildly in bed before able to open his eyes. A quick glance around proves he's the only one in bed and the morning sun is struggling to squeeze through his partially open blinds. He picks up the small note that's resting on Emily's pillow and reads it, *went to church*. Timothy sighs and let's his head fall back on his pillow. He doesn't know if his recent experience was a dream or if he somehow really woke up during the night, only to pass out before morning.

It's almost noon and William and Timothy hold a cup of coffee in front of them with a box of bagels and cream cheese in the middle of the dining room table.

"How is Elizabeth doing?" William asks.

"She was fine last night after everyone left," Timothy responds. William nods and then takes a sip of his coffee. "I don't know what disturbs us more," Timothy continues. "Her outbursts, or the silence. She will sit there with that unnatural grin and that piercing gaze. Her laughter used to warm my heart, now it sends chills down my spine."

William doesn't know how to respond. He cannot talk about raising children or fatherhood. He doesn't know anything about those subjects. Luckily, Emily's returning home, in her Sunday best, gets him off the hook.

"Top of the morning, William," Emily says when she notices him.

"Morning, Emily. You are vibrant as usual," he replies.

"Thank you, William. I try," she says while blushing. She then turns to Timothy. "I tried to wake you this morning, but you were sleeping like a log."

"Yeah, I—I must have been tired," he says not wishing to elaborate any further.

Victor soon enters from outside and advances toward the table.

"Please Father, sit down," Timothy says as he slides an empty cup towards a vacant chair.

"Thank you, Timothy."

"Please excuse me, gentlemen. I must change," Emily says.

"Of course, my dear, Victor says before she heads upstairs.

"Help yourself to a bagel, Victor," William says.

"They do look good, but I shouldn't," Victor says as he pours his cup of coffee from the carafe. He then picks up the tub of cream cheese to read the flavor. "Garden vegetable. Well, that does sound healthy. I suppose I can have one bagel." William and Timothy smile as Victor picks up a napkin and then his bagel.

"So, what happened?" William asks Timothy as Victor spreads his cream cheese on his bagel.

"What do you mean?" he asks perplexed.

"You hesitated when you told Emily you were just tired." Timothy shyly smiles.

"I guess I forgot I had a psychic in the room," he says as William chuckles.

"I'm a medium not a psychic. Psychics read the minds of the living; I talk to the dead." William's response even makes Victor laugh. Timothy seems hesitant to talk, but after a long sip of coffee he begins.

"I don't know how to explain it. I thought it may have been a dream, but I'm not sure now."

"You had an experience?" William asks.

"That's one way of putting it. It was—well, we are all men here. It was erotic. It happened sometime during the night. I thought it was Emily at first, but then I knew it wasn't. That's when I saw a face covered in scales with fangs and a serpent's tongue. It had some resemblance to a female, but more snake-like than human."

"Sounds like a Naga," William thinks out loud.

"What's a Naga?" Timothy asks.

"They are creatures of lore depicted as half human and half serpent originating from India."

"That may be true, William, but I don't think that's what visited Timothy," Victor chimes in. "First, let me just say the Catholic church does not teach or tolerate this viewpoint at all. But I was a scholar in theology and studied multiple versions of the bible before ultimately becoming a priest. There are passages that describe a night creature who is sexually charged and turning into or shown holding a snake. They speak of a demon named Lilith." The chandelier above the table flickers and begins swaying as everyone notices the disturbance.

"That was some kind of—reaction," William says while keeping his focus on the lights.

Emily's scream interrupts their observations, and the three men jump up and hurry upstairs. Emily is standing in the doorway of Elizabeth's room when the others reach her. All of Elizabeth's pencils and art supplies are making laps around the room as they fly around in midair. Her pictures spin off the wall and join the markers and sketchpads as they continue circling the room. Elizabeth glares at Emily with her sinister grin until Victor enters the room with his cross held towards Elizabeth.

"In the name of God, I command thee to halt your mischief!"

"I raped Elizabeth when you were praying to your dead God!" she snarls. The spinning objects soon begin to change direction and rapidly head for Victor. William immediately slams the door shut as soon as Victor steps back into the hallway. The only sound coming from the room now is everything colliding into the door and then falling to the floor. Victor lays his hand on the shoulder of a very distraught Emily.

"You must understand that this creature wants to destroy your resolve. It wants you to question your faith, and it will use your fears and the worst language to achieve it." She nods but cannot articulate any words as she begins downstairs while holding back her tears.

"They are both strong Irish women who are firm in their beliefs, but I'm concerned for their health." Timothy announces in a hushed tone. "I think back now and wonder why their boldness used to annoy me."

"We need to continue regular visitations and prayers. We must be adamant and tenacious if we are to be victorious," Victor reminds him.

"I'm going to check on Emily," he says and then advances down to the lower level.

"May I speak to Elizabeth alone for a moment?" William asks. Victor wonders why he would want to be alone with such a maniacal entity. His first instinct is to deny it, but he also needs to trust, and believe that William is a capable and worthy ally in this fight. Victor knows the value of reinforcements in battles such as these, and that means William must be able to hold his own. Perhaps, seeing how William interacts with the demon now, and understanding his limits, will let him know if he can depend on him when it really counts.

"Yes, but be careful. Demons are clever manipulators," Victor warns.

Elizabeth follows William's movement when he enters her room. He gently closes the door and steps over the fallen artistry tools before sitting down in the chair still at her bedside.

"Good morning, Elizabeth," he begins. Elizabeth let's out a deep and lingering laugh.

"Elizabeth isn't here."

"Where is she?"

"She's in Hell—getting fucked."

"What's your name?"

"Fuck me William," Elizabeth says in her own voice. William remains calm and ignores the demon's deception while continuing with his interrogation.

"Your breed doesn't like to give out their names, do they?" Elizabeth refuses to answer his question and spreads her legs.

"I won't resist. No one is here, No one needs to know." Her innocent voice then changes back into the demon's. "Touch it, smell it, fuck it, lick it, you horny prick."

"You can't get to me," William says in a sure and calm tone. The demon smirks while expressing a deep growl that resembles an amused chuckle.

"You're thinking about it. Imagining it, desiring it. You want to slide it in my tight, soft cunt!" The demon tilts Elizabeth's head to the side. "No? Are you afraid? Undo my straps and I will fuck you." It extends the girl's tongue out and flaps it up and down rapidly. "You can just tell them I got loose and overpowered you."

"You don't know anything about me," William responds calmly.

"Stay with us, William—" the demon says in Sarah's voice. William narrows his brow. How did the demon know about the little girl from his previous case? "—Stay with all of us," the demon continues in its own menacing tone.

"How do you know about that?"

"We know everything about you. Your mother told us after sucking our cocks. Swing, swing, swing from the chandelier."

"Why did you say that?" William becomes uneasy in his chair and the demon can see him starting to crack. He's losing his calm, and no one is there to offer him aid.

"You don't remember?" The demon laughs. "Young William hitting his head on the banister." The demon continues hackling and teasing. "Did daddy leave you, William?"

"You know nothing about me!" William yells while standing up.

"No, William, don't touch me there," the demon says in Elizabeth's voice followed by a long hiss.

William becomes agitated and approaches closer towards the

bed. He doesn't know what his intention was when he reached for Elizabeth, but he didn't get the chance. The demon's lure worked. It rips through one of the straps and then grabs a handful of William's hair and pulls him closer to it. William's eyes become glazed over as soon as it falls into the demon's intense glare.

"Come to me. Come to me." The demon whispers in a seductive tone. "Undo my last strap and I'll coil myself around you." William is now in a trance-like state and becomes unable to resist the order. He begins reaching for the strap, but Angie suddenly appears at the foot of the bed.

"Do not listen, William!" she shouts. Elizabeth's snarl forces Angie to fade, but her appearance allowed William to snap out of his passive state. He frees himself from the demon's grasp and backs up.

"All you have is tricks and bluffs, but no real power," William scolds. Elizabeth giggles malevolently.

"You are a fool for challenging me, William. But I like your type the most."

William doesn't yet realize his idea that the demon is weak leaves him a poor defense against it. He doubts it exists; therefore, he does not take caution when facing it. William turns around to prepare to leave the room, but the next thing the demon says stops him in his tracks.

"Turn back, turn back, thou pretty bride. Within this house thou must not bide. For here do evil things betide." That was the last thing he remembered his mother reading to him.

"How do you know that rhyme?" William says dumbfounded as he turns back.

"We know more about you than you know about yourself."

"Tell me!" he repeats aggravated.

"For here do evil things betide." Elizabeth cackles while William shakes her shoulders just as Victor and Timothy burst into the room.

"Answer me!" William continues shouting.

"William!" Timothy calls out.

"Stop it, William," Victor orders. Victor and Timothy grab each of his arms and pull him out of the room, but Elizabeth gets the last word in before his departure.

"You will be fun to break, William."

Victor aggressively follows William when he storms out of the house.

"I told you to be careful. What happened in there, William?" William stops on the sidewalk before turning to face Victor.

"I don't know," he says after taking a moment to relax. "I don't know why I reacted the way I did."

"Do not let down your guard, William. It knows all the little buttons we have that trigger our reactions," Victor advises. William sighs and shoves his hands in his pockets.

"Before I was sent to live with my grandparents my mother read me a fairy tale. It's the last memory I have of her, and it recited it word for word. There's no way it could've known that."

"It knows it because you know it. Even the things you've buried or forgotten. It will dig them back up and use everything it can against you." Victor pauses before continuing. "Do you have a lot of memories with your parents?" William slowly shakes his head.

"I only have one—and it's not even that good. They were fighting about something in the middle of the night. My dad walked out and slammed the door. I never saw him again. Then I remember my mother reading that story to me. That's it. My next memory is with my grandparents, and I was thirteen."

"What happened to your mother, if I may ask?"

"I was told she died in her sleep soon after my father left."

"You have to realize that just because you can't remember something doesn't mean demons can't find it."

"I never saw or experienced anything I could not handle."

"If you believe you are immune to that creature, then you are already losing. It's been in your head. It will get to you. Do not challenge it. It's the same as inviting it into your home."

"I suppose you think we should just wait for God to show up."

"You don't have much faith, do you?"

"I was given the ability to see what others cannot. I've seen everything—but never an angel. How can an inexperienced mind summon a demon with nothing more than a lit candle? Maybe angels are just metaphors for the gullible."

"Demons want to be found, and they will take every chance they get to torment. Angels, on the other hand, only arrive when they are needed." The men pause with neither uttering a word until Victor continues. "Look, I'm not one to force religion on anyone, but if you aren't on the same side as God, then you can do nothing here." Victor heads back to the house with one last bit of advice. "Get some rest, William."

William starts up his car and then glances up into Elizabeth's room to see Victor securing her straps again before driving away. He feels nauseous, anger, and grief, but knows not where or how these feelings originated. He feels betrayed by his own mind. He will end his visit to the Glass residence for today. He doesn't want to admit it, but this case is different. For the first time, he doesn't know what to do. His solution is to take several swigs of whiskey along with several sleeping pills. He hopes that sleep will give him a few moments of peace and quiet and reverse his uncertainty.

Television becomes a welcomed escape for Timothy and Emily as they flip through 1950's–60's humorous sitcoms later that night. The black and white shows help lighten the mood with their one-liners and eccentric situations.

"I'll be right back," Emily says when the next commercial begins. He nods and gives her a smile as she heads into the powder room from the kitchen. Emily hasn't returned yet when the show comes back on, but the flushing of the toilet eliminates his worry, and his focus is directed to a funny exchange of dialogue.

Emily finishes washing her hands and then dries them on the hand towel before opening the bathroom door. She almost walks into a wrinkled floating head that's gliding towards her with its mouth open. It disappears right away but succeeds in making her let out a bloodcurdling scream.

Timothy jumps off the couch and runs into the kitchen to find Emily with her face against the wall and sobbing.

"Emily, what happened?" he says. She turns around and buries her head into his chest while shaking.

"Some horrible floating head was coming right at me," she says through her tears.

"It's okay, it's gone now," he says, in an attempt, to comfort her.

"It's never gone! None of it," she says while pulling away from him.

Timothy doesn't know how to completely console her since he has a hard time believing his own words. Maybe it's better to turn off the TV and call it a night; it's always good to end the day in bed.

Nine minutes after three-am, the bedroom door begins to close and then open, and finally close once more. Timothy and Emily remain sleeping as their door continues swinging between opening and closing. A disembodied woman with long black hair that conceals her face, crawls toward the bedroom from the hall. Emily's nightstand begins to shake as if it was suddenly caused by an earthquake and her lamp topples over and crashes to the floor. Emily wakes up with a jolt and observes her surroundings. She lightly taps Timothy, but he remains sleeping despite her attempts to wake him. The bedroom door slams shut, and the bed begins bouncing up and down violently. This disturbance succeeds in shaking Timothy from his slumber. Emily holds onto him while screaming as the two are tossed up and down on their bed. The entire house feels as if it's being physically bounced down the block until everything abruptly stops. They remain embraced in the silent darkness hoping their ordeal has ended, but just as they drop their guard the knob to their bedroom door turns and it swings open. The crawling woman enters through the doorway while jittering. Her jet-black hair still covers her face, and the lack of light makes it even harder to identify who she is.

"Elizabeth?" Emily asks softly thinking that maybe her daughter was able to free herself. She pulls away from Timothy and cautiously kneels on the bed while leaning over the side. "Elizabeth," she whispers. "Is that you?" Emily extends her hand toward the woman on her hands and knees and motionless just inside the room. The woman slowly rises to her feet and Emily carefully retracts her hand. The woman is wearing a soiled, shredded dress with no visible pattern or original color. She lifts her pale, pruned hands, with elongated fingernails, to brush her mud-soaked black hair to the side. Her empty eye sockets stare through Emily and her black gums with green teeth send Emily into a terrifying screaming fit. The girl opens her mouth and lets a multitude of cockroaches, beetles and centipedes pour out and drop to the floor as she moans. Emily remains screaming until Timothy turns on his bedside lamp. The illuminated room is void of the horrid woman and bugs. Tired, but too afraid to sleep, the two remain cuddled under the soft glow of Timothy's lamp for the remainder of the night. The lack of sleep will soon start to play havoc on their mentality, but under these conditions rest is all but impossible.

The next morning, William begins his day with his usual cocktail of pills and whiskey. He swallows his drink a little too soon to cause the pill to become lodged in his throat and William is sent into a coughing fit. He reaches for the bottle again and takes several big gulps until the pill is finally washed down. Now his day can begin.

Timothy lets William in when he arrives as Emily and Father Brahmer wait for him in the living room.

"How's Elizabeth?" William asks.

"She is herself—for the moment," Timothy answers. Emily remains silent while gazing at the floor as if she's lost in thought. William tilts his head to try to make eye contact.

"Emily?" he says. She looks up and tries to smile.

"I'm sorry, William. We didn't get a lot of sleep last night."

"Did something happen?"

"The bed was shaking and—we saw another apparition—I don't really want to think about it anymore," she concludes.

The woman, the couple saw the night before, suddenly appears on the stairs, but only to William. He remains focused on her as she moves her mouth as if talking, but no sound is coming out before shortly disappearing again.

"Did she have long black hair?" William asks. Timothy and Emily look at him in disbelief.

"Yes," Timothy responds.

"I just saw her."

"What does she want?" Emily asks. William hesitates before giving her his pensive answer.

"To be found."

"Is she—here?" Timothy asks, but hesitant to hear the answer. William slowly shakes his head.

"She was taken into a marsh and then molested by two soldiers and murdered. Her body was never found."

"That's awful. Poor girl," Emily says sorrowfully.

"Do you know where she is?" Victor asks. William shakes his head again.

"This happened during World War II."

"Oh-my-God," Emily utters in a disheartened tone. "I don't know if I can live here."

"I promise—I'll be here every day," William says.

"We should check on Elizabeth," Victor says while standing

up. William nods and puts his hand on Emily's knee.

"Everything is going to be okay."

"Men love saying that when they don't know what else to say," Emily chuckles. William smiles but cannot disagree with her. After all, he doesn't know what else to say.

William and Victor find Elizabeth sitting up and leaning against the headboard. The windows have their blinds closed and the only light being emitted is from the lamp next to her bed.

"How do you feel, Elizabeth?" William asks as he and Victor pull their chairs to the side of her bed.

"Slightly ill," she responds. "I used to wake up to the sun every morning as a child. Now I can't stand seeing it."

"Have faith, Elizabeth. This too shall pass," Victor says.

"Why did this happen to me?" she asks.

"I don't know," William admits.

"But we will not rest or give up until you are back to your old self," Victor promises.

"Do you know me? You know what I can become, but not who I am," she says.

"Tell us," William urges.

"I love to draw and paint. I like pizza. I think babies are cute. I like to read and watch movies. I'll watch anything that has Gerard Butler in it." William and Victor smile.

"Those are all good things," Victor says. The carefree moment becomes more concerning when Elizabeth begins coughing. It starts out has a tickle that she tries to clear, but it gradually becomes more severe and out of her control.

Victor stands up and puts his hand on her head as he whispers a prayer. A weak moan exits from her lips and an exhausted look comes over her.

"I think I'm going to rest for a little while," she whispers. William and Victor help to lie her back down in bed and pull the covers up to her chin.

"Lord, keep your ever vigilant eyes on this child. Protect and keep her safe from all evil intent," Victor says while making the sign of the cross on her forehead.

William feels sorry that Elizabeth must endure this, but his frustration is with himself for not having a way that will stop her nightmare. She is too young to have her life put on hold and her hope torn away. Hopeless is meant for the older few who saw the worst of humanity has and no resolution to mend it. He wants to help this family, but his ambition lacks patience and it will ultimately lead to his downfall. Despite his just intentions he will continue to make rash decisions, and his next one—may also be his last.

4

No Sleep for the Weary

The autumn weather doesn't always offer opportunities for dining outside, but the late afternoon sun makes the patio of a local bistro an inviting spot for an early dinner. After a long day at the Glass residence, William and Victor decide to meet here before returning home. They enjoy their subs and coffees while discussing the events of the day.

"It was nice to have a conversation with the real Elizabeth today," William says after swallowing his first sip of coffee.

"She's a very strong young woman," Victor admits while nodding.

"Can she overpower the demon on her own?" William asks as Victor shakes his head.

"This isn't a bruise that will heal on its own. A possessed person isn't always in their possessed state. It comes and goes with various stages of intensity. It can last for a minute or an hour. It can be as mild as moving a glass of water or much more violent.

Do not be fooled, William. This demon wants you to lower your guard. It wants to make you think it's not there. The truth is it's always watching, always listening. It gathers its energy and then unleashes it when it desires to do so." The two men take a few moments to finish their meal in silence until a nagging question prompts William's next question.

"I was meaning to ask you why permission is needed in order to perform an exorcist."

"Because it's dangerous. Unfortunately, they are not always successful. The body goes through so much trauma that the host may not survive it. It's a victory for the demon, it took a life, that's what it wanted. In some ways, it's similar to why the police need a search warrant. Anything they find without proper authorization doesn't count in the court of law. Without the church behind me I'm not protected against the demon, or the law if it goes south. In some cases, a minor rite of exorcism can force the demon to leave the individual without too much harm done to him or her; but for stronger demons it won't be enough."

"And you think Elizabeth's demon is strong?"

"I think it's playing with us—mainly with you. But I don't think we've seen what it's truly capable of. It's holding onto a pack of aces, and all we have are two jokers." The two men continue sipping their coffees for several moments. William had expected to have this case concluded by now, but a clear end to this still isn't in sight, and Victor's advice has yet to be taken into consideration.

"I'm usually not on the same case this long. I generally try to avoid getting close to those I have to help," William confides in Victor.

"I thought that was the first step in helping someone," he replies.

"For you it is. For me it's easier if I don't see them as people— just stories."

"Stories about people are the greatest ones. Despite how much hate there is in this world, people still care what happens to one another."

"You may have too much hope," William smirks.

"And you may not have enough," Victor responds.

"When you're young you wish you were older; when you're older you wish you were younger. You are never happy where you are when you are there, and only after you are no longer, do you miss it. That's the true divine comedy."

"So, you're saying no one can be happy?"

"I'm saying that only in retrospect do people realize they were once happy. Currently, everyone is always miserable."

"A little bit of faith goes a long way, William."

"I don't know if I ever had it."

"How do you help souls crossover when you don't believe there is a destination?"

"I don't need to prove it; they are just words. That's all they are, just words. What effect they have is up to those who hear them. I just say them."

"You're right, they are just words," Victor nods. "And words mean something to people, but you are at war with something that doesn't care what you say. It can tell if you mean them or not. Do you think all you have to say is, away with thee, God commands it, and poof the demon is defeated? It doesn't work that way. It doesn't fear you, it fears God, and if it doesn't see God in you, you will always be a toy to it." Victor pauses to gather his thoughts before continuing. "If you think just saying the right words is all it takes then you will fail. But words spoken from one who has God in his heart, and Jesus by his side, someone who truly believes in what he's saying without questions. Well, now that is a powerful weapon. And it's one that you will need. And that's the only thing I can't give you. You have to find that on your own. You can't fake a victory out of this one, William. If you lie to yourself, if you have doubts—you will lose more than just a case." William considers Father Brahmer's words respectively but can't fully bring himself to embrace them.

"I understand you think there's a peaceful and glorious end after life, but I've seen the exact opposite," William continues in a calm and sincere manner. "It's an endless void, unseen, ignored, a lonely, angry prison. To die is one thing, but to know you are dead is another." After Victor ponders William's viewpoint, he comes to a conclusion.

"Maybe the one thing that's different between us is also the same."

"What's that?"

"We both think about death far too early."

William smirks and nods in agreement. His and Victor's

approach may differ, but he has come to enjoy the Father's company and admires his opinions, whether they are objections or otherwise. Their viewpoints, at times, are oceans apart, but their bond has never been closer. A good team consists of those who do not always agree but agree or disagree at the right moments. Their success is heavily dependent on their ability to cooperate and understand how the other might react. Nothing unites opposing forces better than a common problem.

Timothy and Emily prepare to turn in for another night. They try to hope for one without incident, but they have now come to expect that some impending unpleasantries may occur.

Emily passes her daughter's bedroom door, which is opened ajar, and silently contemplates if she should peek inside. Her motherly instinct outweighs her fears, and she gently pushes the door in and then flips the light switch on. At first, she's relieved to find Elizabeth fast asleep; however, in the mirror, she's sitting upright and glaring at Emily with glossy, black, dreadful eyes which reflect no light.

Emily gasps but tries to remain steadfast while holding her ground. A long slender shadow creeping up the wall draws her attention to is just before a huge viper strikes with bared fangs and hissing. Emily cannot prevent herself from letting out a long, ear-piercing scream as she steps back into the hallway.

"What is it, Emily?" Timothy asks wile rushing towards her from their room. She tries to explain in a frantic and breathy tone.

"There's a snake in Elizabeth's room." Timothy advances into the room to investigate and scans the area thoroughly. He looks under the bed and around the floor but cannot see any sign of the serpent.

"Where did you see it?"

"You can't miss it. It was taller than me," she says from the hallway but dares not step any closer toward the room. Timothy picks up the lamp and looks in the corner of the room and around the nightstand, but no sign of a snake is present.

"There's nothing in here, dear." She looks at Timothy from the doorway with tears in her eyes as he cradles herself in his arms.

"I'm not going crazy. I know what I saw."

"It's okay, Emily, it was nothing but an illusion," he assures her while rubbing her shoulders.

"You always say that, but it's never okay," she says. Timothy can't find the words to reply and turns back to turn off the light but is suddenly overcome with horror.

"Oh–my–God—"

Emily follows his gaze and then covers her mouth with her hand to hide her shock. In the mirror, written in what appears to be blood, are the words:

SHE'S MINE

A late-night storm rumbles in the distance with the occasional flash of lightning piercing through the dark rooms. Timothy and Emily are soundly asleep when their digital clock turns from 3:00 to 3:01. A slight trembling occurs from somewhere inside the house followed by the hanging picture, of the tall ships, slanting downward. Long-fingered black handprints appear on the hallway wall as they gradually ascend until twisted clawed footprints begin to take shape. A flash of lightning illuminates a body structure that resembles a hunched over person with arms and legs that's twice as long. This pale-skinned ghoul has a recessed nose and eye sockets, and a wide mouth lined with sharp teeth. It traverses vertically on the wall with ease and without falling or losing its footing as it advances into the master bedroom. The creature disappears from time to time, but its prints remain imprinted on the ceiling as it stalks over the sleeping couple. The lightning illuminates it one last time as it rests just above Timothy like a patient spider.

A snarling growl is the only warning he's given before Timothy suddenly awakes while yelling in agony. The disturbance shakes Emily out of her sleep as well.

"Tim, what is it?"

"I don't know. My face is burning."

She reaches for her lamp to turn it on and then turns back to look at Timothy.

"Oh-my-God, Tim. It looks like you were attacked," she says concerned when seeing three distinct scratch marks stretching from his cheek and down his neck.

"What do you mean, attacked?" he says in disbelief. Emily searches for a tube of lotion among her assortment of creams piled on top of her nightstand while Timothy gets up and observes his injury in the mirror.

"How the fuck did this happen?"

"Sit back down," Emily orders. He sits on his bedside while Emily scoots over to dab the lotion on his wounds.

"Ow, Ow," he responds to every touch of her fingertips. "Ow, ow, ow. Stop. Stop."

"You stop. This will help."

"I'm fine now."

"No, you aren't." Emily continues to rub more lotion on his scratches as he fidgets and squirms.

"Okay, okay, are you done yet?"

"Yes, fine," Emily says annoyed that her attempt to help him was not appreciated, but to Timothy it seemed she was just unaware the pain she was causing him. The sound of running water begins as the two still argue. "You are such a baby," Emily says while capping the tube of Neosporin.

"It hurt."

"I was trying to help," she defends. Timothy lifts his head to listen while holding his hand up to quiet Emily. The two can now clearly hear the running water.

"What is that?" Timothy asks.

"It sounds like the shower," she replies.

"Who would be in the shower?" he questions, but Emily only shakes her head without a vocal response. "Stay here," he advises.

Timothy creeps down the hallway as distant thunder rolls outside. He turns on the bathroom light and then peeks inside to notice the shower curtain closed and the shower running. He carefully advances toward the curtain and slowly lifts his arm to take hold of it. He takes in a deep breath and then pulls the curtain back with haste.

Red water is flowing out of the shower head on a naked girl who's sitting in the tub while holding her knees up to her chin. She looks up and lets out a deafening high-pitched scream from a mouth that resembles a black void.

Timothy yells and backs up as fast as he can into the hallway. From the corner of his eye, he catches a female figure standing beside him and believes her to be Emily.

"Emily—" he sighs and puts his hand on her shoulder. It's only when he turns to face her does he see a woman with long white hair and covered in blood. He lifts his bloody hand from her while jolting backward with another shout. He loses his footing and collapses to the floor even before he knew he had tripped.

The experience shows no signs of dying down and continues to intensify as blood now flows down the walls and begins to flood the bathroom and hallway. Emily runs to kneel beside Timothy while holding him without caring that they are now ankle deep in bloody water.

The mirrored medicine cabinet opens to fling its contents against the bathroom wall with tremendous velocity and doors slam shut while pounding explodes from within the walls. Emily holds Timothy against her chest and yells at the top of her lungs. "Leave our home!"

All the unnatural disturbances such as the pounding sounds, running shower, slamming doors, and flying bathroom toiletries seem to obey her request instantly. The pooling blood also has vanished from the floor and no trace of it is found on the walls or on Timothy and Emily. All is clean, all is quiet, as if nothing had ever happened. Timothy and Emily remain on the floor hesitant to celebrate just yet and for good reason.

A deep, raspy laughter echoes in length from Elizabeth's room. Her door slowly creeks open as a lightning flash shows Elizabeth walking out of the darkness. She has gotten free from her restraints and is now unhindered. Her head, neck and arms crack and jitter as she slowly advances toward her parents.

"Where is he who shall lie beneath me?" Elizabeth asks in a seductive voice.

"Who—" Timothy asks with a reserved meekness. Elizabeth smiles sinfully.

"William," Emily rises to her feet unwilling to tolerate this type of behavior any longer.

"Get out of my daughter!" she yells. Elizabeth opens her mouth to release a swarm of tiny black flies. "Get out of my daughter!" Emily repeats.

"Suck a cock, slut," Elizabeth says in a harsh guttural tone. Emily takes hold of Elizabeth's shoulders and begins shaking her back and forth.

"Get out of my daughter!" Timothy slowly lifts himself up.

"Emily! Stop it, Emily!" Timothy grabs Emily's arms and pries her back from Elizabeth.

"When I'm done raping Elizabeth, I'll come for you,"

Elizabeth barks. Emily's reaction is swiftly delivered with a forceful slap across her daughter's face. Her hand had acted faster than her urge to land the blow and already regrets her action.

Elizabeth laughs cynically while directing her head back to look at Emily. "Bad mommy," she says with a hint of delight. She arches her fingers and lunges toward Emily with violent intentions. Timothy intercepts and wraps his arms around Elizabeth's stomach to hold her back. She squirms and growls while trying to enact her rage on him instead. Timothy avoids her flailing arms and snapping mouth as she contorts her body in extreme poses as she tries to escape from his grasp. Emily can only watch in horror at the struggle between her husband and daughter. Timothy lifts her off the floor and whirls her back into her room. With a gentle push he releases her and then slams the door shut before she can double back.

He holds onto the doorknob with both hands while redirecting all his body weight to lean backwards. Elizabeth attempts to pull the door back open with incredible strength. Timothy is jerked forward, and the door opens a little, but he forces his body back to slam it shut again. He cannot understand how she can be so much stronger than him and with a stamina that is never exhausted. Elizabeth's frustration is obvious as the door begins to splinter and shake while the hallway light bulbs flicker and then explode overhead. Timothy can feel his strength fading and there's no indication the same is happening on the other side of the door. Emily wraps her arms around Timothy and leans her body weight back as well to make Elizabeth use more force and energy.

"Lord, deliver us!" Emily shouts. The resistance Timothy was fighting against suddenly ceases. He and Emily fall back to the floor and all activity finally dies down. The last sound is a thump behind the door from a body that has fallen to the floor. It is completely quiet now, not even the sounds of the storm can be heard. Timothy proceeds to open the door and finds Elizabeth lying unconscious.

"Hold on, darling," Timothy says and then picks Elizabeth up and carries her to bed. He sets her gently down and then pulls the covers up. He then inspects the torn straps and the red bruises on Elizabeth's wrists. They must be due to her pulling at the straps for a long time. Emily walks in after Timothy while crying.

"I hit her. I've never hit her."

"It wasn't our daughter you slapped."

Timothy and Emily embrace in the glow of the streetlight pouring in from the window. Timothy glances between the parted blinds and spots the last of the moving rainclouds has revealed the full moon. This will be another night where neither Timothy nor Emily will drift back to sleep. Not even morning seems to bring them much relief anymore.

Later that morning, Victor inspects Timothy's scratches while Emily and William observe from their seats in the living room.

"Three lines, three scratches mocking the holy trinity, the father, the son and the holy ghost—It's afraid," Victor points out.

"It doesn't feel like it's afraid," Emily says sternly. "It's tearing us apart. I don't even feel whole anymore."

"I know these are trying times, but the bond your family has is strong. This will not defeat you," Victor says empathetically.

"We live in the mouth of hell and I'm playing chess with the devil," Timothy says with embellishment.

"You said there was a benign spirit here, right?" Emily says to William.

"Yes, her name is Angie.

"I don't think she's doing her job," Emily mutters as William smirks at her jab.

"It takes a large amount of energy to pass the demon's barricades. She's able to defy it, but her energy dissipates quickly when matched against such a powerful and dominate force. The other spirits are held back or enslaved by it; sometimes even manipulated to appear grotesque," William explains.

"The fact that Elizabeth was not afflicted yesterday doesn't surprise me now," Victor announces. "It was building up its power to orchestrate this attack on you last night. It knows it needs to try harder to defeat you, but you must not let it."

"Do you think the full moon had anything to do with last night's escalation?" Timothy asks.

"Maybe," William begins. "The moon governs the night and is master to the creatures of the night. It has long been believed that the unnatural gets a little power boost from the lunar phases, and more so when it's full. This is where we get words like lunacy and lunatic," he explains as Timothy and Emily listen with interest. "If it makes you feel any better at least a full moon only happens once a month."

"I deal with something similar," Emily says smugly. William smirks and then turns his attention to Timothy.

"May I see the bathroom where you had your encounter? There might be resonating energy which I can tap into."

"Sure," Timothy agrees.

"We'll be right back," William says to Victor who nods his acceptance.

With a house such as this, so much of its history becomes buried underneath layers of events throughout time that makes it hard for William to pick up on everything at once, but after an event is triggered, that memory is refreshed and easier to sense. Timothy leads William into the upstairs bathroom.

"This is where I saw the girl," he says as he pulls back the shower curtain.

William doesn't immediately see anything out of the ordinary, so he shuts his eyes to clear his mind. When he reopens them, he can now see that the tub is completely filled with blood as some of it spills over the sides to the floor. He turns around and notices blood streaks leading out of the bathroom, into the hallway, and then down the stairs.

"I thought everything took place in the basement, but Adam Faust drained his victims here before dragging the bodies downstairs," William relays his vision to Timothy. "These are all new fixtures, so it didn't happen in this exact tub, just in the same space. He saved the blood—maybe something relating to vampirism."

The drowned girl from the first video is also looking at him from the hallway. She stands rigid and with an unpleasant expression. He remembers seeing her breathing in the water while being held down. He can see it happening now but from a different time. A woman, maybe her mother, is holding this girl underwater until the tiny body stops thrashing. William grasps his chest as his lungs feel deprived of air. He gurgles and catches the sink with his hand just before falling to his knees.

"William!" Timothy says while attempting to catch him. William can see the girl on the bottom of the tub with her eyes open and lifeless until this vision fades back into the present time. William lifts himself onto the closed toilet seat to sit and catch his breath. "Is it your heart, William." Timothy asks concerned.

William shakes his head.

"No, it's not me. I connected with a child who was drowned here. I don't know how long ago, and she doesn't speak."

"Did anyone respectable ever live here?" Timothy asks rhetorically.

"Yeah, you," William answers.

"That didn't help any," he replies.

"I think I'm okay now," William says and stands up. A slow-moving fog glides past the bathroom several inches above the floor. William inquisitively advances into the hallway to see the misty mass hovering just outside Elizabeth's room before disappearing through the door.

"Did you see that?" William asks.

"Yes, what was it?"

"It's an entity trying to manifest. Get Victor, I'll try to uncover its identity."

William enters Elizabeth's room and strides through the flowing mist spreading across the floor. He glances at Elizabeth, who appears to be sleeping, but when he looks away, she opens her eyes.

The mist compacts and rises to form into a human figure of a young, slim, beautiful, naked woman, but with the head of an old hag; whose red eyes and green gums corrupt the attractiveness of her lower physique.

The hag rushes toward William with a screech and pushes him backwards onto the bed. Elizabeth bounces up and down on the bed excitedly as the old hag climbs on top of William and begins choking him.

"Fuck him! Fuck him," Elizabeth laughs sinfully.

William tilts his head towards the mirror to see the hag on top of him as a beautiful woman with red hair. He becomes hypnotized and beguiled by this false beautiful image and loses the ability to resist her. Elizabeth continues shaking the bed against the wall to create loud knocking sounds as the woman loosens William's belt. In the mirror the temptress' hair coils into hissing snakes, but William is trapped in a trance.

Victor hurries toward the room, but Elizabeth shoots a glance at the door to close it before he can reach it.

"William!" Victor shouts. He forces his shoulder into the door when he discovers the knob refuses to turn, but for now, William is helpless and alone.

"The temptress unzips William's pants and pulls them down.

"Yes, fuck him. Make him ours," Elizabeth cheers while wrapping her legs around William's head.

The gorgeous reflection whispers in a pleasant voice to William as he remains paralyzed.

"I am the voice of desire. I am the image of deceit. My kiss is venom. My touch is sweet." The demon temptress closes her fingers around William's boxers and begins to slide them down, but her intention is disrupted by an image that takes shape nearby.

"Leave him be, whore of the night!" Angie demands sternly. She stretches her hand towards the door until the knob turns and Victor bursts through without hesitation. Once her motive was carried out Angie did not remain visible long enough to be seen by him. With his cross held in one hand and a bottle of holy water firmly grasped in the other, he holds Elizabeth at bay while sprinkling the water droplets on the woman defiling William. The nude seductress screeches in frustration as she doesn't want to depart before finishing her carnal act. Vexation sets in and she transforms into a gray cloud except for her head which leads the mass around the room. Victor remains steadfast and directs the cross at her as she soars toward and around him with unnerving wails. He flings more holy water at her image as he turns to keep her in his sights.

"Away with thee and thine will! No victory for you or your ilk will be had this day!" With one last screech she flies into the wall with the cloud exploding and then gently dissipating.

William is released from the spell and begins to shake himself out of his dazed state.

"You stupid fuck! You are our slave," Elizabeth growls at William." Victor responds before William can muster his words.

"Silence all forms of your speech and sounds."

"You have no power over me, priest!" she hollers. Victor lifts the cross and Elizabeth turns away sharply. William pulls up his pants and then is directed to leave by Victor's head nod towards the hallway. For once William obeys without trying to get one last jab in at the demon. Victor backs up while keeping his cross raised. He then shuts the door when he clears the doorway. To William it's a retreat, to Victor it's an end of one battle, but to the demon, it's the beginning of William's defeat.

After William's ordeal everyone convenes back in the living room, but little is spoken about his encounter. It's believed that succubi do not accept rejection and will continue returning until their interest succumbs to their will.

The experiences in the Glass' home and the longevity of this case is starting to weigh heavily on William. There's no sign of progress being made or a resolution that proves an end to this nightmare for Elizabeth and her parents is near. Once thought immune to doubt and fear, William is now beginning to be plagued with the possibility that he's not perfect. He must prove to himself that there's nothing he cannot overcome, but his resilience is fading. More than that; however, is his fear he won't be able to keep his promise to relieve this family of their plight. For these reasons William will never quit but being ill-prepared has its own risks.

Victor is first to break the silence with his observation surrounding the latest turn of events. "I don't want to alarm anyone, but I've witnessed demonic possessions before, but this is nothing like any of those. We are fighting against multiple powerful entities that seem to have a pact with one another. That's not good for us." William figures it's about time to tell the family a secret he had been keeping from them.

"I didn't want to say this before; part of me thought this would have been wrapped up by now. Your house is a crossover point that's allowing a continuous flow of spirits to enter this home freely. Good, evil, lost, from anywhere, from any time. It's like a beckon in the fog. They are drawn to it, they are invited to it, and once here, they become trapped. There is much unrest here."

"What are you saying? That my house can never be cleansed?" Timothy asks in a disturbed tone. William begins by shaking his head.

"I believe a portal exists in the basement. We need to shut it, if we don't more spirits, and the like, will continue to enter freely. It's no different than killing a fly but leaving the window open. More will always come in."

"I can't endure this every night. I just can't. I'm afraid to close my eyes. The anticipation of what's going to happen and the suspicion of being watched are the cause of my anxiety. I never used to be paranoid, but now that's all I am," Emily admits. William can see she's at her wits end from living at this level of activity. He's only dealt with it for a fraction of the time, by comparison, he never had to sleep here. Maybe that's the experience he needs to have; instead of leaving until the light of the sun brings him false courage. If he's to understand what this family is truly living with, he must be immersed in it.

"I can stay here tonight and document what happens," he says. Emily feels relieved at William's offer, thinking that maybe nothing will happen if he's here, but she's also concerned for his safety. She doesn't want someone else to put themselves in danger on her account.

"I would be okay with that but—after what just happened to you, are you sure you want to linger?"

"How can I accurately monitor this activity if it all happens when I'm not here?" William points out. The group thinks about his explanation and then nod in agreement.

"I will bring some extra pillows and blankets to the couch; it's actually very comfortable," Timothy says.

"Thank you, that will do nicely."

"Last night the activity started around three in the morning," Emily says.

"Three, you say?" Victor repeats.

"Yes, does that mean something?" Emily questions.

"Three-am is considered to be the devil's hour, or the witching hour. It mocks the time Jesus died on the cross at three-pm," Victor explains.

"I don't know if I will sleep anymore," Emily says as she shakes her head and trails off.

Mr. and Mrs. Glass retire for the evening leaving William by himself on the couch. He rests his head on two pillows and with a blanket covering his feet and legs while paging through a borrowed magazine under a dim light. He glances at the time on his phone—it's ten minutes past midnight and nothing out of the ordinary has happened so far; he sighs and returns to the magazine.

It's strange how sometimes sleep overtakes someone in the midst of an activity. The magazine slides off William's stomach and falls to the floor; however, the thump doesn't wake him. A shadowy figure reflects in the dark television screen. It stands motionless in front of William, but somehow only appears as a reflection. The figure spreads its arms out and six coiling tentacles slither under and over the creature's outstretched arms. William remains sleeping as the appendages dart into his body. William opens his eyes with an expressionless glare. He rises to a clumsy stand and drags his feet across the floor. His eyes are locked in a wide and never blinking stare as he nears the kitchen. Angie appears near him and tries to get his attention.

"William, wake up." He cannot hear her and continues his sleepwalk toward the basement door.

"Wake up, William!" she says louder. William places his hand on the doorknob and slowly begins turning it, all the while her voice fails to reach him. When the door fully swings open a ghastly, white, and disembodied screaming banshee flies up from the darkness and grabs a hold of William's collar. He's yanked down toward the basement steps, but Angie grabs his arm and pulls him back up. William is in a spirit tug-of-war while Angie continues to beg for him to awake. "You must wake up, William, wake up."

William's eyes blink and he regains control over his own body. He yells and swats at the banshee that's trying to snatch him away from Angie. His hand passes through the banshee as her actions begin to make him levitate. His body arches as he's pulled in two different directions, but Angie proves to be the victorious one when her next forceful tug yanks William from her grip. It descends back into the darkness and William's feet are once again planted on the floor.

A gust of wind shoots out of the basement and collides into him to send his sliding across the floor on his back. After this last attack the door slams shut as if the losing spirits threw a tantrum.

"It knows you are weaker in the basement," Angie says. A deep rumble comes from someplace in the house, similar to the one that started the night before. "And it's not happy right now—" Angie continues. The house trembles and shakes as it gradually becomes more violent. The dining room chandelier sways from side to side, all the faucets and shower turn on, and the toilets overflow.

"The house just woke the fuck up," William exclaims.

"It was never asleep, William," Angie says. "Beware of silence, for waiting makes no sound." A monstrous snarling black dog with red eyes stalks into the kitchen while gazing intensely at William and Angie. William puffs out his chest and stands his ground. He believes being fearless in its presence will take away its power.

"Hellhound, is that all you can do is play with water?"

"No William, don't taunt it!" Angie warns.

The house becomes silent, and the hellhound disappears after his brash comment. There are several moments of stillness with nothing happening until Elizabeth materializes in the kitchen. The demon is allowing her to astral project using its power. She smiles and slowly points to Angie. "Bring me my enemies and slay them before me." Angie vanishes without a word or a struggle. "This will not end well for you, William," Elizabeth laughs and then disappears.

The cupboard doors open followed by dishes and glassware soaring across the kitchen and smashing against the wall. The kitchen table and chairs slide across the floor and then collide into William to pin him against the opposite wall.

The crashing and shaking bring Timothy and Emily rushing down the stairs and into the kitchen. William struggles to push the table away from his torso while ducking and dodging the projectile dishware being flung toward him.

"William," Timothy calls out and ducks below the flying dinnerware to lend his aid. He pulls the table from him, but it immediately slides back into William. He cries out in pain as Timothy attempts to pull the table back again, but astonishingly it seems to have become quite heavier.

Counter drawers open while others fly out of the counter completely. Emily observes horrified at the forks, spoons and knives being shot toward her husband and William.

"Watch out!" she warns. Sharp chef knives are hurled out of the knife block toward William just as Timothy succeeds in pulling the table far enough for William to duck underneath it. He escapes through the legs and then looks back at the knives embedding in the wall where he once occupied. The two men shield their heads as they sprint out of the kitchen. As soon as they survive the trek through the gauntlet, the activity ends.

"Never have I witnessed this much activity or frequency in one place before," William admits. No one bothered to look at the time when everything went haywire, but at least one thing is certain, William's presence does not prevent or lessen the occurrences.

When morning arrives, Victor returns and listens to the events from the previous night.

"This house is physically dangerous to live in," William points out.

"That was one night, William. We've been living like this for slightly over two months," Timothy adds.

"It destroys everything we own, and I fear our sanity is next," Emily says hyperbolically.

"You said you saw Elizabeth in the kitchen too," Victor begins. "What happened there?"

"She pointed at Angie and must have overpowered her because she was gone right away." William thinks for a short moment about that. "It said something to her," William recalls the memory fully before continuing. "Bring me my enemies and slay them before me." Victor looks at William dumbfounded.

"It said that?" William nods and can see Victor is disturbed by the information.

"Is that from something?" William asks.

"Luke, chapter nineteen, verse twenty-seven. It's from the bible."

"I thought it didn't know the bible," Timothy questions.

"Oh, it knows the bible very well," Victor begins. "It just doesn't like hearing about it from us."

"If we knew the demon's name, we could gain power over it. There are books on demonology maybe we can find it in one of them," William suggests.

"True, but that's a needle in a haystack, William. There are countless names belonging to demons and it's not wise to rattle them off from a list. It could end up attracting them," Victor points out.

"Well one thing is for sure." William begins. "When this is all over this case is going to be notorious."

"At least the media hasn't caught wind of this yet; hopefully they won't. We don't need cameras and reporters peeking through the windows," Victor says.

"You're going to tell others about this—about us?" Emily says with concern about her family's name and privacy.

"I document all my cases. Those within my field share their experiences with one another and the industry," William explains.

"I will also have to send a follow-up report back to the church," Victor admits.

"I know you can't think about it now, but someday everyone is going to know about the Glass demon," William says.

5

Roulette with a Demon

William finds the best way to search for information online is with a slight buzz. Red wine works best, but gin & tonic, rum & coke, or brandy old fashioned are all acceptable drinks for the late-night internet warrior. He makes himself comfortable in his home office with a bottle of Pinot Noir and types, demonology into the search engine. He scrolls down the page while skimming through the results, but nothing stands out. He takes a drink and then continues his research on the next page. The first link catches his attention immediately:

Professor Mikael's Demonology Seminars and Teachings

The link takes him to Mikael's profile page belonging to the University of Wisconsin in Stevens Point.

Mikael completed a master's in religious studies with

*a minor in demonology. He's well-traveled to haunted
and cursed locales around the U.S., Canada, and abroad
including Rome, Germany, and England. He has witnessed
first-hand demonic possessions and behavior, as well
as demon-controlled sites. He has had a long career in
communicating with and expelling varies types of demons,
from soldiers to princes of Hell. He has since retired from
the field and now teaches demonology to those pursuing
a degree in religion, theology, ministry, or as an elective
for paranormal investigators or the curious. Providing
invaluable knowledge and experience, Mikael will discuss
topics such as, what are demons, their traits, precautions to
take, and finally, ridding a demonic influence.*

This might be the lucky break William needs. He pulls a pad
of paper toward him and jots down his contact information.

Mikael agrees to meet William the following day, a Saturday,
when class schedules won't interfere with their engagement.
William isn't accustomed to seeking help from others, but there's
been a lot of firsts for him on this case so far. Perhaps, it's time
for him to regain some control of his battles, and what better way
than to seek the council from one who had fought them before.

William admires the posh Victorian house, enclosed by a
short, black cast iron fence, and landscaped with shrubs and
flowering bushes. He looks down at the address he had written
down on the small piece of paper to make sure he's at the right
address. When he confirms it matches, he pushes the paper back
into his pocket and then lifts the latch to the gate. He makes his
way toward the front door and then rings the bell. He waits until
a middle-aged man with glasses and smoking a cigar answers.

"Hello, Mikael?"

"Yes," he replies.

William extends his hand and the two formally greet each
other.

"I'm William Corgel. We spoke yesterday about the case I'm
working on."

"I remember, come on in." Mikael puffs his cigar while
leading William down a corridor and then into his personal
library. This room is larger than most living rooms and is filled
with floor to ceiling bookcases that stretch around the entire

area. There must be at least three thousand of both old classic tomes and newly published books in his collection and Mikael has a strange talent of keeping a mental catalog of every title he owns and where to find it. In the center of the library is his ornate desk with a wingback chair and a floor standing gemstone globe. Mikael heads to the desk and places his cigar in the ashtray.

"Welcome to my library. Now, what can I find for you?"

"Where's your section on demonology?"

"You're looking at it."

"Everything in here is related to demons?"

"All three thousand, four hundred, and fifty-six."

"You know the exact number?"

"I can name them off alphabetically if you want me too."

"I don't think that will be necessary," William replies while observing the vast collection in amazement. "I'm sure what I need is in here somewhere."

"May I make a few suggestions?"

"Yes, please," William begs. Mikael heads to a section to the left of his desk and begins skimming through the titles before sliding a book out with his finger.

"According to Bainsfeld, there are seven princes of Hell based on each of the seven deadly sins. His classification was first published in 1589." Mikael hands him the book and he begins paging through it. Mikael continues skimming through his shelves before withdrawing another title.

"In 1613 Michaelis explains that sixteen demons, which make up three hierarchies, are responsible for tempting mankind to carry out evil acts ranging from murder to infidelity." William places the first book on the desk and then takes the next book Mikael is handing him. William barely has enough time to open the cover before Mikael hands him yet another book.

"The Ars Goetia of The Lesser Key of Solomon is one of the most popular books on demonology. It contains descriptions on seventy-two demons." William sets the previous book down to take this next one.

"That's the revised edition of 1904. The original was published in the 17th century. I—do not have that one, I'm afraid."

"Well, there's certainly a good supply of information here, but I don't know what I'm really looking for," William admits.

"Let's see, I have a few others here that may be beneficial." Mikael takes the books out and hands them to William before he has a chance to set them down.

"Pseudomonarchia Daemonum, 1583. Dictionnaire Infernal, 1818—and the 1863 edition." William holds the three books in his arms with an overwhelmed expression before setting them down on top of the others.

"This is a lot of reading," William says with dismay.

"We might be able to fine-tune these to your specific needs," Mikael begins. "What do you know about this demon that you're facing?" William thinks for a moment before answering.

"Well, the name Lilith did come up."

"Lilith? I see, she was believed to be Adam's first wife before Eve."

"Adam had two wives?"

"Yes, she left him when she wanted to be on top and he said her place was to lie below. She is said to form the demonic race of the succubi."

"Do you have anything about her?" William asks with interest. Mikael turns to another bookshelf and then returns with another book.

"She's not mentioned in any of those, but she is in this one. Demons and Demonology, published in 2000—it's one of my newer books." William swiftly flips through several random pages and studies the illustrations. This one seems a little easier to attain and retain information.

"Do all demons have names?"

"Many of the ranked demons, such as princes and generals, are named and each can control six to twelve thousand soldiers. This book discusses many of these high-ranking demons, along with their characteristics."

"What if I'm dealing with a soldier who doesn't have a name that can be researched?"

"Soldiers may be harder to name, but they are also weaker and would be easier to cast out. From what you have told me it sounds like you are dealing with a general."

"Which means—"

"Which means you are dealing with a very menacing and intelligent entity, and I advise you to use caution." William nods while recalling Victor's similar cautionary advice. "They have been known to jump, you know."

"Jump?"

"Yes, as in changing hosts. They wear and weaken other desirable interests until said persons become unable to defend themselves. I've seen it happen before."

William can't help but ponder Mikael's explanation on his drive home. He can't explain it, but he has an unsettling sensation in the pit of his stomach. Nerves, hunger, dehydration, all plausible explanations for his discomfort; however, it wasn't there before his attempted molestation. He remembers thinking about just letting it happen, that fighting against it might be too difficult. Was that enough to become defeated? His desire to save Elizabeth may be more of a sacrifice, but he'll do what must be done.

Later that night, William rests in his recliner with a straight brandy while reading Mikael's book. Page after page and drink after drink, he stays up far later than he's used to, but drunk and tired make concentration somewhat impossible. William eventually passes out and the book falls to the floor.

Meanwhile, at the Glass residence, Timothy finds Emily standing in the middle of Elizabeth's room while watching her sleep. He advances to her side as they exchange weak smiles.

"When she's sleeping, she looks like our daughter."

"She is our daughter," Timothy replies.

Emily turns around and peeks through the blinds of the window—it's another calm night without a breeze.

"No one knows what is happening here—to us." Her voice is calm and soft. "They all go about their daily routine. Oblivious to the house next door. They complain about their jobs, their chores, their bills. They scold their kids for not brushing their teeth or not going to bed on time. They have so many problems, but at night they all sleep peacefully." Timothy takes her hand in his and pulls her toward him. He doesn't have much to say that will ease her grief and worry.

"Come on, let's go to bed."

When they turn around Elizabeth is sitting upright and looking at them with an expressionless stare. After a moment of silence Emily hurries out of the room trying to hold back her tears.

"Go back to sleep, you," Timothy says calmly.

"I don't sleep—can you?" Timothy starts walking towards

the door without acknowledging the question. "Sweet dreams," Elizabeth adds. Timothy ignores the sinister laughter from Elizabeth's room.

He closes his bedroom door before spotting Emily sitting in a chair while holding a family portrait of them when Elizabeth was younger.

"I'm just going to sit here for a while. You go to bed," she says.

Timothy takes a seat at the foot of the bed and drops his eyes to the floor. He's out of words to say and can't help but wonder if the demon is defeating them. He fears he's close to losing his family and keeping his feelings bottled up in order to appear stronger for them, is driving him closer to his breaking point.

Not much longer during that night, Victor's phone wakes him from a sound sleep. He groggily turns and fumbles with the phone before accepting the call.

"Hello, this is Father Victor Brahmer?

"I apologize for calling at this late hour, Father, but I've just received word," the caller responds.

"It's quite okay. What is this about?"

"I'm calling to inform you that your request to perform an exorcism has been approved." Victor lets out a sigh of relief.

"Thank you. Thank you very much. I will begin making the necessary preparations."

"May God be with you and the family."

Shortly before morning, William dreams about himself as a child. There's something from his childhood that's important, but he's unable to remember the event or discover the clue that will reveal its mystery. What's more unnerving is the fact that the demon seems to know about it in great detail—

Young William lies frightened in bed while holding his covers up to his eyes. The door in the hallway slams shut followed by a loud thump exploding from the wall and then a continuous squeaking. William gets out of bed and hurries into the hallway to find his mother standing with her back towards him.

"Mom!" he calls out. Her joints crack when she turns to face him. William screams out in terror when he sees her bloody face, bulging eyes and dislocated jaw. He takes a step back, unaware of his proximity to the staircase. He loses his balance when his foot fails to land on solid ground, and he tumbles down the stairs.

William awakes suddenly while sitting up urgently in another coughing fit. His dreams attempt to remind him what his mind doesn't want to recall and beginning the day with his usual pills and alcohol cocktail is one way for him to forget it.

It's Friday, a day when many are looking forward to their fish fries and IPAs, but for William, it's the day of the exorcism. Father Brahmer has spent his time in isolation for deep prayers and fasting to prepare himself for this battle with the demon. William arrives at the Glass' home early and invites himself inside to find Timothy sitting on the couch. Timothy acknowledges his presence but remains uncharacteristically impersonal. William too says nothing before sitting beside him. No one knows how today will end or what to expect during the rite. This could be resolved today or continue for another day, week, or month. Hope is faint, dangers are high, and failure is likely. Timothy points to several drawings on the coffee table.

"I managed to pick up several of Elizabeth's work that were on her desk."

"Thank you," William says and reaches for the pictures and begins studying each one in depth before going to the next one. He eventually comes to a shading that depicts a beautiful slender woman in a gown. "Have you looked at these?"

"No," Timothy admits.

"Do you know who she might be?" William hands the picture to Timothy. He admires the picture with a hint of uneasiness.

"This is the woman in the basement; except she wasn't this appealing."

"That's what I figured. This woman could have been one of the murdered victims. Elizabeth saw her as she once was. Which means she developed an interaction with the energy here. She may not have even been aware of it, but that openness allowed spirits and entities to be drawn to and attach themselves to her." Timothy peeks over as William continues flipping through the pictures until he comes to the horses and barn drawing.

"That looks harmless enough," Timothy observes. This is the picture where Elizabeth experienced her nose bleed, but no one else could have known that. Yet, for some reason William remains looking at the image that Timothy was so quick to judge as harmless. William feels an energy in the paper that brings an image of Elizabeth looking into the mirror, but her reflection is the evil doppelganger that consumed her.

Timothy picks up on William's intense gaze of this picture and must question it.

"Do you see something there?" William notices the dried blood spots at the bottom of the page and brings the drawing closer to his eyes to view it. He knows what it looks like to him but decides to get a second opinion. He hands the drawing to Timothy.

"What does this spot look like to you?" Timothy studies the markings before redirecting his gaze back to William.

"An upside-down cross," Timothy answers.

A knock on the door brings Timothy and William to a stand as Victor meets them. He's clothed in a black surplice and purple stole while carrying a briefcase, which houses his bible, holy water, and several crucifixes.

"Welcome, Father," Timothy says.

"How is Elizabeth this morning?" Victor asks.

"She's—not herself," Timothy replies while shaking his head. Victor nods realizing the demon most likely already knows what they are planning to accomplish. Just like Father Brahmer prepared to perform this exorcism so has the demon to resist it. It will be the strongest it has ever been today.

"Have you performed many exorcisms before?" William asks.

"I've sat in on over forty while I was in seminary, that includes the month I spent in Rome for coursework. I've also assisted in ten cases, but this will be the first one I lead." Victor makes the sign of the cross on himself and then blesses William. "Nel nome del Padre, e del Figlio, e dello Spirito Santo. Amen." Victor then looks at William. "Are you ready, William?"

"Yes."

"Good," Victor says before turning his attention back to Timothy. "I will have to ask that both you and Emily remain out of the room during the exorcism. The demon may try to use either of you to stop the rite from moving forward, and once we begin, it's crucial we finish."

William and Victor enter Elizabeth's bedroom and notice her glaring at them with an evil grin.

"Good morning, Elizabeth," William begins.

"Try again," she replies.

"Your time grows short, demon," William taunts, but a glance from Victor lets him know to not engage any further.

"Oh, poor thing—She fell—from that window," Elizabeth snickers. William turns to see a little girl with her neck broken and her head extremely hanging to the side. He jumps back from this disturbing image that fades as soon as Victor raises his cross.

"It's trying to distract and unsettle you. Stand firm, William."

"You have no power over me!" Her temper flares up. The bedroom door slams shut, and the curtains are torn down from the windows.

"Little damaged William; a broken pathetic bastard who nobody wants," Elizabeth cackles.

"Your words have no effect on me," William strikes back, but it's the bait the demon wanted him to take.

"You think you can defeat me? One who needs drugs to sleep, drugs to confront me, drugs to ignore the pain and fear that plague you? Swallow them all tonight!"

"Leave the safety of your host and fight me!" William barks, despite the warnings, and advice he had received he continually taunts the demon.

"Do not coax it, William. Do not invite it to you!" Victor exclaims for fear he may have just put the exorcism's success in serious jeopardy.

Elizabeth lets out a long, deep growl that vibrates in William's chest. The closet door opens and closes continuously with loud and fast slams followed by the light bulb exploding inside the lamp. William is then lifted and flung against the wall; he finds himself immobilized as he's slowly rotated horizontally against the wall.

"You do not know what you are up against. Can you not resist me? Where is your brave speech now?" the demon asks. William is continually turned, while bonded to the wall, until he is completely upside-down. "Your God has forsaken you. I have defeated you. I will claim you," the demon continues.

"In the name of God, release your hold on this man!" Victor demands while extending his crucifix toward Elizabeth. William collapses to the floor and the closet door stops slamming. Elizabeth snarls at Victor, but then darts her head away when she observes the cross.

William joins Victor's side a little shaken, but willing to accept the cross being handed to him. Elizabeth howls as Victor sprinkles holy water on her and then opens the bible to begin the rite.

"God, whose nature is ever merciful and forgiving, accept our prayer that this servant of yours, bound by sin, may be pardoned by your loving kindness." Victor continues his readings while William keeps the cross near Elizabeth as she snarls and shakes violently. "I command you, unclean spirit, whoever you are, along with all your minions now attacking this servant of God, by the mysteries of the incarnation, passion, resurrection, and ascension of our Lord Jesus Christ, by the descent of the Holy Spirit, by the coming of our Lord for judgment, that you tell me by some sign your name, and the day and hour of your departure." Her response is loud, deep, and drawn out.

"Nevvverrr!" Elizabeth twists and turns as she attempts to break free from her straps. She then leans toward William. "You are not a believer. Do you think by holding that symbol you are safe from me? It is weak in your hands."

"I know it as something you dislike. So, I will force it before you," he fires back.

"How long have you've been alone, Corgel? You do not pray to God; you give your soul to Lilith to lick her filthy cunt." Victor raises his voice to drown out Elizabeth's words.

"I cast you out, unclean spirit, along with every satanic power of the enemy, every specter from hell, and all your fell companions; in the name of our Lord Jesus Christ!" Elizabeth redirects her attention and snaps at Victor.

"I fucked Jesus when I fucked Elizabeth."

William presses the cross to her forehead followed by her contorting her body in an unnatural way before lunging at him. The restraints suddenly rip which frees her from the bed and allows her to attack and force William to the floor.

Victor stops his prayer and tries to pry Elizabeth off William, but he receives her swift kick in the gut that sends him backwards. William. He pushes her clamping jaws away, but she's proving to be stronger than he thought. Elizabeth pins one of his arms down and then slaps him hard before digging her nails into his throat and then whispering in his ear.

"I will follow you and then rape you into Hell where your pariah carrion will be fucked by beasts and fiends."

Elizabeth pulls his hair forcefully and scratches him mercifully before Victor returns to make a second attempt to rescue William. "Lie down with us—Give in to us— We will fuck you in the night," Elizabeth continues.

Victor lifts Elizabeth up by the waist and places her back on the bed as she kicks, flails and squirms. He tosses one of her pillows off the bed while keeping a firm grip on its case. The pillow slides out and victor can now use the empty case as a last resort to tie one arm securely to the headboard post.

William sluggishly begins to pick himself up with a multitude of scratches on his face and arms. He uses the dresser for support and peers into the mirror just as a black horned apparition darts out of it and enters his body. Victor is busy tying Elizabeth's second wrist with another pillowcase when he notices the confrontation.

"William!"

William yells and falls to the floor while shaking violently. His eyes become glossy black, and his facial expression resembles that of a predator as he growls and kicks on the floor. Victor finishes his knot that will hopefully keep Elizabeth secured and then hurries to kneel over William. He picks up the cross he had dropped and presses it against William's forehead.

"Begone and stay far from this child of God!" he hollers. The black mass rushes out of William's mouth and sores wildly around the room before disappearing back into the mirror. William flails his arms around himself as if shooing mosquitoes while yelling. "Calm down, William. Calm down," Victor says while helping him to his feet, but the affliction has drained him and left him disoriented. Victor knows this first battle with the demon has failed. "Come on, we did all we can for right now." Victor gently guides William to the door as Elizabeth grins knowing she took the victory here.

"William—" she says in a mocking tone. William gives her a tired glance. "—Did I get to you?" Elizabeth laughs hysterically while William is directed out without a response.

Emily hands William a cup of water, but his shaking hands robs him from accepting it. She sets the cup in front of him and then takes his hands into hers to try to still them.

"Dear, William, your hands are chilled to ice." William feels ill and an instant and lingering sapping of all his body heat. He takes a moment to recompose himself while worry prohibits an exchanging of words.

"Are there two of them?" William finally asks in a shivering voice.

"There are many. They are legion, William," Victor replies. William remains looking at the tablecloth with a blank stare and slowly reaches for the cup of water as soon as Emily retracts her hands.

"It won," William says underneath his breath.

"It's going to take more than one fight. I didn't expect to attain victory on the first day," Victor explains.

"Will it work the second time?" Emily asks.

"It may not, but then we will try it again, and again after that if necessary. Some exorcisms take hours, others take weeks; some even months."

"Is Elizabeth in any pain?" Emily continues.

"She's experiencing lapses in time, as if in a dream. She may get glimpses of what's going on but will be unable to act or react to any happenings. You also must realize that our actions only hurt the demon, not Elizabeth." William avoids making eye contact as he announces his uncertainty.

"It's too strong. How can we fight it?" William's hubris has been torn away from him. Victor knew that someday his pride was going to cause him harm, but despite the need for his humbling experience, he also needs to have confidence, especially now.

"Look at me, William." William hesitates, but finally looks up. "You cannot give in to doubt. You need to put on the full armor of the Lord and calm your mind. A questioning man will fear this demon, but a demon will fear a devout man." William returns to his downward glare without responding. He once thought a brash approach would outmatch the demon, but he can't pretend any longer; he's not ready for this type of activity.

"What do we do now?" Timothy asks.

"We repeat the rite every day until the demon departs—I think it's best for everyone if we continue tomorrow," Victor advises. Timothy and Emily nod in agreement as they stand up, but William is almost oblivious to the conversation taking place around him. Victor glances at him before looking at the Glass couple.

"Walk with me to my car," Victor says to Timothy and Emily.

"Rest here, William; as long as you need." Timothy tells him while gently places his hand on William's shoulder. William is distant but acknowledges Timothy's suggestion.

"Thank you," he replies weakly.

Emily and Timothy accompany Victor outside and toward his car, but Emily mentions her concern for William before he can unlock his door.

"Will he be alright. He doesn't look the same." Victor delays with his answer.

"He has been marked by the demon. I pray he recovers after a good night's sleep; otherwise, Elizabeth won't be the only one who will need our help."

William doesn't remember driving home or why it's already night. He has been in a daze for the last few hours, nothing is clear to him anymore. He finds some degree of comfort at his kitchen table with an open bottle of brandy within arm's reach. His heavy eyes open and close, and his nodding head wakes him from almost falling asleep. One of his other chairs slides gently away from the table. What activity is now happening in his own home? He looks up to see Angie sitting across from him. He drops his guard again knowing she is a kind spirit, but never wondering how she was able to follow him home or if she was the only one that could.

"To feel unnerved is not outside of reason, William," she starts.

"No, not for me." William reaches for the bottle of brandy, but a strict glance from Angie slides the bottle out of his reach.

"That's not going to help you," Angie says with authority. William hesitates to say the words he thought he would never say.

"I lost today."

"That doesn't mean you are yet beaten." William can't find another way to numb his feelings; he lifts himself off the chair to reach for the bottle. Angie shoots another glance at it to make it fly off the table and roll across the carpet. William sighs and sits back down defeated.

"You're better than this, William."

"No, I'm not. I'm completely fucked up. I thought I could walk into this and figure it out along the way. That's how everything else plays out, but I don't know how to help this family."

"That's your first mistake; thinking that you have to do this alone."

"I don't understand its power—or its limits." He finally admits. "There was a time when I thought I could deal with anything."

"How do you know what winning feels like if you've never lost? You've let your pride blind you."

"My pride is my courage."

"There are three things you need to realize right now. One, the demon is real, it is strong, and it can touch you. Two, you will need Father Brahmer's help, and three, you are a warrior of God, but you can still bleed."

"I feel myself cracking."

"Do not despair, sometimes the simplicity of life is hidden in its complexity." Angie places her hand on his cheek and smiles before fading from view.

William glances at the bottle of brandy laying on the floor, he longs to consume the smooth, oaked beverage once more. Close to the bottle is also Mikael's book that he had dropped and never bothered to pick up. He stumbles out of his chair and heads for the bottle but picks up the book instead. He flips through the book until reaching the page showcasing Lilith.

Demon queen of the night who is sexually dominate and predatory towards sleeping men. She is adorned with the ornaments for seduction and visits those who sleep alone to steal their seed through nocturnal emission.

William thinks to himself for a moment. "Queen—" The word has jogged his memory of something he had read before. He reaches over to a stack of papers on the ottoman and shuffles through the pile until he extracts a newspaper article pertaining to the serial killer who once lived in the Glass' home.

Mr. Faust's testimony sounds as if insanity will be his plea. He was recorded saying the following:

"My queen desires blood and rewards me with nightly visitations. It started with her standing over me naked

and beautiful. I do not know how she got into my room or why she was there. Her smile somehow put me at ease. She pulled my pants off and then climbed on top of me. Absent was the will to resist. However, at the moment of intercourse I remembered all warmth suddenly leaving me. Her touch was cold, and her instrument of power felt like solid ice and tiny needles. With every movement she made I felt several tiny stabbing sensations. I had my eyes closed, up to this moment, but when I opened them, I no longer saw a beautiful woman but a horned beast with a female likeness. I began to panic and was overcome with anxiety and paralysis. I do not know how long this lasted. Intense cold and needle-like piercings in my pubic area is the best I can describe the encounter. I must have passed out shortly after ejaculation for when I awoke the next morning I was alone again in my room. Though unpleasant it was I found myself longing for her return. I was mad with obsession and swore I would give anything to spend eternity with her. Two weeks later she returned. I begged her to do what she wished to me, as long as, she never left my side. She promised me immortality under two conditions. That I will remain loyal and faithful to only her and that I would kill for her. I agreed to both."

William thinks out loud. "But the demon isn't Lilith, otherwise it would not have mentioned her—What am I missing?" William continues flipping through the book. "Who are you? Are you in here? How is she connected?" He sighs and slams the book closed. He then lets it fall on top of the papers resting on the ottoman. He needs time to think in peace, and the best place for him to do that is in a nice hot shower.

William has his hands pressed against the tiles with his eyes closed while letting the warm water fall over him. The clear steam rises round him, but gradually becomes black without him seeing the change take place. The bathroom door slowly opens followed by the lights going out. William pulls the shower curtain back to see two red eyes in the doorway glaring at him.

"This is not your home. Leave this place at once!" William shouts. The lights come back on a moment later with no sign that anything was there. Except for one thing. He shuts off the water and steps out of the tub while glaring into the foggy mirror. Written in long strokes is an eerie message:

I CAN
SEE YOU

He wipes away the words to see Elizabeth in her possessed state standing behind him. William quickly turns around, but no one is there. He gets the feeling he's no longer alone. A feeling that is confirmed by the sound of continuous scraping noises coming from the hallway. He grabs a towel and wraps it around himself before going to investigate.

He stands motionless while listening to the scraping sounds becoming louder. A black demonic creature, with no eyes, stalks across the upper part of the wall; it's soon joined by another one that claws itself around a corner. The two creatures slowly advance while leaving tiny paw prints behind them. He tries to maintain a forceful and dominate voice. "You are not welcomed here. I command you to leave my presence!"

The demons growl to bare their fangs and long forked tongues; they ignore his command and continue to advance toward him. William turns around to see another black mass, in the form of a man, standing beside him and he swipes his long nails across William's face deep enough to draw blood. He yells out in pain as the two previous demons pounce on him. His towel is torn off as the beasts scratch his chest and bite his arms mercilessly. Seeing them is one thing, but William did not expect they could make physical contact.

William kicks and punches his way free and then retreats to his bedroom. He slams the door shut while leaning his full body against it to make sure it remains closed. Snarling, clawing, and growling, the fiends attempt to burst through. William grunts and yells while struggling to hold the door closed as loud banging and crashing sounds come from the other side of the door. After a minute the demons seem to give up and all is silent once again. How did they get into his house? Did the demon send them? Can he really be followed? Is he no longer protected, and they were within him? Why does it matter now? William can visit haunted houses all day, but he always returns to his safe haven. He now understands what it's like to live imprisoned in his own home.

How does he help himself?

William slides down the door to rest on the floor while breathing heavily. After his rest he lifts himself back to his feet. The silence is broken when the head of the temptress darts through his wall, with a screech, before immediately taking the form of the red-haired succubus that attacked him in Elizabeth's room. She throws herself at him to make him fall on the bed. She pins his wrists down and then straddles him. Without any clothing on, and the lack of strength to push her off, William loses the fight to deny her. She rapes him in his own bed with fast thrusts. She doesn't stop until his fluids squirt inside of her. She releases him and backs away while smiling. No word does she speak before vanishing from his room. William is slow to recover from the abuse. He approaches the dresser hoping that with enough melatonin in his system he well sleep through this unnatural activity. In the morning this will all just feel like a dream. He gazes into the mirror, but his face transforms into a demoniacally possessed form. He lets out a deep moan while clawing his nails into his face.

"Get out of my head!" he exclaims. He punches the mirror and then pulls a glass shard from the shattered frame before stabbing it into his thigh. He screams and falls against his nightstand while tipping over the alcohol and pill bottles around him. His bedroom door swings open, and Elizabeth walks in with her sinister grin.

"Swallow them all tonight," she says. Against his control, William picks up the pill container and uncaps it. He brings it to his lips and opens his mouth.

He shakes his head rapidly, "Naa—Aaa—Noo—" His eyes wide open and no control over his own actions, he pours every last pill into his mouth and then crunches, chews and then swallows them. Elizabeth squats down in front of him and grabs his chin to bring him close to her face.

"Did I—get—to you?" William can't help it and begins to cry to Elizabeth's satisfaction. "When you die, I will claim you, and you will be in my servitude." Elizabeth laughs and then disappears.

William howls and cries while rolling onto his knees and elbows before forcing two fingers into the back of his mouth to induce vomiting. He then stands up while coughing as he clumsily limps his way out of the room. Every step causes more blood to ooze from the injury that cascades down his leg. He begins to bleed from the mouth and nose when he opens the front door to the outside. The cold wind rushes inside to flip the pages of the book he had left on the ottoman. William can no longer stand. His chest tightens, his lungs fight for oxygen, his heartbeats become irregular. He feels his entire body going into overdrive and then shutting down. With one last yell he collapses on his stoop and rolls down the three steps. He lies naked and unconscious in front of his house with the sound of a distant siren blaring.

Meanwhile, Father Brahmer fell asleep on his couch sometime during a TV show. The TV screen flickers and flash the transitioning scenes and colors on his face as he snoozes. The flickering gradually becomes a stationary bright light that illuminates his dark room. In his dream, Angie steps out from the blinding white light and continues to advance closer toward his point of view.

"William," she says. Victor hears a distant ringing. "William," Angie says again before she and the light disappear to leave his room dark again. Victor can still hear the ringing. He opens his eyes to realize it's his phone. He hurries to his landline and picks up the receiver.

"Hello?"

"Is this Victor Brahmer?" a lady's voice asks.

"Yes, it is."

"I'm calling from St. Michael's. Do you know a William Corgel?"

"Yes, I do."

"He was just admitted and asked for you. He—he's not in good shape." Victor's dream and then this phone call at the same time is not something to ignore.

"I'll be right there."

Victor arrives at the hospital within twenty minutes and hurries to the only nurse behind the front desk.

"Can you tell me which room William Corgel is in?" The nurse checks her computer and then begins to walk around the counter.

"I will take you to him." Victor follows the nurse around the corner and down another hall before her hand gesture directs Victor to William's room. "This is him."

"Thank you," he says and then enters the room. He observes William sleeping in bed from a distance but doesn't walk closer. He sighs and then crosses his chest. "What have you done, William?"

He bows his head and closes his eyes in prayer, but a slight buzzing interrupts him. Victor swats the air around him, but the buzzing continues to intensify. The sound of one fly soon becomes two. Victor swats the air again but refuses to open his eyes or abandon his praying. The tiny annoyance soon develops into a full swarm that drowns out the beeping of the machines. Victor understands that this is more than a pesky fly. He opens his eyes but cannot see what should be very noticeable. "What resides cloaked in this vicinity without permission?" He says in a hushed tone.

A black clawed hand reaches up from the other side of William's bed and falls on top of his stomach. A horrid creature emerges, while snarling, as it climbs on top of William. Victor reaches into his pocket and takes out a tiny metal cross before holding it up to the demon.

"I command you, through Jesus, our lord and savior, to return to whence you came." The buzzing of a thousand invisible flies continue and the lights flicker. Victor raises his tone. "Back, beast to your infernal domain, to where God has sent you and where you shall remain!" The lights flicker on and off followed by the machines hooked up to William losing power. The lights in the hallway are still on meaning only William's room is being deprived of power. "Do not tempt this man any longer. God has ruled for your swift removal, along with all in your company, from this mortal realm!"

The buzzing finally stops and power returns to the machines as the lights turn back on. The demon is gone and Victor sighs in relief, but there is little time for him to rejoice. William begins to suddenly shake uncontrollably as the steady beeps become faster with little pause in between the next heartbeat signal. Victor hurries to William's bedside and tries to hold his seizing body still. "William! Hang in there, William." The fast tempo of the monitor indicates a severe and unnatural rhythm for any heartbeat, but worse than that is the moment when William's movements abruptly cease and he flatlines. "William—" Victor is overcome with fear and worry at the long thin line on the monitor and the continuous siren that accompanies it. He bolts back to the door and out into the hallway.

"I need help!" A doctor and three nurses are already rushing toward the room and quickly hover around William as Victor watches through the window from the hallway.

"He's in cardiac arrest," one of the nurses mentions. Another nurse unsnaps William's hospital gown as the other ready the defibrillator and then places it onto William's bare chest.

"Clear." William's body jolts up after receiving the shock, but the monitor is still showing a flatline.

"Increase voltage," the doctor orders.

"Ready, clear!"

There's no change in the flatline reading.

"Again," the doctor orders.

"Clear."

Victor prays for William while watching helplessly from the window. At any moment he's hoping to see that flatline indicate a pulse, but every attempt to resuscitate William has so far failed. How many times will they try before deciding to call it? He refuses to admit it to himself. Either due to his self-destructive lifestyle, or some horrible evil—William has died.

6

The Corgel Experience

William finds himself, as an adult, back in his childhood room. He discovers his younger self asleep in bed and can hear his parents arguing downstairs. Is this what happens when one dies? Do they see their life play out in front of them? He watches himself as a child wake up and walk past him without knowledge of his presence. He follows the boy to the stairs and see his tears as he spies on his parents' fight.

"Get out of this house!" his mother yells, followed by the slamming of the door by his father. Young William hurries back to his bed and pulls the covers over his head. The stairs creek as his mother climbs them while whispering a familiar rhyme just under her breath.

"Turn back, turn back, thou pretty bride—" His mother walks past his bedroom door without even looking inside. "— Within this house thou must not bide—" His mother enters his father's study and then slams the door shut.

William is observing the events of his past. A past he had suppressed long ago and for a reason he still does not understand. He cannot be seen or interact with anyone. He's not really there. He's only witnessing a replay of something that has long since passed.

Young William wakes up and looks around his room. A loud thump followed by a continuous squeaking is heard.

"Mom?" He gets out of bed and walks into the hallway. This has been a reoccurring dream for William for as long as he can remember—was it a memory instead?

William follows himself as a child as Little William drags his feet to the shut door of his father's study and then places his hand on the doorknob. "Mom, are you in there?" He hesitates, but slowly turns the knob and peeks into the room. He soon freezes in the doorway and then backs up with a look of pure terror.

William cannot see what the boy sees and grows impatient. He storms through the door to find his mother's legs dangling in front of his father's desk with an extension cord around her neck from the chandelier that's loosely swinging from side to side. Blood is escaping from her nose, mouth and ears and her eyes are bulging out from the force of the fall. She must have leapt off the desk which explains the thump and squeaking sounds he remembered hearing.

"—For here do evil things betide." William turns his attention back to the hallway to see his mother next to his younger self in the same horrid form as she died. William observes himself screaming and taking a step backwards off the landing. The small boy tumbles down the stairs and hits his head hard on the banister. He lies unconscious at the bottom of the staircase while his mother looks down at him. "I'm so sorry, William. I wasn't thinking."

William now knows what really happened, and why he didn't remember it, why he didn't want to remember it. His last memory of his mother was after she had died.

William can feel his body being pulled upward before being immersed in a warm light, along with the sound of a steady beeping. His eyes open to a white ceiling and lying in a hospital bed. It takes him some time to understand the monitors and the reason for the bandages where he sustained his injuries. *I'm alive—*

"Mr. Corgel." William recognizes the familiar voice and turns to see Victor sitting at his bedside.

"I was attacked—in my own home," he forces out.

"I know," Victor nods. "Your neighbors called 911 at 7:27 when they heard the ruckus at your house. They thought it was a home invasion or murder attempt."

"Little do they know it was both," William responds weakly. Victor keeps his focus down while rubbing his hands together.

"They asked me if this was a suicide attempt."

"What did you say?"

"What could I say? How could I say it?" Victor looks back up at William. "I just said everything between us is considered confidential and that you are under my watch. I think it satisfied them enough not to file a report with the authorities."

William glances away and remains silent for a moment before looking back at Victor.

"I remember it now. I was eight when my mother hanged herself. She read to me, tucked me in, and walked around the house three days after she had killed herself. That's when I discovered my gift—that's how I discovered it. I found her hanging body in a room she told me never to enter—I must have forgotten it. I had bits and pieces of her, but they were all out of order."

"Traumatic experiences are sometimes blocked out. Our minds do that to protect us," Victor says and then shakes his head. "But alcohol and pills aren't the way to deal with it, William."

"It's never easy to talk to someone who had passed. Sometimes they know it other times they don't. And I have to be the one who tells them that it's too late. Whatever or whoever they are looking for—it's too late. The children are the worst—trying to explain it to them when they just want to play. Do you know what that's like, to look into their eyes? I had to find some way to numb myself—You hide behind your God, but I have to clean up after him." Victor stands up and begins to pace.

"Christ, William, you were dead! You were dead for three and a half minutes. And you know where I was?" He points to the window in the room. "I was right there watching!" Victor pauses and lowers his voice. "I told you the demon quoted Luke 19:27. 19:27 is military time for 7:27PM. That's when you were attacked, that's when it tried to kill you. You've been its target this entire time—and you know what? It did kill you. It killed you, and God brought you back." Victor pauses again. "I'm sorry; I shouldn't have raised my voice. Also forgive me, Lord for using your name in vain," Victor says while crossing himself. Tears swell up in William's eyes and he breaks down.

"I feel more than most—and I hate it. To feel all that pain, sorrow, and hopelessness I sense in those I see. Not only do I have to live through all their pain, but I also have to experience their deaths. I've been crushed, ran over, burnt, drowned, stabbed—I've died so many times I've lost count.

My responsibility is to find a way to help them crossover, to move on, but how do I move on? I never forget, none of it—it just continues to pile up. Anyone can look at me and see that I'm a mess, and I am. I'm a fucking mess, and that will never change. This curse of mine. A hundred years ago I would have been burned at the stake. Today, I live in purgatory, not living, not dead, but enduring both."

"I can't tell you that I understand your life. I don't," Victor sits back down and continues. "I can't see or hear what you can. I'm sure based on your experiences you doubt how a God can forsake his children. I don't have all those answers. I'm just a man, and because I am, I know I'm not strong enough to fight everything that's out there. So, I ask for a little help; and from what I know, and believe, help is available to those who want it. Don't be ashamed that you feel, William. Embrace it and you will be stronger because of it. Don't be afraid to show how you feel, be afraid when you can no longer feel."

"It got what it wanted from me," William says after a long silence. Victor gets up and pulls William's top sheet down to reveal an ornate crucifix on the bed next to him.

"It attached itself to you—followed you. I think I finally got it to retreat."

The nurse enters the room and appears to be excited to see William awake.

"Oh, good. You're awake. How do you feel?" What kind of question is that? No matter the trauma one endures the common response to it is how they feel. He responds with the usual answer which is almost always a lie.

"I'm fine."

"Excellent." The nurse takes down his vitals from the

monitors and then smiles "Everything looks really good for you, William. Let me get the doctor in here and maybe we can get you home today."

"Thank you. I would like to return to work," he says. Victor glances at him in bewilderment. He would have thought this would be what convinces William to leave the case, but he can see a fighting spirit in him and a drive that prohibits him from quitting. Victor just smiles and slowly nods; no words are needed.

To his great relief William is released from the hospital later that day and Victor is there to drive him home. Unimpressive; however, is the typical, depressing, and dull looking cane that the hospital had given him. It's a cane for an old man who walks very little. It reminds him of an object that lacks luster and is void of life. He tosses it in the backseat of Victor's car and then limps to the front to sit down.

The shard of glass that was jabbed into his thigh struck a nerve. The result is a temporary lot of time when the muscles in his leg are too weak to support his weight and his leg will be prone to buckling. William will need to walk with a cane for the next several months.

"Can we stop someplace first?" William asks as he fastens his seatbelt.

"Of course," Victor replies.

"Good, that cane just will not do."

"All is vanity, William," Victor jokes.

"I think I'm allowed to have one vice." Victor chuckles at Williams response, after all, what's so bad about making a tool fit its user's personality?

Victor and William are happy to bring today to a somewhat satisfying end when Victor drops William off at home.

"We will be performing the exorcism again tomorrow," Victor begins.

"What should I do before then?"

"Pray."

"Will I be heard?"

"That depends how much heart you put into it."

William nods and opens the car door. "Thank you, Father." He helps himself out of the vehicle with the help of his new rosewood crafted cane with a silver dome top and rosary beads as a boarder. Other adornments, such as a dove, fish, bible, hands locked in prayer, and several tiny crosses line the sides of the lower portion of the silver top that merges with the wood shaft. At the very top of the dome is a large embossed golden cross. If he can't find God, maybe God will find him.

The first order of business is to make a change at home. He takes out a large yard trash bag and begins tossing all the liquor bottles and pills inside from his bedroom and around the house. He then carries the bag outside and throws it into the garbage.

He returns to his living room and notices the book with its pages still flipped open from the gust of wind the night he was attacked. He's just about to close it but becomes fixated on the content of this page. His eyes and lips make the look of intense focus and concentration. William reads every word on the page before coming to a conclusion. "I've found you—"

The next morning, William begins his day with something he has never done, in a place he's never been. He strolls down the aisle of the congregation room towards the front stage of Victor's church. Once there he admires the eternal light on the wall inside the otherwise dim room. He observes the statue of Jesus on the cross before gently sliding his hands down his cane and then kneels with a bowed head. He takes on the appearance of a devout archangel resting against his sword.

"All I have is dark forces tempting me with gold and desire; saying I will never be who I want to be, succeed in what I want to achieve or attain the salvation from a loving embrace. Demons whispering in my ear; no angelic caress to wash away my tears. I am one man against the world. The strength of fire is bested only by the might of the light that I do not believe resides within me. Console me if I should fall and give me the courage to stand once more.

In my foolishness I tried to defeat the demon with pride and became oppressed and scathed. Am I to become one of its own? Lord, I know I have turned away, but will you take me back and heal my soul? Today, I will be at war with legion; to be among your ranks and not alone in my trial will be all I require. Aid me in my struggle and forgive me for straying—for I know not what I do."

This isn't just another case for William; this is a war. Only soldiers fight wars and William isn't a soldier—until now.

William arrives at the Glass residence about the same time as

Victor. They give each other reassuring smiles and advance toward the house side by side and Timothy opens the door to allow them to enter. Everyone meets in the living room to discuss the plan for the day. William folds his hands on top of his cane as the others sit down.

"I want you to know that we would not hold it against you if you did not return," Timothy says to William.

"You've been through so much, dear. We would completely understand," adds Emily. William is touched by their words. They have been enduring so much unsettling activity and having their only daughter possessed, yet they are able to be concerned about his safety.

"Thank you. I will admit this was out of my wheelhouse almost right from the start, but I am here now, and I aim to carry it through to the end," William says.

"Usually, the church would not allow you to take part in the exorcism, William. But I trust you and I think your part will be essential in this," Victor says.

"Thank you, Father."

Victor stands up and fixes his collar and then picks up his bible and cross. "Well then, I think we are prepared to begin. Please join me in prayer."

Victor leads with the Lord's prayer as everyone listens with their eyes closed and heads bowed followed by everyone saying, "Amen," in unison.

William enters Elizabeth's room alone. He limps while relying heavily on his cane for support. Elizabeth begins laughing when she notices him, but William is unfazed by her unnerving giggling.

"Hello again, William. I heard—you were not well," Elizabeth continues with her antagonizing laugh. William remains calm and standing still with his hands resting on the top of his cane.

"We have unfinished business," he says calmly.

"What's wrong with your leg, William? It looks as if you lost a war." The demon is trying to find a way to disrupt William's resolve, but he is not falling for any of its lures.

"Sometimes one stands better—when they have something to lean on." Elizabeth tries one last thing she think will get to William.

"Lilith told me what she did to you. How did it feel being inside her cunt?"

"An old hag with a mask on," he replies.

"Harum-scarum skeptic, you have no power here," The demon roars.

"You should know. The best disguise is that of a fool."

"God is dead. You cannot defeat me."

"If that's true, why do you fear him?" Elizabeth lunges forward, but her restraints stop her. She growls and then spits.

"Use that to rub your cock tonight."

"The fact that you exist assures me that God exists. And as one of his children I have the power to vanquish you." Elizabeth kicks and contorts her body to try to free herself while roaring. She lunges towards William again, but still fails to reach him.

"When I'm done with Elizabeth, I'll come for you and fuck you in your ass!" Victor now enters the room with the bible resting on his arm and holding up a cross with his other hand. "You cannot save Elizabeth. She's mine. If I leave, I'll take her with me!" the demon shouts.

"She is not yours to take," Victor responds. Timothy and Emily wait just outside of the room while holding each other.

"With this cane—I call you out—by name—" William unfolds his hands and tilts the cane, so the golden cross is facing the demon. It snarls and darts away.

"—Asmodeus!" The demon surprisingly turns back to William and roars.

"How do you know that name!" William advances while bringing the cross closer to the demon. It looks away while snarling. The demon's word games have failed and it was a fight William had to fight on his own. Now that the demon doesn't have a recent victory to give it a power boost, Victor can begin the rite of exorcism.

"Begone, Asmodeus and stay far from this child of God. For it is God who commands you, God who flung you headlong from the heights of heaven into the depths of hell."

"Fuck you, priest!"

The bed begins bouncing up and down and black, formless, smoke entities dart and swirl around the room as the demon calls for reinforcements. Elizabeth's face transforms as if every blood vessel expands and comes to the surface before running black. Her hissing open mouth resembles the blackness of a cottonmouth, and the red veins in her yellow eyes creep like tiny worms traversing her gaze.

"I adjure you in God's name, begone, Asmodeus from this woman who is his. The longer you delay, the heavier your punishment shall be for it is not men you are condemning, but rather God," Victor continues.

All the trapped spirits suddenly appear in the room one by one. The girl with the broken neck and all the maimed bodies of the murdered victims. The drowned girl, the woman with no jaw, they all appear, either summoned to disrupt the exorcism or to watch their jailer be defeated. William is next to say his part.

"God knows you, Asmodeus. I know you, Asmodeus, and together we command you, Asmodeus, along with all your minions, to depart from this woman and this house and to never return. To release your hold on your captives, to let them free from their earthly chains. All who can hear my voice have my permission to depart." The bound spirits slowly begin to heal and become whole before rising in beams of light. This angers the demon even more.

"Shove that cane up your ass!" It continues growling and flailing on the bed. The black spirits remain circling the room. These are not human spirits; they are Asmodeus' soldiers.

"I cast you out, Asmodeus in the name of our Lord Jesus Christ," Victor commands. William puts his hand on her forehead while holding the golden cross against her cheek. He forces her to look at it and not turn away as steam rises from the point of its impression.

"Look upon the symbol of he who holds power over you," Victor says while sprinkling the vial of holy water over Elizabeth and then places his hand on her forehead as well.

"God commands you, Asmodeus to begone from Elizabeth with haste and take all who serve you!" William adds.

Elizabeth roars and arches her body backwards and several loud bangs explode around the room. The flying demonic masses disappear, but one remains. It rushes toward William but stops when he slams his cane in front of him. The black mass then takes the form of a naked beauty with long fiery red hair.

"Do not deny me, do not defy me," she says.

"Such as you were banished from the garden of Eden, so are you now banished from this home, this family, and this man. Return to your banishment, by the order of he who first willed it.

Our Lord!" Victor shouts. Lilith screeches and hisses as her body becomes encased in a fire that doesn't spread beyond her aura. She continues hissing and screeching until the fire consumes her. This only lasts a few moments before only a smoldering black mist rises where she once stood.

Victor and William hold their crosses toward Elizabeth; it is the only foe remaining.

"Your army has left you, as well as your soldiers and generals," William says.

"God and his numerous angels are here to dispatch you, Asmodeus," Victor says.

Elizabeth's arms stretch out as far as they can as her tethers unravel. She levitates upward while roaring before her feet touch down on the floor. William and Victor keep her at a distance with their crucifixes when she darts her arms toward them.

"I—will never—LEEEAVE!" She wails.

"You have been judged and ordered to retreat without delay. You shall not disobey, you shall not tarry. By the order of he who wills your damnation, he who created the heavens and the Earth, you have been banished!" Victor yells with an unwavering tone and irrefutable might. Asmodeus is seen leaping out of Elizabeth's body. Its ogre-like head protrudes from her chest with a charcoal gray complexion. The head is longer than it is wide with pointed ears, deep sunken red eyes, wide nostrils, and a large snarling mouth filled with sharp, white teeth and fangs. Its thick arms shoot forward and its clawed hand reaches for William. The rest of it is still somewhere within Elizabeth, but it's clear he's resisting from some force pulling him out. Its desperate attempt to enter William finally fails, and a single loud explosion echoes throughout the house. The creature is gone, and Elizabeth's body falls to the floor. Everyone can feel the air changing from an overwhelming, heavy cloak to a light and warm sensation.

Victor and William immediately advance to lift Elizabeth up and lean her against the foot of the bed. Her body is weak and limp, her eyes are shut, and her head falls lifelessly on her shoulder. Timothy and Emily hurry into the room and kneel beside their daughter while crying.

"Elizabeth?" Emily whispers while moving her hair to the side to reveal her beautiful face. Victor and William watch in a suspenseful silence. They've done all they can; the time now belongs to her parents.

"Baby? Daddy is here, mom too, please wake up," Timothy mournfully says. Emily picks up her cold hand and holds it in hers.

"My little girl. Come back to us," she says.

The strain on the body after an exorcism is unpredictable. Some come out of it right away, some need days of rest, while others cannot take the abuse and ultimately shut down from a variety of conditions. Her parents sob and caress her head fearing the worst has befallen on their little girl. William closes his eyes and concentrates hard before opening them again.

"Call to her," William says.

"Elizabeth—" Timothy and Emily say together.

"Again," William says.

"Elizabeth. Elizabeth. Elizabeth," the couple repeat over and over.

Elizabeth takes in a deep breath and then opens her eyes.

"Mom—dad," she says before bursting into tears. Timothy and Emily joyfully embrace their daughter while crying.

William releases the breath he was holding and looks over at Victor with a smile. He places his hand on William's shoulder and the two men chuckle in relief. Elizabeth is free.

William meets Victor in his church office the next day. Victor stops typing his report when William slowly strolls in with the help of his cane. Victor stands up and shakes his hand strongly and with a wide smile before the two sit down in the nearby lobby chairs.

"How are you?" Victor asks.

William smiles while letting a moment pass before replying "better," he says.

"You handled yourself very well on your first exorcism," Victor admits, but William only responds with a smile. "How did you find out the demon's name?"

"I found it one of the books I borrowed from Mikael. Asmodeus is a demon characterized by carnal desire, the demon of lust. As I thought back it always insinuated or mentioned some sort of sexual act, even up to its very end. The clues were too many to ignore. Its weakness was not shutting up."

"Demons gain their power by focusing on the weaknesses of mankind," Victor says.

"I'm not sure how, but that book was opened to the exact page I needed in order to put everything together." William explains as Victor chuckles.

"Like I said before, help is available when you need it."

"Lilith was always there," William begins. "She was the first. She opened the doorway and Faust allowed it. She is thought to be the demon bride to Asmodeus. She invited him in and together two demons of lust shared rulership over that space. That house was damned for a long time. Something like that doesn't really, ever go away. The ground remembers."

"It's always an ongoing battle, William, every day, somewhere else, someone will need us again."

William takes the next several weeks to write a memoir of his hellish experience and calls it:

Case 46: The Demon of the Glass House.

The public, media and others in his field quickly learn about it and take an interest into the case of the Glass Demon. Victor's pews have never been so full, and William's cellphone almost never stops ringing. His callers range from reporters, talk show hosts, working professionals, starry-eyed fans or sometimes someone who truly feels they need his help.

Never knowing who he'll meet or where the next call will lead him, he answers with a professional and astute tone. "William Corgel, paranormal medium and investigator." He listens to the speaker before grabbing a notepad and a pen. "Okay, can you describe the type of activity you've been experiencing?"

Two months later, a degree of normalcy returns to William and Victor, but for the Glass family, the memories they endured in that house force them to seek a new home and a fresh start.

The moving truck is parked outside of the house with Timothy parked behind it. William arrives to say his last farewells and meets Timothy, Emily, and Elizabeth on the sidewalk as they exchange hugs.

"That's the last of it. The house is once again vacant," Timothy says.

"Maybe we should just turn it into a park," William jokes as they chuckle amongst themselves, but the truth is he doesn't believe the house will stay calm for long.

"We can't thank you enough for all you've done, William,"

Emily says.

"I wish the very best for all of you," William replies. Elizabeth hugs him again and he kisses the top of her head.

"Thank you, William, and please thank Father Brahmer for me. I know you still talk to him."

"I will," he promises.

Elizabeth then hands him her latest picture of two angels with swords stabbing a demon hovering over a girl who's lying in bed. "You will always be my angel, William."

"Thank you, I will cherish this," he says while smiling and becoming emotional.

"This house will never feel like a home. Not after all that has happened here, but at least I know the new owners won't have to go through what we did," Emily says while looking back at the house one last time.

"Make new memories, and maybe someday you can forget this experience," William adds.

"No, not forget, just move on," Timothy states.

The family and William exchange final waves as the truck begins to drive away with Timothy following behind. William strolls into the street and watches their car disappear around the next turn before he sighs. He will miss them. After all they went through together it's hard not to develop some sort of attachment. This case not only challenged him, but it also molded him. One could say that it even may have saved him. The bonds he made during this encounter will be lifelong.

He directs his attention towards the vacant house. He would be all too happy never to step foot inside there again, but something pulls him to give it one last walk through before turning it over to the real estate agent. This is the only residence he has returned to after completing a job. It is the home that has impacted him the most. Not just professionally, but also emotionally, spiritually, and even physically. In some ways this experience and locale will never be out of his system, his connection to this location has bored itself deep into his psyche. He still has moments when he pictures himself inside these rooms. He will also see and hear restless spirits around this property from the comfort of his own home. The air of the house is still light and airy, but will continue to attract some degree of activity, but so far nothing demonic or malevolent has entered this space. William becomes aware of a soft, warm presence just before Angie appears beside him. She must have decided to remain as a guardian to the family, but now that they have moved, maybe she can finally move on as well.

"You are free now, Angie," William says.

"I was always free, William. I was only here because you were."

"But you didn't know I was going to be here," he replies. She softly puts her hand on his cheek and smiles.

"Of course, I did. I arrived with you. I've been with you since the day you were born. I'm not a ghost dear, William." Angie becomes surrounded in a warm light and two glistering wings frame her profile. "I'm your angel."

William is awestruck and searches for the right words but cannot come up with a worthy response. Angie's appearance had always agitated Asmodeus, and it was her who helped him out of his trance and oppression from Lilith. William never thought about questioning it before, but Angie's abilities was above what a normal human spirit was capable of—she had the power to disrupt evil and their effects.

"When you announced that you were one of God's own, you gained power over the demon; you made it possible for me to act through you." Angie continues. "I was always here to help you, Mr. Corgel. You were never alone."

"Victor said a woman came to him when I was in danger. Was that you?"

"Yes, that had to be your anguish, but all does heal with love." She places her hand on his chest as tears run down his face. She smiles and then kisses his forehead. "Now it is you who is free, William." Her words and touch have lifted the last remnants of evil that was hiding inside him, and he begins to sob. "Do not despair, for I will always be with you."

Angie shines brightly to encase William's entire body before fading away. William has learned that a fear laden soul still contains courage, a troubled, and doubting mind can achieve a calm confidence, and when failure is imminent, hope brings victory.

William's bedroom remains free from pill containers and liquor bottles and Elizabeth's framed picture and an ornate cross hangs over his bed.

With the closing of the case, comes one last task William must complete; it's time to return a book back to its library. He leans on his cane while standing in Mikael's office as his friend returns it to the open spot on his shelf.

"Did this book help you?" Mikael asks.

"Yes, the demon was Asmodeus."

"Asmodeus is a very well-known fallen angel. He, along with Baal are suspects in most possession cases," Mikael explains.

"I never expected to be dealing with two demons, let alone one. I wasn't prepared for this job. I wish I knew then what I know now, but it's over now, I suppose."

"We all wish we knew more when we were younger," Mikael says before lighting up his cigar and continuing. "Is it okay if I share your report with my class? I'm sure it will bring up many discussions."

"Absolutely, that's why we share our stories. Maybe in the future I can call upon your expertise and book collection again."

"I can agree to that."

"Something tells me I may need it again," William says while trailing off into a thought.

"Would you like to be a guest speaker for my class sometime? Hearing the experience directly from you would be of great academic importance."

"I would be honored," William replies while skimming the shelves of Mikael's books.

"Most people don't pay attention to stories such as these. They are too quick to dismiss them as fictional," Mikael says after tapping his cigar ashes in the ashtray.

"Then one day it becomes undeniable," William begins. "It reaches out and touches you. It may not always kill you, but it does leave a scar."

"How's your leg, by the way?" Mikael asks seeing William is still dependent on his cane.

"It'll heal," William responds before withdrawing a book from the shelf that just caught his attention. "The Encyclopedia of Angels," he reads the title.

"Yes, I felt I should at least have one of those amidst a collection like this," Mikael admits.

"One goes a long way," William smiles and chuckles.

Mikael accompanies William toward his car. "I do hope next

time you come across a demon that you give me a call sooner," Mikael says as he swings the cast iron gate open. William laughs and continues to the sidewalk.

"As much as I want to hope that I will never have to deal with another demon; I am in the profession where anything is possible." William opens the car door and then looks back at Mikael. "Maybe we will work together again someday; hopefully under better circumstances."

"You know where I am," he responds with a smile. William gets in the car and rolls the windows down as Mikael leans just inside the passenger door. "Oh, one more thing. I seem to keep losing my cigar lighter. Do I have a ghost?"

"No, you're just forgetful." The men share a laugh before William waves and puts the car into gear. Mikael backs up and holds his hand up in a stationary farewell gesture. Mikael too has been notified that his classes are maxed out and the next semester's waiting list is already full. Just like William said, everyone is going to know about the Glass Demon, with some desiring to know more about it.

For a while William's case with the Glass family and their demon slowly becomes talked about less and less, until it's almost forgotten. Who knows what makes past stories relevant again? Maybe it's a curious mind starved for more information, or perhaps just a news channel that needed a story. Whatever the case, the media brought it back into the homes of the public, and this time it went national.

A reporter is standing in front of the infamous house as the local news team surround the area and a cameraman remains focused on her.

"The Corgel Experience, also known as case forty-six, is the most popular topic among paranormal professionals, believers, and skeptics alike. A year ago, this house behind me, with the green shutters, was the location of what many are calling the most haunted house in modern history and where the exorcism of Elizabeth Glass was performed. William Corgel and Father Victor Brahmer spent over three months battling two demons and a multitude of spirits inside this very home. Both William and Victor have agreed to talk to us about their case, but two questions still remain, where is the Glass family now, and the other question on everyone's mind; is it truly over? The house is still vacant, but it's believed to be at rest."

A new experience for William is watching himself being interviewed on the nightly news from home. "What are your thoughts about the uniqueness of case forty-six?" asks the interviewer.

"I will be the first to admit that the severity of this case is uncommon, but to say it can never happen again would be ignorant. Whether you chose to believe it or not I can tell you that there is real evil that doesn't sleep and wants to be found. My mistake was not taking it more seriously right from the get-go," William answers.

"Do you think you will get another case like case forty-six?"

"Well, I wouldn't be disappointed if I didn't, but I think it's just a matter of time. We deal with it all the time without ever thinking about it. The longer you are exposed to something or the longer something is running or used repeatedly, the closer it gets to messing up. The likelihood that something negative will occur always increases with continuity. For me that was working on forty-five typical hauntings before experiencing my first demonic presence."

"What's your advice to someone who may be dealing with a demon?" William thinks about the question for a moment, but his answer is very clear.

"Never attempt to take it on alone."

Days later, William is resting his hands on the top of his cane while waiting for Victor to meet him in front of the church. The two have become good friends and often meet for lunch or gossip about their work. Victor soon advances down the steps toward William.

"Good morning, Mr. Corgel."

"Good morning, Father Brahmer." William reaches into his pocket and takes out the tiny plastic container of orange Tic Tacs before popping several in his mouth.

"I like the orange ones," he admits.

"Well, that's one addiction I can tolerate," Victor smiles. "How's work lately?" The two begin walking on the sidewalk towards the coffee shop at the corner.

"Haven't come across any demons so far."

"That's good. I saw your interview."

"How did I do?"

"You didn't look nervous at all; you were a complete natural."

"They gave me a lot of donuts," he jokes.

"Perks of the job huh," Victor chuckles.

"I had a dream about Elizabeth last night."

"What did she say?"

"She didn't say anything, but she was smiling."

"That's good. It means she's safe and happy." Victor glances at William's cane. "I thought you didn't need your cane anymore."

"I don't, but I like holding on to it. It gives me hope."

Victor smiles and reaches into his pocket and then hands him a folded piece of paper. "I received this e-mail last night. A lady claims to be visited by nightly spirits and wants me to bless her house. Would you be interested in looking into this with me?"

"I think this is the beginning of a beautiful friendship, Victor."

Later that evening they meet the troubled woman who sent the email. William holds the cane in front of him with his hands resting on top as he and Victor stand at the front door until it opens.

"Good evening, I'm William Corgel."

Who knows where this case will lead—

The former residence of the Glass family remains unsold and vacant. The For Sale sign is still staked in the front lawn and the home looks secure. Besides some minor updating, the house hasn't changed much since the Glass family owned it. The living room carpet has been replaced and all the walls have been repaired and freshly painted. New cabinet doors and counters have also been installed in the kitchen.

It looks perfect for any potential buyer to walk through. Modern, spacious and on a quiet street, it's a steal at the below market asking price. No one would question why the basement door was left open. The fact that it's also riddled with deep gashes and holes seem strange after so much time was taken to make the rest of the house look pristine. But then again, a new door is an inexpensive fix in a house that is otherwise flawless. One should expect some cosmetic work at a lowered asking price after all. But if any potential buyer knew the house's history, they would find it wise to continue their search elsewhere.

Two cars pull up to the curb and a woman holding a folder

meets a newlywed couple expecting their first born. They admire the exterior of the house and immediately feel attracted to it. Something invisible is drawing them in, whispering to them to make them stay. The house is lonely again and needs fresh energy.

The basement door slams shut and a pair of yellow, blood-shot eyes peek through the splintered opening.

Some homes will always be haunted.

"It's nice to step outside of yourself for a little while, but it's always good to come back to who you really are."

THE FORM

A Poem

I awoke to a form sitting on the side of my bed one night.
A form that I never saw before, sitting quietly and still with no
explanation of how or why it was there.
This form lacked any identifying features, no face could I make
out in the dark and no resemblance to a man or a woman that my
gaze could make out.
After a moment I heard it speak without sound as it echoed only
in my head.
"I will possess thee from sleep 'til morning. I will live in your
dreams and corrupt your soul."
Tired as I was, I fell back into a deep slumber—and dreamt.

A hoofprint in the sand of a desolate beach with a red tide. The
sun behind the dense black clouds appeared green and the sand
was a hue of blue or violet.
Beyond the beach was a cave opening that beckoned me closer, yet
my mind warned me to refuse.
I felt the cold sand beneath my feet, but a hot wind on my face as
I drew nearer to this cave.
A shape appeared in the mouth that resembled all the beauty, lust,
and seduction the mind could ever ponder.
Beguiled, I allowed her to lead me inside to what fate I could not
say as morning had arrived.

I awoke the following night to the same form sitting on the side of
my bed.
It sat quietly and still, pondering of what I cannot guess.
"Who are you who must disturb my sleep," I asked.
It answered again without a voice. "I will possess thee from sleep
'til morning. I will live in your dreams and corrupt your soul."
At this moment I fell so tired I do not recall the ability to
respond—and I dreamt where the last one had ended.

The amber glow from the flame-lit torches cast jittering shadows
on the cave walls. My guide had long dark brown hair and I
followed without being told to do so.
I could not help myself but allow my head to tilt downward to
stare. What I saw I did not expect but a tail just above the buttock
I so wished to gaze upon.
She brought me to a room with a large circular bed in the center
and without turning around claimed this is where I would remain
'til the end of my days.
This is where my second dream ends.

It was on the third night that a light from the hall shown into my
chamber.
I do not recall leaving it on, but there it was radiating into my eyes
to rob me of the restful sleep I so desired.
What inconvenience is this?
Some unknown occurrence forces me to unwillingly leave my
comfort to remedy this vexing distraction.

As I return to bed I spot a shadow, that needs no light to exist,
appear in the corner of my room.
It was the featureless form, more human than before, still
observing me in my home.
"What use do you have with me," I implored. But its answer was
always the same.
"I will possess thee from sleep 'til morning. I will live in your
dreams and corrupt your soul."

This night I had no dream as I was unable to return to sleep.
But it was on the fourth night that I awoke suddenly to the same
form sitting on the side of my bed.

I tried to sit up but felt a heaviness on my chest as if I was being
held down by unseen hands.
"Why do you oppress me?" I urged.
But the form purged me of my perplexion with its predicted
reaction. "I will possess thee from sleep 'til morning. I will live in
your dreams and corrupt your soul."

I did not immediately fall back asleep as before but remained
awake and paralyzed to see this form encroach.
Slowly, it stretches its arms up towards me, its hands slither up my
sheets and its fingers curl around my neck.
Its weight falls on me to restrict me, constrict me. I am ensnared
as a captive, coiled, and webbed.

This night I dreamt a dream, so vivid I did not think It was fiction.
My vixen guide pushes my shoulders lightly back and I fall onto
the bed.
An aroma of coconut and the full clear view of her genitalia did
she place near my chin.
"Sweet words can win a girl, but so can a tongue when no words
are spoken."
I felt a yearning to proceed and no objection to refuse.
She is the epitome of seduction. A soft-spoken beauty measured by
an endless secretion of pheromones. I am enslaved by sight, sound,
smell, and taste. I wish for this to never end.

It was here that I had a dream inside a dream, but what I dreamt
was not a dream.
I observed a body in my bed covered with a sheet.
I saw the form was there too, sitting where it always had been.
A voice from somewhere behind me said, "He died during the
night by some unexplainable cause."
At this moment, the form begins to change.
This featureless creature became none other than my vixen guide.

I awoke again relieved this dream was just that, but to my horror I
found myself still in the cave.
I looked to see my beauty sitting at the side of this big red bed.
She looked at me with a grin and said,
"I will possess thee—forever."

About the Author

Jerry J.C. Veit was born in the spring of 1983 to a German and Portuguese family. He developed a love for writing at a young age and a fondness for classic literary works by Charles Dickens, Mark Twain, Edgar Allen Poe, and others.

His introduction into writing began with screenwriting in 2008. After making it to many of the finals in several screenplay contests and writing countless query letters to literary agencies, he ultimately decided to abandon this form of writing. In 2016 he explored self-publishing and transformed all six of his screenplays into novelized scripts that resembled a play. It wasn't until 2021 that he decided to rewrite, reformat, and extend all his titles once again—this time into traditional novels starting with his debut novel, Apocalypsia, and a two-volume anthology of his novellas containing five stories total.

He currently resides in southeastern Wisconsin working by day as a graphic designer at an ad agency, but by night he's a builder of worlds who enjoys writing character-driven stories that inspire, entertain, and hopefully leave an everlasting impression on his audience. He's passionate about writing in the genres of fantasy, dystopias and paranormal, but also penned an inspirational story as well.

9 798987 166635